Ladies Wagon Train

~

The Beginning of the End

A story by R. Steven Hamburg

First Edition
ISBN: 978-1-79432-857-0

Cover art by Rebekah Santiago |
rebekah.joy9@gmail.com

~

As I stated in my first book, I want to give all glory and honor to Yehovah, God of all creation, and to Yeshua HaMashiach (Jesus the Christ) whose atoning blood has given me the opportunity to have life everlasting with Him.

Yeshua (Jesus) is the one whom Yehovah created all things through, and has given all power and glory to. He is my king, and Savior, and He is yours, whether you understand that or not.

~

Acknowledgments

As with the first book I need to give credit where credit is due.

First and foremost, to the God of all creation, Yehovah!

And to Yeshua HaMashiach (Jesus the Christ)! My Savior and King! HalleluYah!

I feel I need to reiterate here, as in the first book: Yeshua (Jesus) is the one whom Yehovah created all things through, and Yehovah has given all power and glory to Him! I admit I don't really understand that. The Father and the Son. No one has been able to explain it to me anyway. But I am fine with that. I am the servant. I do not need to understand. I need to obey. He will explain to me what He wants me to know. The rest is none of my concern.

I believe He gave me this story to write. I am now and shall be eternally grateful because I think it's a fun story, and I am certainly not a writer, so it must be from Him. I have no talent, so any good works that come from this are because of Him.

Baruch Hashem Yehovah

HalleluYah

Blessed is the name Yehovah

Praise to Yah

I want to thank my wife, my most precious gift on this earth, the lovely and gracious Mrs. Hamburg.

It took me waaay too long to write this story. Years! It started out as one very long book and I changed it into two smaller, more manageable ones, and she patiently gave me the time I needed, and put up with my tantrums because of it, with grace and dignity that I did not deserve. Our time is a precious thing. It cannot be brought back once given away, and she gave me her time to let me do this.

Thank you.

I again need to acknowledge my mom. She was the first one to see a copy of the book. I was afraid to let anyone read it for fear of failure and humiliation, but she gave me some very honest criticism, in a very kind way, and she did declare it "A Grabber!"

I needed that. Thank you, Mom. I love you.

I need to mention my editor now. My new editor. She is not the same one as last time. I was blessed to have had Jared help me the first time. However, Ms. Kelsey Bryant (kelsey.irene.bryant@gmail.com) has taken this to a whole new level.

I appreciated her suggestions of little details, things I never would have thought of, and sometimes things I didn't want to do but now I am so glad I did. Always with a suggestion. Always put to me in a kind way. She made this story so much better than it was. If you ever need an editor, look no further than Kelsey. And on top of that she is fast! No fooling around with this girl. She gets it done! Thank you, Kelsey. I cannot thank you enough.

And finally as with the first book, I wish to acknowledge those individuals who intimately know the history of the Oregon Trail, who will most certainly notice the liberties I took to make the story work within my limited abilities.

I hope you will forgive me.

- Steve

Contents

June 1867

The Civil War has been over for two years.

A wagon train consisting of widows, their children, one grumpy old wagon master, and his two grumpier old freighters are somewhere in the Nebraska Territory, headed to California.

They have already survived an Indian fight and a kidnapping and saw one of their own murdered, and they're still going to have to deal with those other men.

They're still out there somewhere. The ones who plan to take them, use them, and then sell them to the highest bidder. And they got a good plan to do it too.

It has been a very hard seventy days on the trail.

It's going to get harder.

1
An Unfair Gunfight

Up in the mountains Walt and his little wagon train of heroes, as Jodi Mesto kept sarcastically referring to them, were crossing yet another high meadow.

After their last raid on a miners' camp, their only goal was to get out of the Rocky Mountains alive.

They had grown to four wagons with eleven women, four children, and now four wounded men.

Sergio was still the worst off from getting shot in his middle. Walt had his cut in his chest and head, and now Harvey sported a wound in his left leg and Billy had been shot in his shoulder.

The wagons were out in the open crossing another meadow, and Walt didn't feel safe out there like that. They were sitting ducks for a rifle shot. He didn't feel safe amongst the trees either. Everywhere he looked seemed like a perfect spot for an ambush. At least they didn't have too far to go now. It'd been three days since their last raid and still no sign of anyone.

The last two raids resulted in two more miners dead, two more miners wounded, and four more unaccounted for. They would have in their possession at least one wagon and most likely several of the mules and packhorses they left behind. And they were probably armed with several rifles, and pistols, and friends. Walt cursed himself for not insisting on taking all the animals. It would have definitely slowed the miners down.

He was sitting up in the driver seat of his wagon so he could look around at the scenery, and at all those potential ambush sites.

Leaning against the wagon boxes, Billy and Harvey peered out from the rear of their wagons, gazing past their horses tied to the axle and trotting along behind them. Sergio couldn't sit up yet, so the ladies had built him a ramp out of boxes of food stuffs piled over with clothes so he could see without having to actually sit up.

It was Harvey who first saw a man on a horse come out into the clearing behind them. He was quite a ways off yet. From that distance he couldn't tell if he was friend or foe. He glanced at Billy, who was looking at the man now, and hollered over to Walt.

Walt turned around. Billy and Harvey were both pointing, so he looked past them and spotted the rider. *This is not gonna be good.* He handed the reins to Lizzy and moved to the back. Sergio was watching the man along with the others.

Then two more mounted men emerged into the clearing, two more after them, and then a wagon.

Everyone was on high alert now watching the men, who seemed to be discussing the wagons crossing the meadow in front of them. Even the ladies driving looked back as they were able.

Finally Lizzy hollered out, "Should we run?"

"Hold the same pace for now. We'll wait to see what those riders are gonna do," Walt told them.

That's when the new strangers took off and started coming hard. They were in for it!

Walt shouted, "Let 'em go!"

"Hyaah!"

"Hyyaaah!"

"Hyaah!" All the ladies cracked their whips and the wagons took off.

4

The race was on!

Walt's wagon was on the outside now as all four lined up side by side. They raced across the meadow, jumping over the rough terrain. Getting onto his knees, Walt yelled over at Billy, "Hold yer fire! Tell Harvey an' Sergio!"

Billy maneuvered around in his wagon to defend it against the approaching men. Harvey was making his arrangements to do the same when he yelled over to Sergio.

Sergio shouted back, "I'm in enough pain already! I'll wait till they get closer."

Jodi turned and saw the men bearing down on them. She cursed, stood up, and yelled at the other ladies who were already doing the same. Taking her whip out, she laid a lash across the rumps of her mules trying to get them to run even harder. They jumped and she gave them another lash and they really started pounding the earth.

The four wagons barreled along side by side, shaking all the occupants around so they couldn't hold on to anything. Not even the side of the wagon or the things packed inside.

The drivers bounced up and down, in danger of bouncing out of the driver's boxes. All the while they yelled at the animals and cracked whips. Some of their language made Walt blush.

The mules pulled with all they had. Nostrils flaring. Eyes bulging. Heads straining forward as if to pull the wagons even that much faster.

The wagons themselves were going airborne as wheels hit little hillocks or clumps of grass, and it seemed at any moment that a spoke would shatter or a harness would break under the strain.

The ladies were driving them wagons for all they were worth, yelling and cursing and whipping them poor animals into a frenzy. Those mules ran like never before.

Walt could see the men were still gaining. And there was the missing wagon right on their heels with four men inside it.

Walt watched the men in the wagon trying to aim their rifles;

then he saw the smoke from their barrels and heard the shots. He looked up to see Lizzy still standing and still whipping them poor animals.

"Get down!" he shouted at her.

She yelled back, "Shut up an' shoot 'em!"

He tried, but he was jostling around so much he couldn't aim. He pointed his pistol and fired with the same efficiency his pursuers had shooting at him.

He saw Billy and Harvey firing away. He saw Sergio lying there on his ramp, now flying up into the air and now slamming back down, all the while calmly aiming his pistol and deliberately pulling the trigger.

They all had the same effect. No one was hitting anyone! The men chasing did hit the wagons, though, which scared Walt to death knowing they could accidentally shoot one of the children or the ladies.

He worried most about the children who were actually flying up and exposing themselves as targets. He yelled at Lizzy, "Swing yer wagon closer to Billy's!"

"Not on yer life!" But then she started to pull it over anyway.

As she edged nearer to Billy's, Jodi began to steer away but Walt yelled at her to get closer. He called to Billy to have Norena pull Harvey's in closer, and Maezy to do the same with Sergio's.

Now they were all right next to each other flying along, crashing against each other, with everyone bouncing up and down inside.

The pursuers quit shooting and slowed up a little as if trying to figure out what was going on. They held their distance about fifty yards away, maintaining speed but not gaining anymore.

The whole parade of wagons and riders still dashed across the clearing at breakneck speed as if it was some kind of rodeo race. But now no one was gaining or losing any ground.

Walt yelled out across the wagons, "No one can hit anythin'! We're gonna have to stop an' let 'em surround us like an' Indian attack.

Then we can fire from here while they're still ridin' around us. It's our only chance!"

"It's no chance! I'm not stoppin'!" Lizzy shouted back over her shoulder.

"You got to! Or they'll kill us all one by one!"

Crashing into each other, the wagons were in real danger of one of them coming apart. Lizzy looked over at Jodi. "We got to try it. Tell the others!"

Jodi called across and they all responded. They were ready.

Drawing closer, the riders started shooting again. Lizzy cried out and lurched forward but immediately sat up with her shoulder bleeding. She yelled across, "Okay, ladies, on three! One! Two! Three!"

All four ladies stood up and hauled back on the reins. "Whoa! Whooaa!"

The animals stopped so fast they skidded with their hooves digging into the dirt.

Caught completely off guard, the riders found themselves riding past and looking at them without even shooting.

The miners' wagon also rumbled to a stop very close, so Walt and the others poured fire into the wagon. The driver was hit and fell over, and the others in the back finally fired back but had two wounded. Jumping over the seat, one of them grabbed and snapped the reins to get their mules moving. He turned the wagon and started running away.

Now the riders chased after their own wagon, and one got shot and toppled off his horse on the way to regroup. About two hundred yards away, they started another conference.

Walt watched them apparently arguing with each other. Their arms flailed around and they pointed at each other and back over to his wagons. So he had all the kids and women climb into the middle wagons, piling the equipment around the sides and burrowing into the center. Sergio and Harvey were now in the outside wagon on one side and Walt and Billy in the outside wagon on the other.

Walt looked over his shoulder at everyone. "I think they'll come at us from both sides. If they change up an' come at jist the one side, we all shoot across the wagons. You women keep them kids down an' behind the equipment!"

Just then the miners started lumbering back toward them with three mounted riders on Walt and Billy's side and two riders and the wagon on Harvey and Sergio's side. The wagon had three rifles pointing toward them with one rider in front and one trailing behind it.

Walt and Billy lined up against the side of their wagon. Harvey was up and ready. Sergio lay there calmly aiming his pistol.

Looking out toward the riders, the men took careful aim, but just as they were about thirty yards away, the miners opened fire.

The two outside wagons took several hits with splinters flying. The men ducked and regrouped, then waited a moment longer and fired.

On Walt and Billy's side one rider immediately fell off his horse and bounced along the ground. Another was shooting back and almost followed his companion's example but gained control and was able to get his animal away. The third rider on their side rode past the wagons firing but hitting nothing.

On Harvey and Sergio's side, the miners' wagon rocked and jumped as it came barreling alongside and all three rifles opened up at one time. Walt and Billy flinched as bullets blasted around them from behind.

The driver of the miners' wagon was now in the back, holding reins through the seat while trying not to be exposed, when he took a bullet, slammed into the side of his wagon, and tumbled over.

Now it seemed everyone had forgotten about the single rider. He was coming up fast, taking aim at Harvey, when Sergio pointed his pistol very carefully and fired. The rider threw his arms up in the air and rode along for another twenty feet like that before falling off his horse.

The miners' wagon kept running along until one of the men in back grabbed the reins and stopped it about two hundred yards away, this time in front of them.

**

The miners all grouped together for the third time. "Look, they done killed Clayborne, Easy, Melton, an' Brett! An' Horton here don't look like he's gonna make it much further!"

"Tain't fair! Tain't right they git to sit there an' we gots to ride by so they can shoot us dead!"

"Well, Estes, whatta you wanna do? Go over there an' work out the rules fer us killin' 'em?"

"Shut up! I'm jist sayin' it tain't fair!"

"Okay, so whatta we gonna do now? We got three healthy an' two wounded bad with Horton there an' Lyle bouncing around here. He looks done fer too."

"Well I hate to say it, but we're through! 'Less you got some other idea. I ain't makin' another pass at 'em like that."

"Me neither. We jist have to git."

"Griffy's right."

"Okay, let's git outta here before Horton an' Lyle bleed out entirely."

"We ought to at least take some shots at 'em."

"Estes, you go ahead. I'm sure they owe us that. I'll wait over there while you do it."

"Shut up! It jist tain't fair, is all! It jist tain't!" He pointed his pistol and fired off a shot at the wagons.

Walt and everyone in the wagons ducked and they all aimed and fired back at once.

"Estes! Are you happy now? Let's git outta here!"

**

The miners turned west, and when they reached the far side of the meadow veered back south and headed toward the end of the clearing from where they first appeared.

The little group watched for a moment and then they all cheered.

Jodi said, "We better check on these men lyin' out there." She glanced at Walt. "It'll take y'all too long to git over there, so we'll go. Keep yer guns ready jist in case."

Jodi and Maezy scrambled out of the wagons and walked over to the two men lying on the ground from Walt and Billy's side. They studied them and then Jodi gave the one closest to her a good hard kick. He never moved other than from the kick itself.

"These two's good an' dead, an' good riddance. Let's go look at t'other." They approached the last man lying there. Jodi gave him a hard kick. "He's as dead as t'others. I say we git outta here before someone else comes along an' wants to ask us why we killin' ever'body."

Jodi hollered at the others, "We don't gotta bury 'em, do we?"

Lizzy said, "Nope, let's git, before someone else shows up. The coyotes an' bears will take care of 'em. I've done all I have to fer 'em."

Walking back, Jodi waved her hand to move out. "Our heroes ain't in no shape to bury anybody, so let's git."

The four men looked at each other and Harvey shrugged. Sergio just laid his head back down. Walt and Billy exchanged another glance, shook their heads in unison, and sat back against the side of the wagon.

The two ladies returned to the wagons and mounted up.

That's when Norena noticed, "Lizzy, yer shoulder!"

"Oh it's fine, jist a cut. We'll fix it up tonight after we git away from here. Okay, ladies, let's move out!"

2
Let's Do What Must Be Done

Clem was sitting up on Cherry and getting impatient. "If we're goin' to do this, ladies, let's git goin'. We need to get started so we can git back to our original purpose. Michael, we'll be gone 'bout ten days, meybe two weeks judgin' by what Mr. Henry Davis here has told us."

Henry beamed and glanced around at being called Mr. Henry Davis. Everyone in the camp smiled back at him.

Clem knew everyone was ready. Cherry was getting antsy and starting to flip her head up and down. They were in the middle of a loose crowd. "Let's move out; we got to git there an' back, an' jist ten days to do it." He looked over at Leah. "Mrs. Knott!"

She was startled out of her thoughts and looked up at him.

"You done right by this boy, I'll tell his ma." Then, turning Cherry's head and without glancing back, he hollered while walking his horse out of the crowd, "Let's head out! Michael, yer in charge!"

Everyone moved aside and let Cherry move out, leading the other horses with their riders, all making up the group to escort Henry home.

Henry rode just behind Clem. He was followed by Mary Williams and Sandy Hollingsworth, their sons Tom Williams and Brennen Hollingsworth, then Joseph Copher and Carl Roch. They brought up the rear, each one leading a packhorse.

They met up with Brent Hafin and Lou Hamilton, who were just outside the camp with the cattle and the other horses they were taking back. They all moved out without saying much. Each in turn looked back and waved. Henry was doing it so much some got worried he would fall off his horse. Clem never did look back. He felt people always made too much out of saying goodbye.

**

Four days had gone by now and Clem and his little group had traveled the whole way without seeing another soul, which was just what he wanted. He didn't want anyone asking any questions about where the brothers were or where these cattle came from. Too many things he didn't know how to answer.

Henry had been giving them day-by-day updates as to how close they were. "Mr. Clem? We'll be at Ma's tomorrow by noon. Ya'll don't have to come any closer. I can go myself."

"Thank you, Henry, but I want to meet yer ma. We came this far. It should be nice, don't ya think? She should be happy to git you back an' all."

"Yes sir. I'm jist worried she might be mad 'bout my brothers."

"Don't worry, son."

They rode the rest of the day without meeting anyone. They made camp that night, and Henry said they could be home just after breakfast if they got up early. Clem promised him they would.

**

It was still dark when they arose and ate a little breakfast of jerky and biscuits with coffee, everyone but Henry. He wouldn't eat and the boys struggled to get him to slow down before they were all ready to go.

He wouldn't hear it. He had the horses fed, watered, and saddled for everyone, ready to go before the others had finished eating. Then they had to wait on Mr. Clem. He was up and wasn't really trying to delay anything, but he was in no rush either. Finally, everyone's nervousness got to him, so he told them to get the herd moving.

It wasn't too long and they came around a tall hill into a little valley. They could see Henry was getting more and more anxious.

He had them turn down a little trail, and then around a bend in the trail, then through a thicket of trees that shaded it so much they lost the sun. As they cleared the trees they could see a small farmstead up ahead.

Henry was so nervous now he could hardly sit his horse. "There it is! An' there's Ma!"

A small, slender woman was walking across the yard and stopped when she looked up and saw them. She shielded her eyes from the sun with her hand, watching the riders come in.

Clem turned in his saddle. "Stay back, ever'one. I'll take Henry up to meet her."

They rode up and he told Henry to stay at his side. As they drew closer, Henry couldn't stop squirming in his saddle.

They were about fifty yards away when she recognized him and covered her mouth with both hands. She stood there as they approached, but Henry wouldn't dismount until he was allowed to.

Finally Clem told him, "Git down and go say hello."

Henry jumped off his horse and ran the last twenty yards to her. Just as he got there, he came to a skidding stop, picked her up in a big hug, and held her for a long moment before setting her down again.

Then he stood grinning down at her. Clearly confused, she peered around Henry for her other sons and, not seeing anyone she recognized, she glanced up at Clem and back at Henry.

The little group was at the edge of the farm with their horses and cattle, next to the pasture fence where a cow and her calf, feeding inside, had wandered over to inspect the newcomers.

The lady held Henry at arm's length. "Henry boy, where's yer brothers?"

"I'm real sorry, Ma, but they's all dead. They died jist like you said they would, in a gunfight with Mr. Clem an' the other ladies." He jerked his thumb back indicating the man sitting on his horse. The lady gave him a quick look and then turned back to Henry.

He kept right on talking. "They didn't shoot me. I thought they was ghosts, jist like Mitch always said was out to git me, but they wasn't. They was jis—"

"Shush, boy, hush up. Don't say nuthin' fer me, okay?"

She looked over at Clem now, who had dismounted and was standing behind Henry, and then past him to the group at the edge of the farm, still on their horses with the herd milling around right behind them.

"Hello, that yer family?"

Henry spoke up. "No, Ma, that's—"

"Henry, shush, I need to talk to the gentleman. I want you to be quiet fer a moment."

"Yes ma'am." Henry stepped back so his ma could look directly at Clem.

Clem took his hat off. "Ma'am, I brought yer son back. I'm, well, it's a little complicated."

"You a lawman?"

"No, ma'am. I'm takin' a wagon train of folks out to California an' we met yer sons, an', well, we had a problem, an' there was trouble."

"I'm sorry, mister. My boys was bad; they finally got what was comin', I 'spect. Are they all dead?"

Clem nodded, turning his hat in his hand. "Yes ma'am. I am very sorry to say that, but it's true. They really gave us no other choice."

She let out a big sigh. "I'm sure they didn't. Did they kill some of yers in the process?"

He had to clear his throat. "Well, no, ma'am. I, uh, I didn't give 'em the chance. They drew guns an'...we already had 'em covered an'...well, I am sorry."

Clem kept turning his hat as he talked. He felt terrible for the woman, knowing that she was facing the man who killed her boys, yet at the same time knowing what they were like.

14

She let out another shaky sigh. "I'm sure they was at fault. I am very sorry fer whatever they done to bring this on you. Thank you fer sparin' my Henry." She glanced down and away for a moment and then raised her head, looking at Clem.

Her eyes were moist, but she smiled a little. "You must be very tired. Would you care to bring yer family up to the house? I still got coffee on, an' I can make up sumptin' to eat if you haven't eatin proper. Perhaps you'd be willin' to tell me the details of what happened. I'm sorry, mister, but I'd like to know, please, if you don't mind."

"Yes ma'am, I will, an' we're not hungry, we're good fer now."

She nodded slightly, then turned and smiled at Henry. Hooking her arm through his, she rotated him around to walk to the house. Clem looked back and motioned for the others to follow.

The boys took down part of the pasture fence, moved the cattle into the pasture with the cow, and brought the horses up to Clem. He stood there waiting and told them to take the horses over to the corral. The ladies followed Clem to the house.

They climbed onto the porch and were just ready to knock when the door flew open.

Clem stepped back, reaching for his pistol, when Henry stuck his face out with a big smile and invited everyone into his home. He waved his arm and stepped back to let them all in.

It was a clean room. A woodstove stood in the far corner with a coffeepot on it, and a pie sat on the table. The lady was setting out plates and had turned to get some cups when they entered her little house. She stopped and welcomed them in.

"Would y'all like a piece of pie?"

They all thanked her. "Maybe later," Clem said.

She motioned for them to take a seat. "I'll be with you in jist a moment."

The ladies sat around the table and Henry stood back beaming with an even bigger smile than they had got used to seeing on him since they met him. Henry's ma set down cups for everyone and began to cut the pie as the boys poked their heads in.

"I'm sure the boys could eat a piece of pie."

Henry darted to the door and waved them in. "Take a seat. Ma's pie is the best you'll—"

"Henry, let ever'one get settled, please. I'm sure they all seen pie before an' know what to do with it."

She stopped for a moment, holding the knife in the pie, when all of a sudden she let it go and stood up straight. "Excuse me, ladies, would you be so kind as to serve the boys? I need to step outside fer a moment."

She quickly walked out. The boys all paid attention to the pie, forgetting where they were and why.

Clem stepped out and watched her pace around the yard, arms crossed over her chest. Turning, she saw him and came back to the porch and into the house. He stepped down into the yard and was leaning against the hitching post in front of the house when he heard something behind him. Pivoting, he looked up and there was the lady standing on the porch with two cups of coffee.

She set them on a little table between two chairs and seated herself, then beckoned for him to come up. He just stood there staring at her.

"Mister, would you please come up here an' sit down. I would 'preciate it if you would. I don't want to stand down there in the yard, but I'm willin' to if need be."

Clem continued to stand looking up at her. "Yes ma'am, I guess I will."

He came up the steps, walked past her to the second chair, and sat down. Hands folded together between his legs, he gazed out into the yard not saying anything. He wanted to tell her about her boys but wasn't sure how to start.

She sat back in her chair looking out into the yard as well. Then without a glance at him she started talking. "I told you earlier my boys was bad. They was bad as snakes. I'm sorry fer it. I tried fer a long time to help 'em, but after a while I jist give up. They was jist like their pa. He could be nice, but he had a part that was most pure evil. Mitch was prob'ly most twenty when I s'pose I finally give up. I used to ask the Lord all the time to save 'em, an' to help me know what to do. I guess He wasn't listenin', or He had other plans 'cause He didn't change 'em. Finally I started askin' jist to help my Henry. He did that. I'm not mad at the Lord. I know whatever He does, it's right, an' good, an' just."

Tears dripped down her cheeks now. She kept wiping them away but they kept falling. "Did they git buried?"

"Yes ma'am. I am real sorry."

"Thank you, but I'm real sorry they came across y'all. I'm real sorry fer whatever they did. Would you be able to tell me, mister? I really want to know."

Clem pondered how to begin. He cleared his throat. "It was 'bout two weeks ago." He proceeded to tell her everything he could remember as softly as he could put it. He even told her about how he was going to take Henry with them but the ladies stopped him.

"I'm sorry."

"Ma'am?"

"I'm sorry. It was my boys what caused this problem, an' then you got so upset. I am truly sorry, from the bottom of my heart." She had tears streaming down her face again. She looked at him and then down to the yard.

Clem gazed at the yard, not knowing what to do. He just told her he was going to kidnap her only remaining son and now she was apologizing to him. He wanted to get up and walk around but he didn't want to upset her more.

"You can git up an' leave if you like. I know men like to walk around at times like this. I'm okay now. It was all my fault."

"No, ma'am—"

She sat up and pointed her finger at him. "Yes sir, it is. Please, I need to say somethin'. It's my fault Henry was out there with 'em. I shoulda kept him here at home, but I wanted him to learn to stand up to his brothers, which he would never git to do if I kept him sheltered. You were kind to Henry, I know. I know you had yer anger towards him an' all, an' I'm not sayin' you was right 'bout that, but in the end you did the right thing."

"Ma'am, it's not—"

"No! It is jis that! You didn't take him, an' you didn't turn him over to the law, who prob'ly woulda killed him sure, an' you made sure he got home. Seems to me you done right by him, an' don't start up with me agin, not now. You saved me too."

Clem didn't know what to say, so he didn't say anything, he just sat there.

"What was I gonna do without my Henry to take care of me? You seen him with the horses by now. It's jist not natural. The Lord did that fer him. It's jist not natural.

"Simple he may be, but he's smart in his own way. So he could make a livin', prob'ly a good one. An' he's been sweet on this girl that lives the other side of the valley. She's a little simple too, like Henry. An' I've never been sure I should let 'em start courtin', but now that his brothers is gone... Well, now he can be his good honest self, an' if they have young'uns, don't mean they'll all be simple like them two. Not all mine was, an' her brothers are not. Her pa, Axel, spoke to me 'bout it before, but I was always scared 'bout Henry's brothers. Folks round here knowed they was bad but they didn't know how bad they was. Axel knows Henry's not like that, an' who else is there fer his daughter? We both agreed Henry could provide with what he knows 'bout animals. Mister, you saved Henry an' you saved me an' Axel's little girl too."

She paused for a moment. Clem just stared into the yard. Then she started up again.

"Anyways, now my Henry can be the man I know he can be.

Honest, an' happy, an' a good father to his young'uns. Help round the town. An' if his young'uns turn out to be simple too, well then that's the will of the Lord. An' I'm not gonna argue." She began to cry quietly again.

He waited for her to get herself under control. "Thank you, ma'am, yer a kind woman."

"You don't know who yer talkin' to, mister."

"I b'lieve I do. I've been with Henry now 'bout two weeks an', well, he is the talkative sort."

"Oh, what did he tell you?"

She was staring at him now, eyes still wet.

Clem looked back at her. "He told me you love him very much. An' that you were outnumbered with hard men, includin' his pa. An' that you had to do what you had to do in order to save yer son from gittin' killed."

"He told you 'bout that?"

"Yes ma'am."

"An' you still brought him here?"

"It's his home. Where else could we take him?"

Her eyes wandered and finally settled on staring out into the yard. "Whatta 'bout California. He could start over there."

"We talked 'bout that. We all knew, an' you know too, he wouldn't go without you."

She stood up all of a sudden. "You never drank yer coffee. Let me git you another cup. Those ladies in there are prob'ly waitin' on us."

Taking the two cups, she walked back into the house. Clem wondered when he had a conversation like that before. *Had to be with Veda. Sure takes a lot out of a man.*

She came out with two new cups of coffee and, putting them on the table between them, she sat down again. Mary and Sandy followed and looked around before Mary sat against the porch rail and Sandy leaned against the house itself. The boys filed out with Henry and ran over to the barn.

"Ladies, why don't you git yerselves a chair an' sit."

"Thank you, but we've been sitting for two months now; it does me good to stand a while," Sandy replied.

"Suit yerself." She turned to Clem. "Drink yer coffee."

"Yes ma'am, it's good! Thank you."

"Yer welcome." She watched the boys go running from the barn, around to the corral, then out to the pasture to look at the cattle, then back to the barn before disappearing inside.

"Them boys got energy to burn," Henry's ma remarked.

"Yes they do. They're jist boys. An' yet it wasn't but a month ago I had 'em in battle with a band of Cheyenne Indians intent on killin' 'em."

She turned sharply toward Clem. "Why would you do that? They's jist boys. Not but fifteen years old meybe!"

He told her about finding the Hod wagon under attack, and then how the Indians lured them away from the rest of the wagon train and attacked.

"If it weren't fer them repeaters I bought, we woulda all been killed fer sure. I shoulda known better. I jist 'bout got all them boys killed."

"But you saved that lady an' her two young'uns."

Clem didn't say anything. She decided she wanted to change the subject. "Where did the cattle come from? An' why did you bring 'em here?"

She immediately noticed this made everyone very uncomfortable. The ladies straightened up and glanced at each other and then anyplace but at Clem or herself.

She looked over at Clem and then turned back toward them, then to Clem again, as if wondering if she'd said something wrong.

Clem just kept staring into the yard, but with a little more concentration than before. "They're Henry's."

She waited a moment for something else to come out. "I see; they had no other brands er nuthin'?"

Clem eased up a bit now. "Nope, might want to brand 'em up though, so's no one would try to claim 'em. As a matter a' fact I better give him a bill of sale fer 'em. Make it all legal an' all. After all, it was me what found 'em an' brought 'em to our camp. So I guess by rights they was mine an' I give 'em to Henry, so now they're his."

"An' why did you give 'em to Henry?"

"Why? Uhh, well, 'cause. 'Cause...he saved our girls is why. That's why. Now please don't go askin' me to go into all that detail again. It was terrible an' I would rather not start talkin' 'bout it agin, if you don't mind."

The light in her eyes showed she was enjoying watching the man work his way out of his latest predicament. "I see. So they're all his now."

"Yes ma'am, they're his now. Done an' done. I got to write out a bill of sale though. Do you have any paper on hand by any chance?"

"Paper? Oh, well yes, as a matter of fact I do. It's old paper but I b'lieve it's blank." She got up and went into the house.

The other ladies watched her go inside with a little relief. They glanced over at Clem smiling and tried to stop and appear casual when she returned with some old yellowed paper.

She regarded the ladies with her eyebrows raised, then laid the paper on the little table and handed Clem a pencil. "So how much does my Henry owe you fer these cows here, hmm?"

"Cows, heifers, an' a few bulls, ma'am. I don't think we ever settled on a price." He gave a big sigh as he thought about it. "I believe what with him helpin' us to rescue them girls an' all, well, I guess I would take two good horses from the herd we brought back with us an' we'll call it all even."

"Sounds pretty generous to me."

"Generous? I dunno. Why, I thought you mighta got a little testy at me fer chargin' anythin', what with him savin' our girls an' all."

"Uh-huh."

"I figure I'm gittin' off real lean here, but then I do feel we did put in some effort, to git him back here with his cattle an' all."

"I see. Well, I'm sure he'd agree with whatever you wanted, an' he's out there havin' too much fun with them other boys right now, so I guess he wouldn't mind me sittin' in fer him an' agreein' to this contract of yers. I still think it's overgenerous, but then if yer satisfied I guess we can all call it a done deal."

She reached over and stuck her hand out to shake Clem's. He started to take it when Sandy, leaning against the house, spoke up.

"Clem, if I may. Do you really think we need two more horses?"

He stopped with his hand hanging in midair. "Mrs. Hollingsworth, I do believe we need to show somethin' in the way of a fair trade, fer all others who might happen to ask questions later on."

Sandy stood up away from the house now. Henry's ma was sitting back watching the two.

She continued. "I understand, but do we actually need to take the horses with us?"

"Ma'am? I don't unnerstand. Yer not suggestin' we say somethin' an' do the opposite? That would be, well, it might be—"

"No! Clem's right." Henry's ma raised her hand to be allowed to speak. "Please, ma'am. Mrs. Hollingsworth, is it? I b'lieve it would be better fer everyone if we did it Clem's way. I b'lieve it would be best fer Henry at least. Fer one it would help him keep track of how he ended up with the herd, jist in case he was to mention it to anyone else. An' I can speak fer him now an' say that we are very happy with the deal."

Sandy smiled down at Henry's ma. "Well, then, I have no further suggestions."

Clem adopted his famous sour expression. "Hrmmph, well then, I guess I'm glad I still git to act in the role of Wagon Master. At least sometimes. So if there's no other concerns from anyone, I'll write up this bill of sale, an' it's all done."

"Good. Henry will be delighted, an' I am too."

Clem finished writing his bill of sale and put down the pencil. "Done an' done. Now, meybe I'll have a piece of that pie, an' might I git a little more coffee with it?"

"Of course, I'll be right back." Henry's ma got up and went back into the house.

Sandy Hollingsworth looked over at Mary Williams sitting against the railing and said in a low manly voice, "Get to feel like the Wagon Master." Then she turned to Clem. "You haven't let down your mantle anytime that I know of. But I am glad that you're willing to at least listen now and then to another suggestion."

He looked up in utter surprise. "Now an' then? Why—" He stopped in mid-sentence when Henry's ma returned with the coffee and a piece of pie. Another half piece lay on the plate together with the first.

"Here, to seal the deal then." She handed him the pie but remained standing.

Beaming at getting served the extra piece, he took a big bite and talked around the mouthful. "Thank you, it's very good."

She smiled down at him and turned around to address the ladies. "So, I hate to ask this because it seems ever'time I bring up a new question ever'one gits real uncomfortable. I hate causin' a rift. But here goes anyway. How long are y'all plannin' on stayin'?"

Clem spoke up around the pie. "Oh, that's a easy one. Gotta git back as soon as we can. I s'pose we'll leave out this afternoon an' make camp where we did last night, then back to the wagons in 'bout five days."

She faced him. "Really? You can't afford one extra day? It's been so long since I had nice adult people I could talk to fer a night. Jist one night?" She turned back to the ladies. "Leave first thing in the mornin'. My Henry will escort you out of the valley. Keep you on track an' save a little time that way. It'd be mighty nice to have company fer one night."

Clem was paying complete attention to his pie now. He waved his fork hand. "Well, I'll let the ladies decide."

Sandy spoke up. "Yes, we would love to. It'd be so nice to sleep somewhere other than under that wagon, or just plain sky for once. It's been, I don't know, two months now? It all just seems to run together and then everything just goes boom! And we have something like last week. It's more than a body can take almost."

Henry's ma appeared delighted yet sympathetic. "You poor dears, I can't imagine. How 'bout a nice hot bath, an' then we can settle in fer the night an' make up some beds, fer you two anyway. You men will jist have to make do in the barn, or anywhere else you like out of the house."

Clem was finishing his pie, scraping the plate to get every last bit. "We'll be fine, make up a bed in that barn."

"Good. I'll git them boys to fetch some water so you'll be able to have a proper bath. Now in the meantime, perhaps you ladies would care to tell me jist how this all got started?"

Sandy spoke to Mary. "I believe you'd be the best to tell that story. After all, it was yours and Leah's plan that got us all started down this road. I just hope that all the excitement is over with now."

"Amen! Well, I guess I should start at the beginning."

Clem was draining his coffee and cut it short to stand and raise his hand with the cup. "Hold up, ma'am, if you would fer jist a moment. I know this tale far too well, so if you'll excuse me, I'll take a walk around yer farm while y'all sit here an' bring Mrs.—uhhhh—Davis up to date."

Henry's ma lifted her hands to cover her neck. "Oh gracious! I'm sorry! You've been here since mornin' an' I never introduced myself. I'm a terrible hostess. My name is Emiline. Emiline Davis. Folks call me Emmie. I hope ya'll do the same."

"Emiline. What a beautiful name, and Emmie, please don't apologize, it's been quite a morning for you no doubt," Sandy said.

Her head dropped and she looked down at the porch. "Well, it has been one to remember."

Sandy turned to Clem. "Okay, you were leaving. Mary, you were going to tell Emmie exactly how we ended up here in her front yard, and I will hush up."

Clem excused himself, stepped off the porch, and struck out across the yard, heading for the barn while the ladies gathered to explain and listen to the story of the Ladies Wagon Train.

3
Clem Bentone

Clem feared that the story would make him appear more than he was. Or worse than he had planned on. Either way, he didn't want to listen to them talk about him and everything they had been through already. This trip had turned into a whole lot more than he wanted, and he still feared what was up ahead.

He wandered into the barn; it was decent enough. Not big, but well built. He headed out back and around a shed, a chicken coop, a corn crib, piles of lumber that should have been stored in the barn, and odd tools and such that showed there'd not been a man around, or at least a good one, to get this place in order. Not that he ever kept his place in order much. He was always gone.

He went out into the pasture and checked on the cattle. The horses were out there now, and they all seemed to be right at home.

Fetching Cherry, he saddled her up and took her down the road to look at the countryside. It was nice to get away from all the trouble and decisions. He just wanted to enjoy the afternoon for a while.

It was getting toward evening when he returned. He found the ladies still out on the front porch when he rode up. "Must have added some to the story."

Emmie Davis waved her hand at Clem. "Oh pooh. We done heard that an' talked 'bout a dozen other things since then. We was startin' to git worried you mighta got lost when we saw you come up the lane."

"Lost? I never—well, I wasn't lost, just enjoyin' the countryside. I was enjoyin'—the day."

Mary laughed. "He was going to say the silence."

Emmie smiled. "I'm glad he didn't. You hungry? We fed the boys but it's still warm, waitin' on you."

"Yes, thank you." He dismounted and handed the reins to Brent, who had come to lead Cherry away.

"I'll fix her up an' put her in the corral with t'others, after she has sumpthin' to eat, Mr. Clem."

"Thank you, Brent, I 'preciate that."

Clem stepped up onto the porch and into the house and sat at the table. Following him, Emmie stood with hands on her hips glaring down at him, then cleared her throat to get him to look up at her. "Warsh basin is around the side, got towels an' plenty of soap. I think the others would appreciate it if you were to warsh a little under yer arms too."

He looked at her for a moment with an expression of minor disgust and then rose without saying a word and walked out and down the steps, and around to the side of the house. She watched him go.

***

The other two ladies held big smiles on their faces. She looked over at them and smiled. "He seems like a nice man. Is he?"

They exchanged glances as if they needed help to decide. It was Sandy who spoke up. "Well, he can be, I suppose. He is a very good wagon master. Thought of everything, and more even. And he's brave as a lion. Maybe a little too brave with the boys but, well, they're all he's got. I certainly don't envy him. He drinks a little, or I should say a lot more than most of the ladies would prefer."

"Oh?"

"Yes, he's gotten downright soused a couple of times, to be honest, but then, he has so much on his shoulders. He has to care for us all. Then the Indian attack. Then, well, I am so sorry about your sons."

"Thank you, but as I told Clem, sometime there's nuthin' you can do. I fought fer them boys fer so long, an' finally I jist give up. I never should have. I let 'em down. But I jist felt like I couldn't go any further. 'Cept my Henry. But them boys, after their pa died, there was no controllin' 'em at all. All I could do was protect Henry an' even then I let him go with 'em that last time."

"Clem told you, he saved those girls. It must have been God because if your Henry wasn't there, it could have been much, much worse."

Clem came around the house with his hair slicked back and his shirt sticking to him from wet skin underneath. "Did the best I can. Hope I'm not too offensive to you ladies."

"I'm sure yer wonderful, thank you. Now would you like to eat in here or on the porch?"

"Porch, please; I've always enjoyed sittin' on the porch."

"So be it. Make yerself at home an' I'll fetch you sumptin' to eat."

***

It was fully evening now and Mary was taking her bath inside. Sandy was done and getting herself ready. The beds were made up in what used to be the boys' room.

While the other boys were preparing a tub out in the barn for all of them, Clem was still on the porch with Emmie sitting in the chair beside him.

"It's been quite an' undertakin', you with all these ladies, then Indians, then my sons. An' you still have 'bout halfway to go yet?"

"Yes ma'am. I jist hope it's much quieter than it has been. This has been all the excitement I need fer one lifetime." He let out another big sigh. "It's been real nice here. Thank you. To be honest, we didn't know what to expect bringin' him here. It was a pleasant surprise."

"I suppose I unnerstand that. What with you meetin' my sons the way you did, an' hearin' 'bout me an' his pa. I shouldn't of done that, but I b'lieve I'd do it agin if he was to come at Henry like he did. I make no apologies fer it."

"No need. You did what you believed you had to. Sometimes we git caught up in things we'd never seek out an' yet we got to deal with 'em. They don't leave us alone. They demand you deal with 'em. I'm sorry. I can't imagine how hard that musta been."

"Not that hard, I'm sorry to say. He was a evil man. Bought me when I was fifteen. Bill favored me and when Ma died, Pa said he didn't need me around no more, so he sold me to Bill, an' Pa told me I'm a married woman. Bill wasn't evil always. Jist most days. Then after Henry was born he got mad 'bout him being simple an' all, an' never would leave him alone. Set the boys agin him too."

Emmie alternately crinkled and smoothed her apron. "I really think that day he was gonna kill Henry, so I ran an' got his pistol an' told him he could leave or I'd kill him. He cussed me an' started to walk towards me an' I shot him square in the chest. I cut Henry down an' told him to stay put an' don't say nuthin' to his brothers, an' I tied that rope around Bill's feet an' jumped up on horseback, an' I drug him out into the pasture into a little shallow hole."

She looked out into the yard remembering that day. Then speaking a little softer she continued, "I got some rocks an' branches over him to hide him as best I could. Didn't care to bury him. Jist didn't want anyone else to find him. Them boys figured I had sumpthin' to do with their pa leavin', but I never owned up to nuthin'. I jist kept tellin' 'em that he was gone, an' as far as I cared good riddance. They found him sometime later an' knew I done it but never said much 'bout it."

"I'm sorry."

"Me too; I shoulda done it a long time sooner. Saved Henry most of them beatins. You've seen him. He don't never do nuthin' to deserve a beatin' like he got from that man. I was a terrible ma fer lettin' him git it like that. An' lettin' Bill make them boys that way."

"Can't do what you want sometimes when yer all alone."

Emmie didn't say anything.

They sat there not talking for a while. Finally, the two ladies came out and announced they were going to bed. They said their goodnights, but Clem and Emmie stayed on the porch mostly in silence as the boys came up and said goodnight and went off to the barn.

"Guess I'm takin' a cold bath tonight."

"Yep."

"So do you like it here?"

"Not really, too many bad memories. But I can't leave nowhere. Where would we go? I got Henry to think 'bout, his future, an' Axel's daughter."

"So sell this place an' leave. You an' Henry, an' his wife, could go anywhere you want. Go home."

"I sometimes thought 'bout goin' home, but then why would I want to see that old man? He'd jist want to sell me agin."

"You could come out to California like these here ladies. Henry will have friends out there by then. You'll know these two ladies. Might even be able to take a train in a few years from what I'm hearin'. Start over. That's what these ladies is doin', what I'm doin'."

"Can't take horses on a train. Besides, I'll be gone before they bring a train as close as Denver."

"Well, maybe I jist might come back this way an' see if yer still here. Show you the way out there if you'd want to go see it."

She looked at him in honest surprise. She blinked a couple of times and then stared out into the night. "Really? You can't do that. You come back here all this way. Pshaw, why would you do that? I don't even know if I could find anyone else wantin' to go out to California."

"I thought maybe jist you an' Henry, an' his wife, if they're married. Prob'ly join up with another wagon train. I'd rather not lead another; my leadin' days are done with this one."

"That's a long way to come to help one old lady an' her son."

"Don't know what old lady yer talkin' 'bout. Besides, I got nuthin' to do once I deposit these here ladies out there where they want to go. I told 'em I'd help lead 'em around a little once we got out there. But then I'm free as a bird. Go where I want an' don't got to answer to nobody."

Her gaze flitted to him again, then back out into the darkness. "Don't know what to think 'bout that. That's a mighty big thing fer a person to do fer somebody you hardly even know."

"Oh, I think I know you all right. An' I certainly know Henry."

She stared at the barn, which had one lamp hanging out front showing the way, but otherwise it was just dark. The stars were out but wispy clouds drifted past, so you couldn't see them real clear. Clem was also looking out into the night. He was real relaxed, sitting back in his chair, legs stuck straight out in front of him.

"I think these two ladies here are pretty impressed with you. I heared yer a first-rate wagon master. I know Henry speaks highly of you, an' he's a good judge of people. He knows when people is good or bad. I can always trust him."

"Well, like I said, my wagon master days will be over soon enough. Think 'bout it if you don't like it here. This would be a short trip out an' I actually do owe Henry a favor."

"Now why do you owe him a favor?"

"Well, it's hard to say. I guess I don't know. I guess...well, he helped me. I came pert near to—well, I was gittin' tired of people an' their ways an'...I don't know that I can explain it. I don't know how to say it, I guess. I jist know I do, is all. So meybe you'll think 'bout it."

"Let me ask you a question, an' you got to promise not to say anythin' to anyone 'bout it. Promise?"

He looked over at her and raised his right hand. "I give you my word."

She eyed him doubtfully but must have decided he meant it. "Okay, I heard these ladies say yer a first-rate wagon master, but you can also be a real curmudgeon, an' that yer meaner than you need to be, an' you drink too much, 'specially fer a Christian. I b'lieve they was tellin' the truth, based on how they feel anyway, so why you bein' so ornery? You ain't been nuthin' but nice here."

He watched her throughout the question, but he never flinched. Then he got this slight amused smile that seemed to surprise her; she probably thought he was going to be real upset about being discussed like that. He looked into the night again and let out a big sigh.

"Yeah, they're right, mostly, but I got my reasons."

She kept her eyes on him. "Good, I'd like to hear 'em."

He glanced over at her. She was smiling at him now. Then he looked back out toward the barn. "You women always want to hear why someone does sumptin' wrong, so's you can help, I s'pose, huh?" He regarded her again.

Her smile grew. "Yep, now go on, so I can help."

He couldn't help but break out into a big grin himself.

He turned his gaze out again into the night. "Well, you see, it's like this. Normally, at home I'm friendly, but out here, with them, I can't be friendly—it'll git people killed, most likely me first. An' if I was friendlier I'd be havin' to have a meetin' most ever' night with someone 'bout sumptin' they don't like. If the men was along, they'd fight amongst themselves first, then the husband would have to come over an' we'd have a meetin'. Now it's jist women, an' their young'uns. That's fer one."

He looked at her. She was at full attention. That made him a little uncomfortable. He waited a moment for her to glance away so he could stop, but she wasn't moving, so he decided he had to go on. He looked out into the dark. It was always easier to talk when he didn't have to make eye contact with a person. Unless he needed to threaten them, or make sure they understood whatever.

"Well, fer another, I've had a hard enough time dealin' with folks when my Veda was alive. Now she's dead, an', well, I jist didn't care 'bout folks like I used to. I know that's wrong, but, well, folks is hard enough to like when you got someone to come home to; when yer alone, it's double hard."

He glanced at her.

She was gazing at him, waiting; she wasn't about to let him stop now. "I know, go on, you ain't finished yet."

This surprised him, and he turned his eyes back to the darkness and continued.

"So, well, I tend to drink more than I used to, s'pose a lot more. An' as to bein' mean, well, I never figured I was actually mean—rough a little meybe, not mean. Gotta tell the truth, even when it's gonna hurt, but I try to find ways to soften it. An' I'm not a Christian, not like them anyways. I'm a different kind, like they was in the Bible, not like modern folks. So, well."

He stood all of a sudden and looked down at her for a moment with a little smile on his face. "I guess I'd better git off to bed. We gotta git goin' early in the mornin'. Love yo—"

He froze. His eyes were as big as saucers! His mouth was pinched tight as if he had just bitten a lemon. He stared at her and then looked out into the dark for a moment and then back to her. She gazed up at him a little bit shocked.

He cleared his throat and started up again. "I—I didn't mean... It's just, I was married once, and it was a habit sorta, an' well, I—I'm sorry, I didn't mean to say it."

She was smiling up at him now. "It's okay. I was married once myself, meybe not to a nice man, but I unnerstand."

He still had that scared expression on his face. He smiled weakly and stepped around her, then stopped and looked down at her again. "I think it would be best if we kept this conversation between us."

She still looked up at him all smiles. "I figured."

He couldn't help but smile. She just seemed to know him. She made him uncomfortable, but also comfortable, all at the same time. That made him uncomfortable. It was confusing. "Well, we'll be up before light, gotta git goin' as soon as we can. I got 'bout sixty other people waitin' on us back at Scotts Bluff. "

"I'll have breakfast ready."

He smiled again, he just couldn't help himself. "Thank you, goodnight."

"Goodnight, an' thank you."

His smile went a little broader now, more relaxed. He stepped off into the dark.

***

She sat watching him walk across the yard, trying to follow him in the dark. She couldn't really see him but now and then. Then she saw the lamp come down and disappear into the barn.

She sat there thinking, *My my, come out to California? "I'll come back an' git you"? "What old lady?"* Well, well, well...

She broke out into a very contented grin. Then she rose and went into the house.

***

Clem was up an hour before light. When he started to jostle and poke the boys awake, they weren't so eager after a warm night in the soft hay. They eventually got up, and after stretching and yawning and tucking shirts back in and pulling boots back on, they fed the horses. Then they cleaned up the barn at Clem's direction, putting things in order while the horses ate. Finally, they saddled up the horses for the trip back to the wagon train.

Clem made sure everything started out right and then headed over to the house. He noticed the lights were on and the door was open. The sun still hadn't come up. He smiled about that, and thought it was going to be a good day.

Emmie came to the open door as he climbed up the steps. She had a cup of coffee that she offered to Clem.

Looking at the cup in her hand, he smiled. "Good mornin'."

"Good mornin', Clem. Did you sleep okay?"

"Yes ma'am, slept fine."

Henry bounded up the steps of the porch just then and made a point to smell the coffee in his mother's hand.

"Ma, Mr. Clem jist drinks tea, he don't drink no coffee."

Clem turned to Henry. "Thank you, Henry, but coffee will be fine this mornin'. We got a long way to go an' sometimes I like to drink coffee. Not ever'one drinks tea."

Emmie smiled. "I'm sorry, Clem, but I don't have any tea or I'd git you some."

He looked back at her, trying not to be annoyed at her son, and reached for the cup. "Coffee will be jist fine this mornin'. Breakfast smells good. I'm starved." He peeked past her into the house.

She stepped aside and waved him in. "Well then, you better come inside an' eat. You got a long trip ahead of you."

He entered to a table filled with pancakes, potatoes, bacon, biscuits, and jam. And he saw a pile of fried sliced beef also.

The two ladies stood at the woodstove frying eggs.

"Good morning, Clem."

"Good morning, Clem, how'd you sleep last night?"

"Like a baby, thank you." He was all smiles.

They looked at each other with the same thought. He just didn't look right like that. Sandy said, "We actually got to sleep in beds. It was won-der-ful. We took the liberty of asking Emmie if she might fry you up some beef, and of course she did. And look over there." She pointed at the table.

Mary stepped over to it and lifted a little towel covering a basket. "She stayed up the whole night and made us some wonderful fried pies to take with us on the trip back."

He grew an even bigger smile and turned to Emmie. "Thank you, Emmie, that's real nice of you."

"Weren't nuthin'. I was up, couldn't sleep. I guess with all the excitement of you folks comin' in an' all the news an' things."

The two ladies gave each other a sad look.

Emmie saw it. "Now don't start agin. I don't mean jist 'bout my boys. I mean Henry mostly. I'll be honest. I'll miss my boys in spite of who they was. But I jist can't seem to bring myself to mourn 'em. Maybe later, but I jist don't feel like it right now. I don't know. I always knew this was goin' to happin to 'em sooner or later. I'm jist glad they didn't hurt none of you nice people in the process. An' I got my Henry back safe. That's the best part."

"We are so sorry, Emmie, if there was any other way—" Sandy began.

Emmie cut her off. "There wasn't. It couldn't be helped. They brought it on themselves an' they didn't have to. It's done."

Clem was watching them, looking for a way to change the subject. "Well, let's eat before them boys git here an' take it all."

Mary glared at him. "Clem Bentone! You can just wait a moment and let them boys eat along with you."

He looked worried. "Wait? You've seen 'em eat. They won't leave a crumb fer a hungry man."

Emmie chimed in. "You hush. Henry, go git the other boys before this one here starts in an' doesn't leave 'em anythin'."

"Yes ma'am, right away." He dashed out the door and started hollering as he jumped off the porch and ran across the yard.

The boys all came crowding in almost immediately afterwards and sat at the table, staring at the food like hungry wolves. Clem cleared his throat loudly and spoke up. "Ehhmm, gentleman?"

They all turned their eyes toward him excitedly.

"Have y'all warshed up?"

"What?" It was asked in unison, pleading looks coming over their faces.

"Well? You best git to—"

Lew Hamilton was up and bolting for the door before he finished the sentence. The others quickly realized the implications of arriving late at the wash basin. They were on him like wildcats hollering to wait

36

up, or to be next at the basin.

Sitting back, Clem laughed gently at the ladies, sipping coffee when he reached for a biscuit.

Emmie took a swipe at his hand with a wooden spoon. "Now hold on, Mr. Bentone."

He looked up at her standing there with that spoon in her hand, menacing him with it. "Have you warshed up yet?"

He was shocked. "What? I never did nuthin' yet. I wasn't even workin' this mornin', jist given—"

"Hush now. Go on an' warsh up like you made them boys."

He sat a moment with his hand out to get the biscuit. His face changed expressions and then just as he tossed his napkin down on the table, Lew crashed in followed by the rest of the posse of boys. They grabbed chairs and resumed their looks of hungry wolves.

Clem stood up, causing them all to look at him again. "Y'all jist sit back and don't touch a thing till I git back." He moved from the table, seeing them all look like they just had their food taken away from them forever. He gave them a stern frown. "I mean it." Eyeing them, he backed away, turned, and strolled out the door.

The boys watched him go, then looked at each other, truly heartbroken. The ladies gazed at the crestfallen boys in amusement. "Y'all can grab a biscuit!" Emmie said, and they grabbed. "But nuthin' more!"

"Yes ma'ams" rang out around the table as boys grabbed biscuits, tried to beat the next one to the butter, and stuffed them into their mouths.

When Clem returned, he surveyed the scene of boys sitting patiently waiting for him. Suspicious, he looked at the ladies, who looked back in mock confusion, which made him all the more suspicious, but he never said anything.

He sat down and, showing his hands to Emmie, reached for a biscuit—and that's when he noticed they were mostly gone. He stopped with his hand in midair for a split second, and then he snatched two and placed them on his plate.

The boys all started to grab biscuits again when he held up his hand and cleared his throat loudly, stopping everyone. "Let's say grace fer this food."

They all reluctantly took their hands back, folded them in front of them or in their laps, and bowed their heads.

He said a small prayer and upon saying amen, he quickly reached out and grabbed another biscuit, then asked for the butter.

The boys were caught off guard, but that was only for a second before they all seized biscuits themselves. Then the noise of "pass this" and "pass that" drowned out everything else as the ladies were busy frying eggs and placing them on each plate held up to receive them.

Clem never held up his plate. He went about his business of buttering biscuits and pancakes and adding slices of beef next to potatoes without ever glancing up at the ladies offering eggs.

Finally, Emmie brought the skillet to him and asked if he would like some eggs. He looked up with a smile and sat back and thanked her.

She smiled back and slid three eggs onto his plate.

He thanked her again and sat forward while she winked at the two ladies standing at the stove. Grinning at each other, they watched the boys devouring everything they could before someone else got it.

All of a sudden Joseph sat up and said, "Wait!" Everyone stopped. He peered at the ladies standing by the stove and asked them, "Did y'all git to eat yet?" At this, everyone else looked up at them.

Emmie smiled and said, "No, but it's all right. Y'all need to eat now, and we will once you git back to your chores."

"Okay." That was all he said before he and everyone else set to the food again without another thought.

It took just a few minutes and every plate was clean. Most had taken to wiping the plates with the last of a biscuit or a pancake. Then they all sat back much satisfied, surveying the clean plates before them and their friends, and beaming.

Clem cleared his throat again and held up his coffee cup. Smiling, Emmie brought the coffeepot over.

"I'm sorry it's not tea."

"I'm happy with this, thank you."

Everyone smiled at them. He raised his cup as a toast to them. "Thank you, ladies, one an' all, it was delicious."

All the boys followed suit. "Thank yous" went around the table with clinking of cups one to another.

Clem sat for a moment after the table was cleared and then finally, reluctantly, he stood up. "I am very sorry to say, but we have to be goin' now or we're gonna be late. We've spent far too much time already, but it has been wonderful, an' I believe no one is in a hurry to leave. But we really got to go."

Emmie was regarding him with her hands folded in front of her. "I know, you git goin' now. You got things to tend to, an' I don't want to be the one responsible fer holdin' you up."

"I'll write when I git somewhere, if you wouldn't mind."

"I'll find someone to read it to me."

He turned and walked out the door, hollering at the boys to make things ready.

They already had.

The ladies stayed inside and finished eating and insisted on helping clean up in spite of Emmie's protest. Finally, there was nothing else to do but say their goodbyes.

They walked out to where the boys had the horses near the porch saddled and ready.

Clem sat on Cherry and grinned at the ladies as they came out. The ladies smiled back. He looked down at Emmie, who was standing on her porch watching and smiling. He touched his hat, turned Cherry toward the entrance to the ranch, and started to walk her out.

Stepping down to the ground, Emmie followed them. Henry walked amongst the horses, reaching up and shaking hands with the boys and saying goodbye for the hundredth time, before returning to his mother's side. He waved at the boys and they waved back at him.

As Clem reached the edge of the ranch, he turned in his saddle and waved to them. Henry squeezed his mother's hand. "I knew he would, Ma, I knew he would."

Emmie didn't say anything; she just waved back at Clem.

He moved back around and then she waved at the two ladies, who had turned to wave at her. And then all the boys. She kept watching Clem.

Just as he was about to disappear into the trees covering the lane, he turned in his saddle to glance back one more time. He raised his hand and was gone.

She stood with her hand up until the last one disappeared into the trees and left it there for a moment longer. Then she turned and looked up at Henry. Her eyes filled with tears that she had to wipe away. "Well, Henry. We got work to do, startin' with goin' to see Annabel Reinhart. Whatta ya say to that?"

4
Starting Over

Sandy Hollingsworth came up beside Clem on his horse. "Clem? We should be back in camp by tomorrow, shouldn't we?"

"I s'pose."

"Emmie turned out to be real nice, don't you think?"

"Yep, an' if you'll excuse me, I got to keep track of where we are." He nudged Cherry to put himself a bit further out in front of the little group.

They were riding back northward through the westernmost part of the high plains. East of them was the great grasslands of Kansas and westward the foothills. The footstool of the great Rocky Mountains of Colorado. This country had a rugged beauty of prairie land broken up by deep canyons filled with a mixture of scrub oak and pine.

Sandy called after him, "Oh, I'm sorry! I'll leave you to your thoughts." She held up and let Mary catch up. The ladies exchanged big smiles.

"It'll be nice to get back home."

"Home?" Sandy was confused. "Oh! You're right. The wagon train is our home for now."

Mary nodded. "For what, maybe three more months, maybe a little more?"

"I suppose. So how are you getting along?"

"Oh, I'm having the time of my life sleeping on the ground, doing laundry when I can get to a creek somewhere."

"Cooking outdoors, beans, bacon, and biscuits."

"And Mr. Clem Bentone, he makes everything better."

"He does help."

Mary laughed a little now. "I know. He tries to make it better. We asked him to take us across."

Sandy looked at her in an odd way. "Frankly, I never thought he would've agreed. I was surprised when Leah told us she found someone."

"Yeah, well...he agreed, that's the main thing."

"You said that in a funny way. Did Leah have to talk him into it at the last or something?"

Mary gave her a knowing look. "Something like that. If you remember when we first met him, he was even grumpier than he is now."

"Oh, that first meeting, when he tried to scare us all away. I thought that was a strange way for someone to introduce themselves, but I figured he was trying to eliminate the scaredy cats who would want to leave after getting started. I was so glad no one left—showed him we're strong enough."

"That's right. We've had Indians, kidnappers...it has to be better from here on out. I think he was worried more than he needed to be."

"Probably. Something tells me, though, he's going to be in a little better mood from now on till we reach California." Sandy grinned.

"Mrs. Emmie Davis?" Mary raised an eyebrow.

"Mrs. Emmie Davis." They both laughed. "She seems to be a wonderful person."

"And they seemed to hit it off all right."

"And they're both single now, so there would be nothing wrong, if two people were attracted to each other." Sandy glanced ahead at Clem's back, now quite a few yards in front.

"Think of the irony. Clem was going to kidnap Henry and then he never would have met her!"

They laughed again.

"This has been a strange trip. I wonder if they all go this way," Sandy remarked.

"It would explain Clem C. Bentone."

They laughed again and kept up this banter until they stopped for the night.

***

"Mr. Walt, how far are we from that Oregon Trail?"

Walt looked over at Zebulon riding next to him in the first wagon this morning. Billy was driving the second wagon with Lizzy at the reins of the third and poor Sergio as a passenger in the last driven by Jodi Mesto. Harvey rode herd, keeping the horses following the little wagon train.

They were almost at the base of the Rockies now and the heavy pine forests were giving way to the scrub oak of the high plains.

"Should see it in a day or two. Gittin' anxious?"

"Yes sir, an' a little worried 'bout who else we'll run into out here."

"Zeb, I think they're behind us fer good. But we need to keep a good lookout jist in case. Might be we run into somebody else. Might be they grabbed them ladies by now."

"You think they might have?"

"No tellin'. When we git back to the trail we'll start to ask around again."

"There's people to ask there?"

"Oh yeah, we'll meet lots of people on the trail before this trip is over."

***

Eddie Hod saw Michael standing just outside of the wagons looking over at the hills that Clem and his troop had gone into. Walking up beside him, he stood there gazing at the same scene as Michael, who for his part never turned from his vigil.

Eddie stood in silence for a moment with his friend and trail boss, just staring at the sky starting to darken in the distance, the hills, and the tops of the trees that grew below alongside the river.

"When do you expect 'em back?"

"I really don't know. Mr. Clem won't be dawdlin' on the way. He'll want to git goin' agin. I want to git goin'. Fort Laramie is jist a few days away, then the Rocky Mountains, an' then the desert. Never seen desert."

It was about six o'clock in the evening when the outriders first spotted Clem and his bunch. Watching this group come up from the south, they wanted it to be them but knew they would have to wait to confirm before letting anyone else know. Finally there was no doubt. Oscar took off to tell the others, and Joseph rode out to meet them.

***

Clem had been walking around the camp for a while now. He had gotten something hot to eat and was making the rounds, getting a feel for how the ladies and the children were holding up.

Michael had let him walk, leaving him to his own thoughts. They had their initial meeting after they first arrived, and then Clem wanted to walk by himself, so Michael found other things to do.

Now Clem returned to him. "Ever'thin' looks good. You done a fine job while we was gone. 'Preciate that. I'm goin' to bed. I'll see you in the mornin'." Clem was tired, physically and emotionally. It had been a strange trip.

"Yes sir, goodnight. Good to have y'all back." Michael left Clem preparing his bed next to Hugh's wagon and strode away toward Eddie, who was watching them from his campfire.

***

"Well, what'd he say?" Eddie asked Michael.

"Not much, that's typical though. But he seemed happy—for

some reason, that seems odd to me—anyway it'll take a couple of weeks to find out ever'thin' I can 'bout that trip. We'll git more info from the men an' the moms than we'll ever git from him. We're up early again; you got first watch covered?"

"Yep, we're good. I'm up till midnight, then Lester's watch captain. He's on till four, then he gives it to Gabe."

"Good. 'Night."

"'Night." Eddie headed to get a cup of coffee, and then on to his horse to go out and start his round as watch captain.

His head was healing. He felt good. He still had a nasty purple scar from the Indian attack that he tried to cover up with his hat, and people were kind about it. He knew he'd get a lot of looks in Fort Laramie, but there was nothing he could do about that. Just tell them the truth. It was a great story. Then he started thinking about his dad and the story turned sad. He loved his dad.

He mounted up and rode out into the night.

***

"Good mornin', Mr. Walt."

"Mornin', Zeb, thank you." He accepted the coffee offered.

The cup was warm in his hands, and that felt good on this cool morning. He looked toward the eastern sky as the deep reddish orange of sunrise started to lighten into purple hues just before the sun appeared over the horizon.

"Mr. Walt? How soon till you think we see someone?"

"Prob'ly today, by tomorrow sure. The trail gits pretty busy, 'specially movin' west, I s'pose. I haven't spent a lot of time on it, mostly crossin' over headed north or south."

"So how do we ask folks we see 'bout them ladies?"

"Well, we'll jist ask if they seen any wagon train with nuthin' but women an' young'uns along."

"What if we ask the wrong people?"

Walt glanced up at him. The boy looked worried. "I know, we jist have to play it by ear."

"Think we'll find 'em?"

Walt gazed eastward down the trail. They were camped just off the side of it where the mountains gave way to a large, flat plain. The road, the Oregon Trail, wandered off toward the fort and disappeared over the edge of a hill.

"Yes, I don't know why, but I do, an' I can't tell you where we'll find 'em. But we'll find 'em one way or another."

Harvey walked over using the cane one of the ladies grabbed from the miners. He was mighty glad they did. "What's the powwow 'bout?"

"Talkin' 'bout the next step of our plan with Zeb here."

"Okay, Mr. Zebulon, what's the plan?"

"Good mornin', Mr. Harvey. I was askin' Mr. Walt what we do next."

"What'd he say?"

"Start askin' whoever we meet if they seen anyone."

"An' if they have?"

"I don't know; Mr. Walt?"

"Well, depends on what they say. I'm sorry, but I say we should head back to Fort Casper—they should know somethin', or at least they should have heard of 'em, if they even really exist. Beginnin' to wonder."

"If they haven't?"

Walt looked at Zeb and sighed. "We've been back in them mountains long time. If our ladies haven't met them outlaws yet, then they've prob'ly been past here by now, an' if they have met 'em, we're jist too late an' I—I don't know what we'll do. Harvey, what'dya think?"

"I think shot up like we are we can't fight off them women we're tryin' to save let alone a gang of armed men. Hopefully, we find the ladies before they do."

A new voice entered the conference from behind the men.

"Before who does what?"

Harvey turned to regard his young friend. "Hey, Billy. Jist talkin' 'bout what's next."

"What's next?"

"Head east, find the ladies, evade the outlaws, live happily ever after."

Billy smiled. "Good, let's git sumpthin' to eat an' head out after 'em."

***

Michael and Clem were riding out in front of the wagon train, their preferred place when Michael wasn't making his rounds.

They rode along quietly admiring the majesty of the high plains— the rugged canyons, the rolling hills with the grasses reluctantly giving way to scrubby sagebrush. Cactus with their beautiful pink and purple flowers began to appear. And off in the distance those Rocky Mountains. They didn't make Clem feel any better.

Every so often Michael would pull off and make another turn around the wagon train, talking to the ladies and the children. He made sure the wagons were being handled properly, asking how they were holding up or if anyone needed maintenance, even though every night Clem and Michael inspected a couple, trying to keep ahead of things.

After making the rounds he would head out to his outriders and talk to them, then back in toward the herd drivers, and then finally back up to Clem.

***

Just after noon, Michael was back with the wagons while Clem was out checking the other outriders, questioning them on what they observed. Ever since the night those two Cherokee decided not to kill the boys but teach them instead, he used every opportunity to quiz his men and subtly remind them of just how dangerous this land could be. Tom Williams and Eddie Hod were the outriders in front—the best place to be in the whole wagon train as far as the men were concerned.

"Eddie, take a look over there."

"Where?"

"Over there, over that hill that way. Whatta ya see?"

"Why don't you jist tell me what you think it is. Oh, the fort! You think it's the fort!"

***

Clem had the wagons circled up that evening with the fort off in the distance clearly in sight. Several of the ladies had expressed their desire to push on through the night and make camp there somewhere in the early morning hours, but Clem either ignored them outright or simply insisted on staying one more night on the plains—partly just to reinforce the fact that he was in charge and not about to start listening to anybody's opinions on anything where he had already made up his mind.

He called a meeting that night after everyone had eaten and was trying to get settled in. This always irritated most everyone because he could have done it earlier, long before they were trying to settle children down after letting them have some free time to play from so many long hours in the wagons.

"Ladies, I wanted to call this meetin' to answer the many questions I would be gittin' from ever'one if I didn't tell you all first. So, 'bout the fort. There is no fort. Never been one as far as I know. It's jist a town that grew outta a tradin' post."

He started to pace back and forth a little. He hated having to hold these formal meetings. "There is a garrison stationed there, so I s'pose that's why they call it a fort. When we arrive you'll notice it looks jist like most small towns 'cept fer a long white two-story buildin' what sorta dominates the town. That's the barracks where the soldiers are bivouacked. I don't know where the officers live, never asked. S'pose in several of the houses near there. There are several stores and a couple of saloons, and two liveries, obviously one jist fer the Army. I s'pose there's a church or two. Never asked 'bout that neither. Like I said, not

48

much different than any small town."

He stopped now and purposely looked around to see if anyone was even paying attention. At his last meeting he noticed the ladies seemed decidedly disinterested. Tonight at least they appeared to be listening—and a little irritated—but that never bothered him. "We'll be stayin' jist two days. We already got plenty of rest and we need to git movin'. Them Sierra Nevadas is waitin' on us an' I don't want to head up inta them anywhere near late fall or early winter. Snow will kill us. So that's all I got. I'm goin' to have a drink an' git ready fer bed. If you got any questions, bring yer own cup."

With that he turned and headed over to Hugh's wagon, where he was making his home on this trip.

Everyone stood watching him for a moment, trying to decide if they really needed to put up with him anymore tonight or just let him go. They all decided it wasn't worth it and went back to their own wagons.

***

The wagon train pulled into Fort Laramie, Dakota Territory, seventy-four days after they started. They had been some of the hardest seventy-four days Clem Bentone could ever remember: an Indian fight, a kidnapping, and then taking Henry home.

Now he did become mighty fond of the widow Emmie Davis, and in a very short time. They just seemed to fit with each other. But that only added to his worries.

5
Dakota Territory

The day Clem's wagon train pulled into Fort Laramie, Walt's four wagons were about a week west, headed straight for them.

They had waited two days at their camp looking for someone on the trail with any knowledge of the Ladies Wagon Train. They didn't see anyone. Not from either direction. Finally, they all decided to head eastward back down the trail to make one last attempt to find them.

"You heroes comfortable back there?" Jodi chuckled to herself. She just loved digging at them.

Walt decided he had enough. "I can't see nuthin' from the back of this wagon. Hold up, I'm comin' up."

Jodi stopped the wagon. As he was getting up, the wagon jerked and Walt lurched forward. He grabbed the back of the seat just as it stopped and slammed him into it.

Jodi looked around at him. "Oh, I am sorry! Dumb ol' mules don't know when to stand still, an' I should be watchin' better."

"Yeah. No problem." He looked up at her, grinning at him while he steadied himself. "Please put the brake on while I climb up."

"Oh, you mean this here thing? Gladly."

He hollered out to everyone else, "Let's take a break. I know I need one. We all can use a little walkin' around some, I s'pect, an' we'll move on after we git a little somethin' to eat."

50

After the wagons pulled to a stop at the base of a low, grassy hill, Walt hiked to the top of it and disappeared over the crest.

Lizzy walked up to Jodi. "You better let him be. I'm sure he's tired an' still mendin' from his wounds, so jist meybe he'll want a little quiet fer a while."

"What are you sayin'? You sayin' I'm botherin' him?"

"Yes, I am. So you need to back off. As a matter of fact, you've been on the lead wagon more than yer share, so you can go ride in the back of the last one, with Mr. Sergio. I'm sure you'll be able to entertain him."

"He don't even speak English."

"He speaks it very well."

"Not when I'm talkin' to him."

"I'm not surprised."

Jodi gave her a sour look. Lizzy returned it with her own sour smile.

A few feet away by another wagon, Billy looked at Harvey. "We can't leave her here, can we?"

"No, my friend. Maybe...no, we can't do that." He let out a big sigh and shrugged.

Sergio watched the two of them discuss his impending situation. He was able to move on his own now if he took it slowly. As he eased out of the wagon, he grumbled, "What are you two complaining about? I have to ride with her now."

"Yeah, sorry, we all need to take our turn at the rack."

Billy eyed Harvey with a puzzled expression. "The rack?"

"Never mind. We all have to take our turns ridin' with her. Sergio fer the next week."

"Week?"

He looked at him. "That's fairest; we got a long way to go. Then we'll start switchin' off."

Sergio shook his head and started to walk over the hill where

Walt went earlier. "This quest just got a lot harder."

***

Sunrise was about an hour away and Fort Laramie was two days behind them. Clem was stretching and surveying the group. The men were at their positions and ready to start pushing the herd. Mounting Cherry, he gave her a nudge to walk her out, and they set off.

They all felt pretty good beginning the next part of their journey, even though Clem made sure they all understood the trail was going to get tougher, but he wasn't expecting any more trouble. That's what he told them anyway.

Leah and several others had different ideas: trouble was waiting for them.

They knew the Rocky Mountains were coming up soon, and that was the most probable site for an ambush to take place, in their minds. No one said anything to anyone that hadn't already been mentioned in the informal meetings they had started holding prior to leaving.

They had become real proficient at getting ready so early, and most were up by the time the boys arrived.

That left them time before climbing into the driver's seats to check with each other to see how they were doing or if anyone needed to trade out the young'uns for a time, or to let the young ladies trade wagons and ride together to have a chance to talk. Or sometimes the mothers would double up and let the older daughters drive a wagon themselves. Anything to break up the monotony.

Clem was glad for it—anything to help. Morale was always a major problem on such a long journey. Bringing together so many different people, making them share their lives in such close quarters, and under such tough circumstances, driving wagons pulled by two or four or even sometimes six mules at once, day after day, mile after mile, with no end anytime soon.

Anything they did to keep themselves happy and that didn't slow the wagons down was just fine in Clem's eyes, even if it meant keeping that stupid piano.

***

The Ladies Wagon Train was on their way, again.

"What's our next destination?" Michael had ridden next to Clem for a while now and could tell he had been lost in his thoughts, but Michael was ready to make another round of the wagons, and the ladies and his men would be asking him.

"Next? Fort Casper, 'bout four long days. I want to push 'em a little more now 'cause we got behind, an' that'll catch up to us when we hit the Sierra Nevadas. They can git snow in September easy, an' if we git caught in it we can be in real trouble."

Clem looked around as if getting his bearings. "So we got Fort Casper, then we'll leave the Platte an' start followin' the Sweetwater River, an' on to Independence Rock an' a real surprise fer you there—ice, under the grass."

"Ice? Out here?"

"It's true. There's ice under there. I got no idea how it got there, or how it stays, but it's there an' we'll dig up some when we arrive. Have a cool drink of sumpthin'.'"

"I'm continually surprised by what we find out here."

"It is kinda amazin'. Then we're on to the Devil's Gate, an' then the Rocky Mountains. It don't git any easier."

"Devil's Gate? Why they call it that?"

"Don't know; gotta call it sumpthin', I s'pose."

"Yeah, s'pose. So we're goin' through them high canyons in them Rockies I heard 'bout?"

Clem looked at Michael and smiled. "Most people think that. No, it's jist a real high, flat pass called South Pass; don't know what it's south of. Not really a hard climb neither, jist a real long, steady pull, an' then you wouldn't even know we was over till you look back. It's a gentle slope but the animals feel it all right, an' folks do too. Don't know why, but folks is known to git sick up there; strange, that. Anyways, we're halfway then, or close enough to call it that."

Clem stopped talking and thought about that. *Halfway.*

The idea always made him feel a little queasy, and it wasn't the pass neither; it was the thought they still had just as far to go as they'd come.

He snapped out of his thoughts. "I thought we'd lose at least a couple of young'uns by now, or a couple of the ladies to the cholera or accident or sumpthin'; I'm surprised by that too. Bunch of things surprised me with these ladies, but other than Mrs. Saddenwasser we lost no one, an' that was jist evil men at the wrong time." He shook his head. "All in all I say the Lord does seem to be with us so far."

"Yes sir, hallelujah."

"HalleluYah is right."

***

The thick prairie grass and soft rolling hills of the Midwest were gone now, replaced by grasses growing in tufts and bunches, sagebrush, and the reddish buttes and brown hills of the West.

It was why so many people used oxen—because the grasses went away and the forage was harder on horses and mules.

Clem was confident that if you took care of your animals, keeping them fresh, changing them out often, they would hold up until they made it across the desert to the Sierra Nevadas. That was why he brought extra mules along and kept them in the herd in spite of the extra work and enticement for Indian raids.

It was a calculated gamble, but not having any men, and having all these women, he wanted speed. He would gamble on less brute strength.

***

Dickson's men arrived at yet another little protected hollow up in the hills, overlooking the trail near where the Platte and the Sweetwater Rivers came together.

Just below their camp, the trail started off by leading whoever was on the trail into a constricted area with the river on the far side and the hills closing right down against it on their side.

At the eastern edge of his spot was one particular little mound that jutted way out, causing the trail to bend around it before coming into the small plain. They would set up in the middle of the trail so their ladies wouldn't see them until they came around the hill. Then it would be too late.

If they had to attack, Dickson's men would be able to kill the ladies in the lead wagons quickly, and then the whole wagon train would come to a stop. If the wagons decided to sit still and wait them out, the men would be able to climb the hills swiftly and have the advantage of shooting down on them.

They really had no escape. The best they could do was come out into the plain and circle up to try to withstand the attack. Or give up. That's why he had the white flag. To stop them and let them see they had no hope.

From their camp up in the hills they had a great view of anyone or anything approaching from either direction. It was the perfect place to finally make their move, where all the planning would come to a head. If it was to be a war, they got a fine place to start one.

The camp was only two days by wagon train west of Fort Casper, or one long day by horseback, but he felt that was far enough that they didn't have to worry about any help coming from there. No place was perfect, but Dickson felt real good about his selection.

***

The second wagon train, the one carrying the four new friends and the ladies from the mining camps, was headed east toward Fort Casper and was about two days away. They were slowly rolling along looking for signs of a fight and trying not to make such good time that they might miss something.

They never did notice they were being watched by several men up in the bluffs.

***

"Do you think we should take 'em? Wouldn't hurt to add some more women to our haul, would it?" It was Fred speaking. Ralph, Jack, and Frank all looked at each other; then Ralph spoke up.

"Yes, Fred, it would. Look, they got four men with 'em. You think they're jist gonna give up an' let us take 'em?"

Fred shrugged. "Jist a thought. We got a few days till our ladies git here. It would be done an' the bodies carried out of the way before the sun sets."

"We're too close, Fred. Jist let it go on by."

"I'll let Dickson know 'bout 'em an' see if he has anythin' to say."

"Do that."

He walked back to his horse, mounted up, and rode off down a gap in the back of the hills. Turning eastward, he headed to the main camp just back of the buttes and came in to see the men watching the little wagon train.

"Hey, boss. What'dya think 'bout us takin' 'em out? It wouldn't take long. They got some women we could use an' add to our group we're gonna sell."

Dickson turned to look at Fred as he dismounted.

"Thought 'bout it. But I don't want nuthin' to disrupt our plans now. Not when we're this close. Our wagon train will be here in meybe six days. I wouldn't want someone else comin' along an' snoopin' around lookin' fer their friends. Jist let 'em go—their good fortune."

Fred's face grew dark. He looked down, then around, and tried again. "Okay, if yer sure. I jist thought we could take 'em an' it would be all over before suppertime, real easy."

The men were looking at the two of them now, wondering if Dickson would want to do this.

Dickson looked annoyed but then... "You know, Fred, when I think 'bout it, yer right."

Now Fred's eyes lit up. "Yes sir, now yer talkin'." He turned to the

56

other men and waved his hand at them to get to their horses. "Let's go git 'em, boys."

They started to rise from their spots, some overlooking the trail and others around the campfire, but then they hesitated and turned to Dickson. He was standing up with a determined look on his face. "No, let's not go git 'em, Fred. I was bein' sarcastic; I already said let 'em go. I meant it."

Fred stood there glaring at Dickson. He'd been made a fool of. Glancing around, he saw everyone else was grinning at him.

"Fred, you got it?" Fred looked back at Dickson. Dickson had his hand resting on the handle of his pistol in his holster.

Fred's hand started to move toward his own gun. When Dickson saw the motion he immediately gripped the handle fully, ready to pull if Fred didn't stop.

Fred noticed Dickson's move, realized what he was doing, and stopped. He slowly raised both hands. "Yeah, I got it. We leave 'em alone."

Dickson didn't change his countenance or move his hand. "Good, now git back to t'others an' make sure they got it."

Fred didn't say anything more. He returned to his horse and glanced at the men who were obviously tense and watching him. No one was smiling. They all stood where they were and watched him mount up, turn his horse away, and head back to the other camp.

Dickson watched him ride out, then looked back over at the men. He still had his hand on his pistol. "Good, now we all unnerstand each other. Unless there's someone else who wants to talk 'bout my decision?"

No one said anything.

"Good." He walked over to the campfire and poured himself a cup of coffee. "Good."

***

"Walt, did you see a wisp of smoke up in those hills?" Selma was looking up enjoying the ride when she thought she might have seen something.

Walt drove the second wagon today, behind Sergio, who was in the first one. Selma Yule had joined the group during the third raid on a miners' camp.

"No, did you see sumpthin'? I can holler up at Sergio, ask him to stop."

"I don't know. I was worried 'bout Indians, to be honest. Don't they use smoke signals or somethin'?"

"Yes ma'am, they do, but they're fairly pronounced. I can't read 'em, but you certainly would know when yer lookin' at one."

"Okay, I guess I was gittin' worried fer nuthin'. What's next?"

"Fort Casper."

"How much farther is it?"

"We can be there early day after tomorrow, I think. We can ask 'em if they seen anyone. I don't know, meybe they haven't gotten this far." He sighed. "We'll talk 'bout it when we make camp tonight, but I think we should give it one more day an' ask at the fort an' then look at our plans agin. We're this close."

6
Flag of Truce

The cavalry captain's coat was so thick with dust it had actually become part of the very fabric, changing the color from a straight deep blue to a grayish blue. It had been brushed repeatedly trying to clean it, but to no avail. He started thinking it was the dust that held it together.

He was thirty-five and had dark hair with just a wisp of gray at the temples, and he was tired. It was a hard life out there, and the increasing Indian raids weren't making it any easier. He was happy to be moving the fort closer to Fort Laramie.

Walt had asked if he'd seen any wagon trains in the last couple of days with a whole lot of women and no men.

"No, sir, we haven't seen anything unusual, but then we've been mighty busy ourselves lately. Indians been causing a real ruckus, and frankly I'm getting worried. It's not a good time to be traveling in such a small train as you got here. I'd recommend you wait until the next one comes along and join up with it. There's safety in numbers and you got no numbers, and a lot of women yerselves. You all Mormons?"

"No, sir, jist happen to be made up this way. Kinda accidental, but yer busy an' we ain't got time ourselves. We need to find our friends as soon as possible."

"Well, we ain't seen anyone like you're asking about, but they coulda come through here and we coulda been out, so we wouldn't know if they were here or not. We been out a lot lately 'cause of the Indians. Matter of fact, you're the first wagon train, of any size, that I've seen coming back from the west since I been out here."

"Really? Well, thank you, Captain. I think we'll head out first thing tomorrow mornin'. We spent too much time comin' this way as it is. Good luck with yer move."

"Thank you. You know, you should wait. There should be another wagon train along any day now. They're not coming through like before, but still, the next one should be only a day or two. Sometimes they come in groups. Groups are safer."

"Yes sir, thank you again, Captain, good day."

"Good day to you, sir."

Walt walked out of the cabin that served as the captain's office and home, then across the yard to the wagons. Everyone was taking care of chores until he walked up, when they all stopped to listen.

"Well, I think we missed 'em."

Billy and Harvey both sadly shook their heads in agreement.

Walt waited for them to say something but seeing they were in no mood, he continued. "I jist hope we're not too late now. We wasted three days and we have to make that back up before we can hope to catch 'em. We're gonna have to push hard the next few days till we git west an' find some other wagons or hopefully, with the Lord's grace, we find our wagon train."

While he spoke, Walt strode over to the fire and made himself a plate of bacon and cornbread.

Emerald came over and poured him a cup of coffee. "It was not wasted. We were so close it woulda been foolish not to come here to ask. But now whatta 'bout these Indians the captain seems so worried 'bout? Maybe we should stay an' wait fer another wagon train to come along."

"Miss Emerald, yer more than welcome to wait. No one will be upset. But we have to git goin' first thing in the mornin'. As fer the

Indians, we'll jist have to avoid 'em. We don't need any more fights 'less it's with them kidnappers."

"Well, I hope the Indians are accommodatin'."

"Yes ma'am, me too. Now if you'll excuse me, I need to git these wagons ready fer tomorrow."

"Of course, good evenin' to you."

"Good evenin', ma'am."

***

The little wagon train pulled out early the next morning—just two days in front of Clem's wagon train coming in from Fort Laramie. Walt was anxious to catch up to the wagon train that was actually behind them now.

He was going to run the wagons hard for the next few days. He wanted to try their hardest to get as far as they could while there was enough light to see. The plan was to let the animals rest once they caught up to the wagons they chased.

***

Dickson's men, camped up in the rocks, watched them go past, headed back west this time. No one asked if there was any change in plans. Though they let them roll on by, several conversations occurred as to who they were and what they were doing out here.

The consensus was that they were Mormons and had gotten lost somehow. Everyone thought that was pretty funny, except Fred. He was getting more than a little ribbing about the last time they came through. Although he took it quietly, he was keeping score. He wouldn't forget.

***

Michael had everyone up by three thirty this morning, catching many by surprise. "Come on, let's git up, we got to git movin'. Time's a'wastin'."

His mother, Leah, wasn't having it. "What are you doing here so early? We don't get up till four, which is more than early enough without you trying to keep us going with no sleep."

"Yes ma'am, new orders. We've gotten behind schedule an' we need to try to make it up as much as possible."

"Pshaw! Doesn't mean anything. We got here in just two months and we're behind schedule? I don't believe it."

"Ma, please git up. I have to git t'others up."

He walked off and encountered a similar reaction at almost half the wagons he came to.

Clem stepped out into the middle of the circle. No animals were in it tonight because of the relative safety of being next to the fort. He hollered while rotating in a tight circle, "Ever'one, you got to git up! Yer trail boss is doin' his job an' you have to honor yer pledge you made back in Independence! Now let's git goin'! We've lost valuable time. By the time we hit those Sierra Nevadas, we could hit snow. Then we'll have to wait until next May to cross over. An' nobody wants to live with me till next May."

"Amen!" He turned but couldn't see where the voice came from, but he recognized it and grinned. Mary Williams.

He started up again. "We don't have time to waste! Please, ever'body, let's git goin'!"

Sandy leaned in. "Leah, did you just hear him say please?"

"I believe I did. He must be feeling ill again."

The two ladies started to laugh a little and noticed Clem looking their way. They waved at him as he walked over to the horses. Glancing back at each other, they laughed a little easier now.

The whole camp was up and moving before long. They were feeling pretty good about themselves in spite of the possible dangers ahead and the soon-to-be rougher trail.

They would tackle both problems as they came.

The first one was the hardest. They'd have to make a decision if they came across men who wanted to basically force them to marry them, or marry someone else for a profit. And many were beginning to discount the idea that someone would try to make them into prostitutes. They felt that was just people becoming hysterical.

The wagon train had split into two camps on this matter. It was becoming a concern of Clem's, who was clearly on the one side but tried to keep himself out of that conversation.

Leah, Mary, Millie, and the other ladies of the group who planned on the survivors being turned into prostitutes instructed their sons to be extra vigilant. They asked Clem to bring them in a little closer than they used to be, and he agreed, partly because there was not so much landscape in which to hide, but also because he wanted them closer in case of attack.

The first day went by without anything to be alarmed about. They did see Indians on a hilltop overlooking the trail, so they herded the animals into the center of the wagon train by forming a three-sided box or corral.

Clem had them practicing this more often now. They couldn't keep the animals there because they couldn't maintain that formation on the trail for long, but it was wise to learn how to do it quickly when needed.

***

Jed was sitting on a rock, up on a hill, just up from the trail. He watched the road and had to shield his eyes from the rising sun. Thinking he saw a rider for a moment, he crouched down, keeping behind the rock as much as he could.

Sure enough, there were two riders. It was them. It was time. He slid down the side of the hill, jumped on his horse, wheeled it around, and kicked its sides.

He took off looking for Bill and saw him sitting his horse, right in the middle of the trail. After he waved his hat, Bill turned and galloped off ahead of him.

***

Tom Williams and Brennen Hollingsworth were out in front of the wagons this morning. They stayed much closer than before because of

Clem's orders. Coming to a bend, Brennen told Tom that he would go on up alone; Tom could wait back a little, just in case someone was around that bend.

Tom wouldn't agree. "Nope, we're in this together. There won't be anythin' anyway."

They rounded the bend, and sure enough, everything was normal. Then they saw them—twelve men on horses lined up across the trail.

They all had rifles, the butts resting on their legs, pointing up in the air. The boys pulled their horses to a stop. The men were about two hundred yards down the trail. One man in the middle raised his hand in a salute but otherwise no one moved.

The boys sat there for a moment and then veered their horses around, expecting to get shot at any minute. Kicking them in their flanks, they started running back toward the wagon train. They just turned the corner again when they saw Mr. Clem leading the wagons up.

They were right there! Too close to turn around now! They both waved their hats in the air. Clem raised his hand to stop the train and watched the boys ride in hard, waving their hats and obviously upset.

"Riders! Twelve men blockin' the trail! Jist around the bend!"

They skidded to a halt where Clem had stopped. He sat on Cherry, already looking up into the hills and across the river trying to assess the situation. Michael was approaching from behind. The wagons were about twenty feet back. He knew they heard.

Millie Hafin was in the first wagon. She didn't move but she knew the others would be coming to find out what was up. Sure enough, Wheaton Lindy soon stood at the side of her wagon, looking toward Clem and the boys.

"What's going on?" She glanced up at Millie.

"Riders blocking the trail up ahead. Better go tell the others to get rifles ready, and tell the boys to come in."

Wheaton didn't say another word. She turned and ran to Georgia Carsten's wagon, which was the next one back. Stepping away from it, she waved at the other women and the boys to come up to listen.

It didn't take but a moment and everyone in the train was gathered around.

"Riders blocking the road up ahead! About twelve of them that we know of. I saw Clem looking up into the hills, so we need to get ready and get the rifles out. Get the children inside and hunker down. We all know what to do, ladies! We'll start now and wait to hear it from Clem!"

All the women hurried back to their wagons and started giving orders. The littlest ones disappeared into the wagons. The boys held their position where they were supposed to be, and those watching the herd began bringing it up against the back of the wagons.

***

"Well, Fritz, I guess we find out 'bout ol' Clem now." Hugh had gotten down and was standing next to the driver's box of his friend's wagon, looking up at him.

"Yeah, looks that way. We're in a bad spot too. They had this place picked out, waitin' fer us to come along an' step into it."

"Well, let's see what Clem wants to do."

"I don't like what his options are: die or let them ladies git taken."

"Fritz, yer turnin' out to be a dark cloud in ever' situation."

"They're twelve men with rifles."

"They ain't killed us yet. I'm gonna kill some of 'em if it comes down to it."

"It's prob'ly gonna."

Hugh got angry and slammed his hand against the side of the wagon, startling the mules. "I ain't gonna give up none of these ladies an' none of these young'uns to the likes of them, an' I ain't gonna go dyin' without takin' some with me. There's only twelve that we know of.

I'm sure they ain't hidin' any; too many to make up a gang that big."

"I ain't sure of nuthin', 'cept—wait, here comes Clem. Let's see what he's got to say."

Clem stopped and spoke to Millie Hafin and Wheaton Lindy as he rode back alongside the wagons. They got out and followed him back.

He dismounted between Leah Knott's and Karen Roch's wagons and motioned everyone to come to where he was.

"Okay, folks, I guess by now y'all heard what's up ahead. This might be what I've been worryin' 'bout, or it might be jist a big misunderstandin'. Either way we can't sit here in this narrow area. If they mean us harm, they could climb these hills an' shoot down on us, an' then we got more trouble."

"Let's send riders back to Fort Casper to get help. We can hold out till then!" Karen Roch hollered out.

Clem turned to her. "No, ma'am. I don't believe we could. They'd git the high ground an' be shootin' down on us, an' our riders wouldn't git to the fort till noon tomorrow. Then by the time they got soldiers back here we'd be dead or gone, at least most of us.

"We can't climb them hills neither, they'd jist go higher, so we're stuck. I hafta go see 'em and see what's on their mind, and we'll go from there. When I go out there y'all follow me up, an' when you clear that bend you form a square. I want three wagons wide in the front an' the rest lined up behind. You know how. Bring the animals in but leave the back open. We don't want 'em stampedin' an' no place to go. All the men come in an' climb into a wagon. You ladies drivin' will have to lay down in the boxes agin an' drive the teams while tryin' to stay hidden. The rest git yer rifles ready."

"We're ready now, Clem." Several held up their rifles.

That surprised him. "Oh, okay, good, so you know what to do. If it all goes bad an' I'm able, I'll give a signal to bring the wagons out at 'em. You bring 'em hard. If they want to attack us then we'll not oblige

66

'em by stayin' in one place. We'll be tryin' to keep 'em at bay till we can git outta this mess. If I don't make it, Michael's in charge an' he'll git y'all to California. He knows what to do with my share."

He let out a big sigh. "Let's say a prayer."

Everyone bowed their heads and Clem said a short prayer seeking the mercy and grace of Yehovah.

"Okay, Michael, you bring 'em out slowly but keep 'em movin' forward. We should know sumpthin' real quick. You can stop if you see me comin' back, or if I give a signal to run at 'em, come hard."

"What kind of signal?"

"I don't know, but you'll figure it out."

He walked over to Cherry and mounted up.

Clem slowly rode to where the trail disappeared at the hill. He stopped and looked back. Everyone was loading up in the wagons, getting ready to move out.

Michael waved and turned to start the wagons.

Clem raised his hand in a salute and then disappeared around the bend.

He saw the riders immediately and wanted to stop, but he kept slowly trotting out to meet them. They hadn't moved. They were sitting on their horses blocking the way.

***

About a hundred yards from them, he slowed Cherry to a walk.

The men saw him approaching, and three of them came out from the middle of the group, one raising a white flag. He had it all along, but Clem never noticed it until he raised it up high, waving it gently back and forth.

Clem halted for a moment and watched them walk their horses toward him. Then he nudged Cherry again and started walking her up.

When he was about twenty yards away, he stopped again. They kept on till they were about ten feet in front of him.

They were dusty and dirty from living out in the open. He knew the one in the middle was going to be the boss, and they were killers, he could tell that.

They sat there smiling at him because they knew they had him trapped and there was nothing he could do about it.

The one in the middle brought the flag down and tossed it in the dirt in front of him.

"Well, Ol' Leather, we been waitin' fer this day fer 'bout two months now. Glad you could keep 'em comin'. You did right smart 'bout it too."

"Whatta ya want with us?"

The leader dropped his smile. "I b'lieve you know exactly what we want, Ol' Leather. We want them women. We want y'all to surrender yerselves an' we'll take over from here. We're gonna take care of 'em till we can find 'em suitable husbands to marry up with, up in the mountains yonder." He nodded back toward the Rocky Mountains. "Then we'll sell 'em to their new husbands. It'll be kinda romantic, don't you think?"

The others chuckled. The boss looked back and forth at his two men, smiling at them, and then back to Clem. His smile left him.

Clem regarded the three of them and then leaned over and looked behind them at the men backing them up. Then back again to the boss. "They're under my protection. They ain't gonna leave with you, an' they ain't gonna marry nobody but what they want to, so you can turn around now."

Dickson answered, "Hard talk fer a man as old as you, leadin' a bunch of farmers' widows. I believe we should ask 'em what they want to do. 'Cause they need to know, old man, if they turn us down, a whole lot of 'em will git killed, includin' you an' most of them boys you got with you. We know you ain't got no men, other than two ol' mule skinners."

The man leaned forward onto the neck of his horse, staring hard at Clem. "Now you need to unnerstand, old man, that yer still alive only 'cause we admire what you done so far gittin' 'em out here. But that's over now. We're not killers. We'll let you leave, right now, an' you can go tell whoever you want, whatever you want to tell 'em—I don't care—an' we'll leave you alone. But if you stay you'll end up gut shot. You'll want to leave then, but it'll be too late. We don't have to be so generous. You got no escape. If you try to send fer help, we got men watchin' the trail behind you already; they'll shoot 'em long before they ever see any soldiers out here."

Clem was trying to give the boss his hard look. He didn't want him to know how scared he was.

The man had clear blue eyes and black hair with gray at the sides and showing in his week-old stubble. A small scar branded his upper eyebrow. Clem noticed a small bead of sweat running down the side of his face.

"Fort Casper was already sendin' troops this way to watch out fer us 'cause they heard 'bout you."

"Liar." Dickson waved his arm as if to shoo him away like a small, bothersome child. "Now, no more talk. You go tell 'em to git ready or we're gonna come down hard on you, old man. You'll not be given a second chance. We didn't come out here to bargain. That there flag was jist to let you know we don't have to kill you, it's up to you."

They glanced around Clem just then because Michael was bringing the wagons from around the bend. As they emerged into the open part of the trail, they started forming into the square they were taught to make.

The men fixed their attention back on Clem. "No more time, Leather. What's yer call?"

***

Michael had the wagons in the square pattern, three wagons wide in the front, keeping them just far apart enough to prevent them from bumping into each other if they had to make a run for it. He had eight wagons on one side and nine on the other forming a long corral to keep the animals in the center, with the back end open. Walking them slowly toward the meeting in the middle of the trail, he could see three men talking to Clem about fifty yards in front of a wide row of other men.

***

Dickson knew he had them. They had nowhere to run.

Clem looked at the ground trying to think of something. Then his eyes darted past the three of them at the men behind, then off to his left and up toward the top of the little hill bordering the trail. He stopped, and then he flinched and started to smile. While holding Dickson's gaze he pointed up the hill. "Whatta 'bout them?"

Dickson was staring hard at the old man. He looked to his right and up the hill to see what the old codger was looking at.

The other two also glanced up when *bam!* Dickson heard a gunshot and flinched. *Bam!* He heard a second gunshot as a lightning bolt hit him in the chest. The pain knocked him straight up in his saddle.

Then a third gunshot split the air. *Bam!* He flinched again but didn't feel anything. His chest screaming in pain, he started to pull his own gun out of his holster when he heard a fourth shot. *Bam!*

He turned to look for Old Leather and there he was, pointing a pistol directly at him, smoke curling out the barrel.

It was all so strange, everything moving so slow. He saw Old Leather aiming his pistol straight at him. The old man had this terrible, frightened look on his face. It was so sad that Dickson almost felt sorry for him. Then he saw the fire and smoke from the barrel and felt the lightning hit him again, followed by the sound of another gunshot from somewhere way off in the distance. He doubled over in pain and heard a sixth shot.

Now he was looking at Ralph, who was falling off his horse, but ever so slowly, and there was Ralph's horse jumping out of his way as he fell. He realized he was falling himself between the two horses, but there was no sound anywhere, and he was falling so slowly it wasn't even real; it was like—nothing.

He tried to clear his mind. As he lay on the ground watching his horse jump up and away from him, he saw the sky, and there was Old Leather turning his horse around. *He shot me. He shot me! He can't do that! We had a flag of truce! You can't shoot people... It's not right. Why...you...can't...*

***

Clem had shot all three of them twice, one right after the other, in a moment of panic after a crazy idea came to him. It was his only chance. He had looked up that hill and pointed. *Please look! Please!* And they did.

He was watching the last man falling when he realized he had to get out of there.

He yanked Cherry's reins, turning her in a tight circle, and jammed his boot heels into her haunches. "Hyaaah! Run, Cherry! Save us!"

She jumped out from under him and was digging in her hooves when he heard rifles firing behind him. Whipping his reins across Cherry's shoulder, he heard more shots, pistol shots now. He worried they would shoot Cherry. "Hyaah! Run, Cherry! Run!"

***

Michael heard the gunshots, and he knew that was his signal. Raising his hat and waving it, he yelled, "Yeeaahh! Run 'em! Run 'em hard!"

Millie Hafin stood up in her driver's box, snapped her whip over the mules, and cracked the reins on their backs to get them running. They were already walking, so getting them to run was not as big an ordeal as before.

In the front middle wagon was Wheaton Lindy, with Georgia Carsten on the outside of her nearest the river.

All three ladies were standing now and yelling at their mules and cracking the reins across their backs. "Yaahh! Yaahh!"

The momentum from the mules up front starting to run and all the ladies standing, shouting, and cracking whips had the whole train running now.

The ladies in front dropped down into the driver's boxes but kept popping up their heads to yell at their mules and crack the whips, even though they were banging back and forth inside the boxes.

***

Dickson's men saw the wagons picking up speed. They didn't circle up! They were coming right at them at a full run now. The men could hear shots but no one seemed to be in any apparent danger. It was just as Dickson predicted. They couldn't kill a man.

They drew pistols and started shooting, first at Clem and then at the wagons barreling toward them.

***

Clem rode at the wagons as fast as Cherry could carry him. She was apparently unfazed when rifles from his own wagons started shooting at the men. He thought for sure they were going to kill them both!

He steered Cherry toward the three wagons coming at him and drove her between Millie's and Wheaton's wagons, right into the herd running inside the corral they made. He plowed straight into the herd, bringing Cherry to a stop almost immediately with the animals beating against her chest and sides.

***

Millie saw the three men lying in the road, but she never even tried to steer out of the way when she felt the first bump and the wagon jump. "Take that, Masser Hafin!" she yelled as she bounced into the air. She felt the back of her wagon bump and jump up. "You take that, Masser!" She bounced again and cracked her whip. "Hyyaaaahhhh!"

The two wagons next to her didn't have any room to move out of the way, so they ran over the men lying in the trail. The rest of the wagons followed the three leads, and most of those near the front of the line felt the same bump and jump. Several knew what it must have been and it made them sick to their stomachs.

The herd neither knew nor cared. They just ran on through.

***

Dickson's men urged their horses forward. Both groups were closing ground fast. Jed moved slightly to his left and Fred moved to his right as they approached the wagons. Horse followed Jed and the men split into two lines, one racing at each side of the wagons.

Willy was with Jed's group now, looking at a young woman in the back of the first wagon on his side. He could see she was fearful but determined; then he saw the rifle coming up and she fired.

Something hit him and he felt the pain instantly, but he held on to his reins and aimed at the next wagon he passed because he didn't have time to shoot that girl.

Seeing another rifle appear from the next wagon, he stuck out his pistol and pulled the trigger. He saw the rifle slant upward and then that wagon was gone past, and the next one already had a rifle firing away at him.

He felt like they were all firing at him! He got past that one, fired into the next one, and then was out of ammunition, and just like that he was riding past the last wagon following Jed.

It seemed to the men that all the rifles from the wagons erupted continually, with a cloud of smoke surrounding them as they galloped by.

Yancy, the last one on his side, saw Charley and Frank both jerk and sit up in their saddles. Charley rolled off the back of his horse and Frank fell off the side as he ran by. He was past them before they hit the ground.

Everyone was shooting into the wagons with pistols from point-blank range, but each man only had three or four shots left after firing at Clem. In contrast, rifles fired at them almost nonstop. Every wagon had a rifle sticking out the front or the back.

It was a deadly fire and four more men took a bullet.

***

Lou Hamilton was trying to aim, but all he could do was point and fire. Brennen, Eddie, and everyone else were having the same problem—they were bounced around too much by the wagons. They could see the faces of the killers as they rode by. Those men were scared! They pointed pistols right into the wagons and fired. The boys could see fire and smoke coming out the end of the pistols pointing at them. Tom raised his rifle at the next man to approach and pulled the trigger. He could see the man's face turn from excitement to horror as he sat up on his horse and fell off to the side.

***

Two were shot dead and one wounded on the one side while the other side had two wounded, but they still fired as they rode past. A third was shot and hoping to stay on his horse and not get shot again. He'd quit returning fire; he was just trying to hang on.

The riders quickly found themselves past the wagon train and rather than stopping and turning around, Jed kept them going until they reached the bend where they first saw the wagons come out.

A couple of men started to slow up, but seeing that Jed kept riding they had to follow or face the wagons by themselves. The wagons were still firing, but from the rear as they sped away.

***

Clem had both his feet pulled out of his stirrups when Cherry hit the herd, but he was able to hang on to her as the animals rushed by, even though they seemed to try to drag him off.

Only a second later he found himself coming out the back of the herd and breaking free of the animals beating against him. But then he was out in the open and all by himself looking at the riders, who were stopping and starting to regroup.

And rifles still fired at him from his own wagons behind him!

He wheeled Cherry around and whipped her with the reins again, yelling at her to get back into the herd. Once back inside, he moved to come alongside Hugh's wagon.

74

Pulling Cherry next to it, he jumped onboard shouting at him, "Gimme a rifle!"

Hugh had almost jumped on top of him when he first saw a man landing in the box next to him. Grabbing the reins again, Hugh nodded down toward the bottom of the driver's box.

Clem snatched it up, ready to fire when they attacked again. He immediately fired off a couple rounds and only then did he notice they weren't attacking. He could see the riders yelling at each other, but they weren't coming after them.

***

"They're gittin' away!" Fred shouted at Jed, but he just sat there watching them go. A small amount of blood trickled down the side of Jed's face and his sleeve turned red from a wound. He looked at his arm and then back at the wagons.

Fred waited a second and, realizing Jed wasn't going to go after them, he decided he would take charge of the men. "They're gittin' away! Follow me!"

Fred kicked his horse to make it jump out to chase them and was about two lengths away when he noticed no one followed him. He reined in the horse and sat there looking at the wagons running away, feeling defeated. Then he turned the horse around and came back to the group, glaring at Jed. "Yer lettin' 'em git away!"

Jed reached over and grabbed the reins of Fred's horse. "Shut up! It's over! We only have seven men left. And three are wounded!" He didn't think of his own wound. "We ain't got enough to fight no more! We only got four men able to fight against them rifles. We got to let 'em go!"

Fred wasn't going to hear it. He looked at everyone and hollered that they were letting them get away.

Horse hollered back at him, "Go git 'em, Fred! Jist ignore them rifles! They must have twenty on that one side, so I'd attack t'other if I was you."

"Shut up, Horse!"

Horse pulled his pistol and aimed it at Fred. "I do got one bullet left."

Fuming, Fred stared at Horse for a moment with that barrel pointing at him, then turned around to watch the wagons rumbling away. "We shoulda gone after 'em. Now what?"

Jed watched them run away into a dust cloud left by the wagons and all the animals and then around a small curve in the trail. "We'll git 'em, Fred, but not today. Dickson's plan was no good. We'll git 'em another day, soon enough."

"Well, we shoulda attacked again. Whatta 'bout Dickson an' t'others?"

"Fred! We're done. Leave 'em be. Someone will bury 'em, what's left."

***

Clem's wagon bounced along with Hugh yelling at his mules and cracking the reins. Hugh had taken a bullet in his side but seemed okay in spite of it. Clem gazed at the kidnappers just sitting there watching his wagons leave.

It looked like they'd had enough. "Keep goin'!" he told Hugh, who kept hollering at his mules while leaning to one side because of his wound.

Clem called Cherry to the edge of the wagon, then jumped onto her and moved her up between the wagons and the herd. "Keep 'em runnin'!" he yelled at each wagon he passed.

More than once a rifle came out aiming at him before they realized who it was, and more than once he thought he was a dead man.

Finally, he was between Millie and Wheaton. He shouted at Wheaton Lindy, "You need to move back into single file! Pull in behind t'others, the rest will follow! Keep 'em runnin' till I say whoa!"

They were sitting up again but never answered, just kept snapping the reins and cracking their whips and hollering.

"Hyyaaahhhh! Hyaaahh!"

Then she slowed just a little, and as Millie moved out front she shifted over and behind her. All the other wagons started to maneuver around each other to return to a single line.

Throughout the whole maneuver they kept the mules running. The herd kept alongside wherever they could fit in.

He pulled Cherry out in front of them now. Michael appeared from his right, bringing Cloud up beside Cherry.

"Keep 'em runnin', Michael!"

Michael looked over and yelled out, "Yes sir!"

Clem pulled Cherry away to his left and let her fade back till he was trailing Hugh's wagon again.

He looked behind and saw no one was coming after them.

They would be back, he knew it, and he wouldn't get away with another trick like that again.

He let Cherry move up a little and stayed there trailing the wagons as they kept the mules running.

7
Run for Your Lives

Clem let the mules run for another twenty minutes until they got lathered up and were starting to fade.

Coming up front again to Michael, he hollered out, "Slow 'em down, let's walk 'em a bit before we stop 'em!"

Michael nodded and gave the signal.

They kept going for yet another twenty minutes until Clem finally brought them to a halt in the middle of a wide plain with good visibility on all sides.

"Michael, circle 'em up! Bring 'em into a circle!"

Before long Michael had all the wagons in a circle, with all the animals inside corralled up and the men posted, standing on the ground this time right next to the wagons, rifles ready.

It was all over, just like that, and they were still free—for now anyways.

***

After circling the wagons, the women checked on their children and on everyone else.

Timmy Hollingsworth, seven years old, was shot dead. Sandy Hollingsworth sat in the back of her wagon holding him, not saying anything, just holding him in her arms. He was Brennen's little brother.

Oscar Hindle was sixteen years old. He was one of the older men, and one of the most beloved of all. Mrs. Hindle was beside herself with grief.

Hugh suffered badly from a wound and was being treated by Millie Hafin. The bullet had gone through most of his body and was easy to extract from his back. He had been offered ether but chose Clem's whiskey instead, and after being sewed up, he groaned terribly and nursed the bottle they left with him.

Leah Knott had a small wound in her right arm, more of a cut than an actual bullet hole. It wasn't very deep and she had it sewed up, using only a small amount of the ether Clem brought along.

The one who had everyone worried the most was Maddy O'Hara, Willa O'Hara's eleven-year-old daughter. She had been shot in her leg and the bullet shattered the bone in her shin halfway down.

Clem told the ladies, "The only way to save her life is to amputate that leg at the knee, an' pray an' hope against an infection."

He explained how they had to put some ether on a cloth, hold it to her face to breathe it in, and then add drops periodically to keep her subdued. Even with that, several people would have to hold her down, or have her strapped down, because she could thrash about due to the effects of the drug.

Maddy wanted nothing to do with amputation. "Ma, please wait! Can't we clamp it tight to keep it from moving? It can heal that way, crooked and all. I don't mind." She kept telling her ma it was better than amputation if she was going to get married someday, crying, "Please, Ma, no one wants a peg-leg wife. Please, let it go and see if an infection starts up. If it does, we can operate."

Her mom relented. "All right, Maddy, but I'm going to watch it intensely for the next few weeks. If there is even the slightest hint of smell, or any sight of gangrene, we'll operate immediately."

Maddy thanked her profusely.

They decided to give her the ether, but they promised her it was just to set the leg. There would be no operation.

They put her in the drug-induced half sleep Clem had told them to expect, not fully unconscious but not awake or coherent. She was placed on a couple of wagon planks put over two kegs so everyone could cluster around her to help hold her down.

Several ladies lined up on either side. They tied her arms and legs to other planks lying on the ground to help hold her in place; the ladies stood on those.

Then with Mary Williams on one end and Rachel La Fayette on the other, they pulled the leg out as straight as they could, holding her by the foot and ankle. Maddy was moaning terribly and trying to squirm out from under the ladies who restrained her.

Once the leg was straight, it was Georgia Carsten who pushed and massaged the bones into place as best she could figure they should be, while the two ladies held the leg out. Then the poultice was applied, followed by many small splints and finally lots of cord wrapping it tight to keep it all together.

Once they were done they all gathered around her, laid hands on her, and prayed for healing.

***

Clem had insisted on waiting until everyone else was stabilized before he allowed anyone to look at his wound. He'd been shot in the back near his shoulder blade, and they had to cut him open to get the bullet out.

They wanted to give him the ether, but he refused the same as Hugh. He took two long pulls on his whiskey instead and lay down on the back gate of Fritzy's wagon.

Lying on his stomach, he held a cord that was wrapped around a board on the ground, with two boys standing on it like they did for Maddy. He had the cord bound around each hand to pull against during the surgery.

Throughout the procedure he kept complaining that Mary Williams was taking her time digging around inside, as retaliation.

He continued to complain while she sewed him back up, so she finally told him to hush up or she would be forced to add more stitches.

***

They formed a burial crew and laid little Timmy and Oscar in one grave side by side with twin crosses. They were in the shade of a large rock beside the trail where they could be seen but not disturbed.

After it was over, Michael asked Clem, "Could I talk to you about what started the shootin'?"

Clem looked at him and then over at the wagons with the boys posted weapons out, looking for war, and the ladies who weren't taking care of others standing right alongside, rifles ready. He shuddered and returned his attention to Michael. "Give me some time, son. I don't know what—" He stopped in mid-sentence. Then he looked back at the wagons again. "Give me some time, please."

Michael went and told his ma and the other ladies who had been asking.

After supper Clem held a meeting. "We have to keep movin' and stay vigilant," he told everyone. "I don't think we'll see those men again fer a while, but I can't rule out that I could be wrong either."

He turned and faced Mrs. Hollingsworth and Mrs. Hindle, the mothers of the two dead boys. They stood side by side, arms crossed as if they were holding themselves, with their children surrounding them.

He took his hat off and held it in front of him. "Ladies, I do not know how to tell you, I am so very sorry. This is my fault. I shoulda—"

"No." It was Sandy Hollingsworth. She held out her hand toward him, eyes full of tears. "It's not your fault. They didn't have to attack us. They could have left us alone and let us go on our way. They're murderers. They killed my little boy." She stopped, trying to overcome her grief.

Anna Hindle spoke up. "Sandy's right." Her voice was shaking. "They could have left us alone. They killed my Oscar." She dropped her head for a moment and lifted it up to look at Clem, who was in near tears himself. "I—we understand we can't stay. We have to move on; Oscar would understand and tell me to go. He's fine now. He's sleeping and will rise again to see the throne of glory, but, today, we have to move out and leave him here." She turned to Sandy again and, reaching out, squeezed her arm. Sandy faced her and they embraced each other, crying softly with their children gathering around and hugging them from behind.

Clem turned and motioned to Michael as he walked away. He had them leave right after the meeting.

Brennen drove his mother's wagon, while Harry Hindle drove his mother's, and Tom Williams took over for Michael's mom, driving her wagon for her. Clem lay face down looking out the back of Fritzy's wagon and had them ride far into the night before they stopped again. They kept that pace up for the next two days.

Every night they had their sentries out, but not as far as before, and they changed them every two hours now.

No one complained.

***

It was evening. Everyone was busy taking care of their chores. It was just like any other ordinary night—which, after that fight, Michael felt that any ordinary night seemed so unordinary. He had been waiting for Clem to bring up the subject, but clearly Clem didn't want to talk about it, so finally he felt he needed to try him again.

"So you jist made it up right then?" Michael asked him.

"I didn't know what to do. I knew they were gonna kill me, an' prob'ly you, an' most of the men right then. I don't even know how I came up with the idea. I jist looked up there on the hill, an' then a thought came to me while I was lookin'. I don't know, meybe it was the Holy Spirit, I jist don't know, but I started to act like I saw sumpthin', and asked them to look, and they did."

He looked down for a long moment. "Then I shot 'em."

Michael watched him, wanting to help but not knowing what to do.

Clem raised his head and looked Michael in the eyes. "I never gave 'em a chance. I killed 'em under a flag of truce, Michael. That's murder."

"That's not murder! They was gonna kill us all! They gave you no choice."

"Don't matter. They was evil no doubt, but to kill someone under a flag of truce? I'm pretty sure ever'one else would call it murder."

"I'm glad you thought of it—you saved us all, at least all the men anyway. They woulda killed us sure; they wouldn't need us fer nothin'."

***

Later that evening, Michael was with his mother at their wagon.

"He thinks he murdered them?"

"Yeah, I told him it wasn't...don't know if he agrees."

"They meant to kill him, and you probably, and most of the boys, if not all of them. And we can imagine what would have happened to the girls. He saved us all. I'll give the other ladies my opinion on that matter. I can't say what they'll think, but that's what I think. Thank you, Michael."

"Yes ma'am. Goodnight, Ma."

***

The Ladies Wagon Train had been pressing hard now to get out of the area, and Clem felt vindicated going with the mules instead of oxen, for the purpose of maintaining speed.

Before they left Independence, he presumed there would be problems that would necessitate holding over for several days at a time, so he wanted to cover as much distance per day as he could. And now with the kidnappers having shown themselves openly and losing that battle, he wanted to make even more speed if at all possible.

Because of their ability to maintain such speed, they found themselves passing yet another wagon train, and this one actually moved over and back in behind them without any incident or nasty looks.

That was a little unusual because most times, people would act as if they had the right of way and the ones following should simply stay behind until breaking camp in the morning.

About ten minutes after they passed the wagons, the wagon master from that train came riding up to the front of their line hailing the leader.

"Hallo! Whose yer wagon master? Hallo!" He waved his hat in the air.

Clem was back on Cherry this afternoon because he insisted on riding as much as he could while still healing. He looked over and there, off to his right holding position just outside of his lead wagon, was this man earnestly trying to get his attention.

The man clearly wanted to talk, but he wouldn't come over, not until he was invited. Looking at him, Clem thought this was going to be trouble for some reason, but he couldn't just ignore him.

Clem finally waved at the man to come over but didn't stop Cherry to talk. He didn't have the wagons stop either, even though they hadn't taken a break today and it was well past noon already.

The newcomer brought his horse up alongside Cherry and rode silently now as if waiting for Clem to greet him. But receiving nothing other than a silent rider paying a great deal of attention to the trail and ignoring him, he introduced himself.

"Hallo, sir, my name's Silas Kuhns, from Sumneytown, Pennsylvania."

Clem glanced at the man and nodded but didn't say anything.

The new man waited.

Clem kept riding as if he were alone again.

The new man tried again. "And whom might you be, sir?"

Clem didn't say anything for half a minute, then finally looked over at him, not even trying to hide his dissatisfaction at having to entertain somebody. "My name's Clem, Bentone."

The newcomer ignored the glare. "Hallo, Clem Bentone, nice to meet you, sir."

Silas waited for the usual response in return. He got nothing. However, he was not to be dispatched so easily. "So, where are you all headed?"

Again Clem tried to ignore the intruder, and just when he was about to repeat the question, without looking over Clem let out a big sigh. "California; I don't know where yet."

The new man didn't seem to take any offense. "California? Don't know where? Well, I suppose you will know when you see it then." He got no response. "We are headed to Oree-gon—that's northward of California, you know."

Still silence in return. The new man finally gave up hope of his new neighbor talking, so he went ahead and asked about the information he wanted to know, gleaned from some riders they met yesterday. "We heard there was a real gun battle, with outlaws, just a couple of days ago."

Clem never glanced over. "Don't know what you heard, an' I don't care to discuss such things."

Silas ignored Clem this time. "We talked with riders who came up on us yesterday; they was on horseback. We heard someone killed several men. I was wondering if you heard about it or saw them, the ones who got killed. I have responsibilities to the people I'm leading out here, and any help you could give me on such things would be greatly appreciated."

Clem never acknowledged he heard him at all, so the man tried again. "I never met anyone who had been in a real gun battle, other than men from the war, of course. That's quite a different thing than what happened to these men."

Still no response, so he tried yet again. "There are soldiers that are paid to fight, and sometimes die, obviously, whereas these men were killed for reasons unknown, by persons unknown."

Then, looking around, "I presume the killers can return."

Clem kept his gaze on the trail in front of him. He glanced at the gentleman for just a second and then went back to watching the trail.

Clem finally relented, without looking at the new man. "They can return, but you seem to have plenty of men along to fight if needed. You needn't worry 'bout them. They shouldn't attack such a large train with so many men, an' as fer us, we can take care of ourselves."

Clem looked at him now. "Those men are killers, an' we aim to git as far away from here as soon as possible. We'll be ready fer 'em if they attack us, but till then, I suggest you keep vigilant."

Silas Kuhns from Sumneytown regarded Clem. "Sir, I do not understand why you're so reticent to talk, and why you wouldn't want to stay with us. Safety in numbers is what they say."

Clem realized this was already turning into an investigation.

The new man lost his friendly, smiling countenance and grew serious. "What about the soldiers back at Fort Casper? What did they say about it?"

"You'll need to talk to them. I haven't talked to anyone since we saw 'em; don't intend to."

"Sir, I do not understand you. Why would you not want to help a fellow traveler?"

Clem looked at the man again. "Out here you need to help yerself, sir, an' I don't have the time to teach how to handle yer wagon train. I tell you to be vigilant. From that you will need to make yer own plans. I'm not here to guide you neither. We'll be turnin' south soon enough. You'll be goin' wherever you plan to go, an' I think you should have nuthin' to worry 'bout from them. I can't say anythin' more."

Silas actually bristled now. "Fine. However, I do have one last question. Were you involved in that attack? Is this the frontier justice I've heard about? Did they attack you? You were able to fight them off? And what now?"

Clem looked back at him, this time openly showing him a little sympathy. "That was several questions, all of which I have no desire to answer. An' I do thank you fer yer offer, but we will be fine, an' we're movin' much faster than yerselves, an' I'll not slow down. I have discussed this with the women, an' they're in complete agreement. There really is nuthin' else to say." He kept his eyes on him, hoping to end this conversation.

Silas was exasperated. "Very well then, God's speed and protection go with you." Touching the brim of his hat, with a very sour look, he turned his horse and moved out of the way, letting the wagons rumble past him with a slight nod to Margaret Reynolds, who watched the whole conversation from the front row of her wagon box.

As the wagons passed, Mr. Kuhns nodded or touched the edge of his hat, and the ladies in turn nodded toward him.

After the last of the wagons, he waited on the herd to go by, and then he cantered back to his own wagon train.

8
Regroup and Keep Going

Jed was moving the men out of the area.

He needed to regroup and get the wounded to a doctor. None of the others cared to help them more than tear up an old shirt for bandages and give them some extra whiskey to drink.

The men never had a thought to bury those who died. They did go back to take the horses, and Jed took control of Dickson's saddlebags with the money, but the dead themselves were left where they fell.

Jed knew the cavalry would be out soon, looking for whoever done this and sending out telegraphs to all the sheriffs and marshals in the area.

He wouldn't start tracking the wagon train just yet. He knew where they were going, and they would catch up to them fairly quickly when they were ready.

He didn't dare move into some small town either, where everyone would be asking a lot of questions, so that left Denver. In Denver they could spread out and hide until he was ready to move out again. It was his best choice to regroup, get healed, and get more men, and he wanted the rest of that money from Dickson's house.

He was already working on his next plan. There were plenty of mining camps in those Sierra Nevada Mountains, maybe more than in the Rockies. So he knew approximately where he would hit them again;

he just had to pick his last spot very carefully. He wouldn't get a third chance.

***

The fourth night heading back to Denver, he decided he had to tell the men his idea, or Fred would start working on his own plans. "Okay, so here's the new plan. We'll be in Denver in a few days. We git Willy an' Bill patched up by a doc. We got money back at Dickson's house, an' I know how to git it—thank you, Dickson Ross, you big blowhard. The fastest way there an' back is stagecoach. I'll take it back there an' be back in Denver in 'bout two weeks, maybe three."

Fred heard enough. "No, why do you go git the money? How can we trust you?"

Jed was ready. He whipped out his gun, stuck it in Fred's face, and cocked the hammer all the way back. "'Cause this is my job now. You say even one more word, an' so help me you won't git to finish it."

Fred never moved. He finally looked away, and everyone knew Jed was the leader now; no one was going to dispute it.

Jed surveyed the group, then resumed where he left off. "I'll be back in plenty of time. We'll catch up, an' then pass up, our lady wagon train, an' this next time, we'll not meet 'em out in the open like this— we'll kill 'em in the lead wagons an' stop 'em before they can move. Then they're ours."

He looked at them all again. He could see they believed him. He was the boss. "I think we need to find a couple more men. So, once we git them two healed, an' we git two more, settin' up a proper ambush, we should have more than enough."

Everyone seemed to be happy, except Fred, but Jed knew it was just a matter of time for him. He had to be patient, and Fred would cause a fight with someone and either get killed outright or, if it seemed in doubt, he would help out and shoot him himself.

All the men calculated what Jed was telling them. One more chance, but it probably meant another three months on the trail, and they were all thinking the same thing: *Three more months with these snakes an' liars is gonna be hard, but it's gonna be a huge payoff in the end!*

***

It had been ten days since the little wagon train, with Walt and company, had left Fort Casper. They'd met a lot of people along the way, most everyone heading west, same as them, but no one had seen the all lady wagon train, or knew anyone that had. No one even knew of anyone bearing a close description to them.

Walt came to a conclusion that he didn't like, but he was unable to produce a better reason for his growing dread. They either missed their signs somehow, which would probably be impossible, or they were actually out in front of them. It couldn't be anything else.

He knew they wouldn't have stayed that long in Fort Laramie. They could have turned off to Denver. It was an actual possibility, but a very remote one.

As Walt drove the second wagon, he decided he would bring up the subject tonight. He hollered at Jodi driving the first wagon, "Let's pull up fer the night, I'm tired."

She yelled something derogatory back at him, which he didn't listen to anyway. He hollered behind to Harvey, who was driving the third wagon, and he in turn hollered to Billy in the last one.

Standing up, Walt shouted to Sergio, who was with Jodi again, and pointed toward a little area not far from the river. Sergio said something to Jodi, who turned toward the small plain. Everyone turned their wagons, and pretty soon they had all stopped and the men and the ladies were unhooking harnesses and leading animals to a picket line to tie them up for the night.

After supper and everything was cleared away, Walt said he wanted to discuss their next step. He went over his thoughts and asked for others to give their opinion. Jodi Mesto was the first to speak up, as usual.

"I think we need to go back east. Back down the trail we came, back at least to where we came outta the mountains, an' then decide from there. They ain't in front of us, at least if you were anywhere near correct before you came up into the mountains."

"I agree with her. They couldn't have moved that fast unless they were coverin' forty mile a day. An' they couldn't be doin' that." This was Lizzy.

Now Harvey spoke up. "Jodi's right. We need to turn around, as much as I hate to say it, but we'll never find anyone this way. Either we're way out in front or they gone off somewhere else an' we missed the signs. Either way we're wastin' our time here."

Walt watched everyone else while those three were speaking to judge their reaction. They were all nodding in agreement as each returned his look. "Well, I guess we turn around in the mornin'. I'm gittin' pretty tired of this back an' forth, but I agree. I don't think we're gonna find anyone headin' west. So I guess it's back to...where? Where we came out? Or do we go all the way back to Fort Casper? Any votes?"

No one said anything. They were all getting frustrated from going back over the same trail again.

Billy spoke up. "So what if we don't find anythin'? Let's say we go back all the way to Fort Casper an' no sign of 'em? We need to do this thorough, once an' fer all. I say we go all the way back to Fort Laramie an' find out what they knew, or if they even showed up a'tall, then we head back this way askin', an' we jist keep on goin' to California. If we don't find anyone, well, enough of this back an' forth; either we go all the way back to Fort Laramie, or we go out to California an' resign ourselves to the fact that we missed 'em!"

Sergio watched them all as well, studying everyone the same as Walt, trying to judge opinions. They all seemed so tired. Then he spoke up. "We all need to stop and think for a moment. There are eighteen people here who have overcome a lot of adversity, the four of us coming out here to help, and the fourteen ladies with the children, who survived and even thrived in a deadly environment. We should not be feeling upset with our accomplishments. God hasn't forsaken us. He has protected us. If you listen to anyone who reads a Bible, like I know Señor Walt does, then we see that all the patriarchs have endured much worse than what we have so far. We really have not been given anything we cannot handle."

They all gazed at him and several smiled. Walt smiled and nodded to his new friend.

"Well, Sergio's right. Thank you. We need to count our blessings. An' also, right now we need to git some sleep. So do we all agree?"

Everyone nodded, even Jodi; she was done with it.

"Good, this is the final plan then. No changes, no matter what. We head back east, all the way back to Fort Laramie, an' see if they even came out this far, then back this way an' on to California, no matter what. So fer now, goodnight ever'one."

Rising, he walked to his bedroll, lay down, and covered himself up to go to sleep.

Everyone else followed suit, heading to their own bedrolls, either on the ground or in the back of a wagon. Soon Harvey was snoring away, and everyone either chuckled or sighed, resigned to another night of him. Shortly, however, they were all sleeping, serenaded by the sound of his sawing.

***

Leah Knott noticed the ladies in their wagon train were suffering from what she thought was all the stress they had been going through, starting with having to get up at four o'clock every single morning.

Four o'clock came so awful early when you didn't get to bed until nine or ten o'clock that previous evening. They worried about making it to the mountains before the snow, and every day a conversation took place about how many days they were away from those mountains, and the desert before it, and if there was going to be another attack, or when.

They seemed to be getting lazy when it came to keeping their wagons in line and closed ranks. They weren't paying as much attention to the upkeep of the wagons themselves as before.

Maybe it was the deaths of the two boys. The boys all mourned Oscar and reminded each other how it could be one of them at any time. Oscar was one of the men who had survived the Indian attack. He was always so happy and looking at the good side of things.

Maybe it was from having to open Maddy's leg every day to inspect it. She couldn't help but cry, and sometimes scream out in pain, it was so sensitive, so excruciating, to have them cut her again and again to drain the swelling, when just to touch it was painful in itself.

It was a miracle they hadn't needed to take her leg.

Everyday, just so they could look at it, they had to unwrap the splints and then unwrap the new bandage, and her ma would have none of her pleadings to leave her be. She and Mary Williams would closely examine it. They would smell the wound, trying to find signs of infection or rotting. The poor dear suffered badly, but she still had her leg.

The children had the job of gathering buffalo chips now for the next morning's fire, since all the trees were gone because of the previous wagon trains. If they didn't find any, it meant another morning with a cold breakfast of jerked meat, hardtack, and dried fruit with a little coffee. They were always able to come up with a pot of coffee and some hot water for Clem's tea, and that would be all there was to a breakfast.

Many times at dinner, or lunch as many people referred to it now, it was the same menu, minus the coffee.

But there was a hot supper most every night for everyone except the outriders. They had to keep outside until they were relieved by the next man, so they ate whatever was handy whenever someone brought it out to them, usually after everyone in the camp had eaten.

But for those who got to stay in camp, the main supper hour

being over meant time to mend clothes. How on earth the young'uns could get their clothes torn so often by just riding in a wagon or on a horse was a constant topic of discussion.

And then there were the repairs to the wagons. A problem with a wagon seemed to crop up every day; at least that was the opinion of the ladies. They always needed a lot of hands to help with repairs, so the ladies were called on to brace a wagon or use the lever to lift up the wagon box to replace or repair a wheel. They would all crowd in shoulder to shoulder, grab the long pole, and strain at lifting, but they did it.

It always led to good-natured ribbing about the driver and her inability to stay out of the holes or off the rocks, but they got the wagons fixed, along with the clothes, and everyone got fed.

And all these things had to be done before they could finally get ready to make a bed on the ground, wrapped in a blanket, hoping it would not rain, again.

***

This night was a wet night, and everyone was in a miserable mood. It had been drizzling on and off all day long. They had a wagon get stuck in a rut again just after breakfast. Then, trying to help push it out, it seemed that half the ladies at one time or another slipped down into the muddy road. The cold dinner at noontime was followed by cold supper after they stopped for the night. They didn't even get to make coffee, which just added to everyone's sourness. And the gunfight was still on everyone's mind. Mrs. Hindle and Mrs. Hollingsworth were trying their best to stay a part of the community, but it was hard to get them to come and talk with someone during the evenings. And no one wanted to press them too much on the matter. All in all everyone was really growing tired of life on the trail.

Leah was getting worried by the changes she saw. She went to talk to Clem about it.

"Of course I'm aware of it," he said. "But there ain't really nuthin'

I can do fer you, other than keep you rollin' along. We have to keep movin'. I've seen folks jist give up."

He had worried about this from the beginning, what with having all women and no men along. He told her, "Yer really doin' much better than I expected an' I'll keep an eye out fer signs of trouble, but fer now I can't have you start gettin' down in the dumps. Others'll notice and it will make things much worse'n they are now."

This was daily life on the trail, except for Saturdays. Even with the strain of day-to-day living, and actually having gunfights with men who were willing to kill them, Clem insisted on taking Saturdays off and just resting.

And they actually began to appreciate taking that day off. Sleeping in was so nice: Not having to harness the mules by five o'clock. Letting the children sleep in. Not having to prepare something to eat with not near enough time to do it, all before they would hear Michael and one of the boys telling everyone it was time to get loaded up, time to move out, again.

***

The operator handed the deputy sheriff the telegraph and stood on the boardwalk watching and waiting for his reaction.

Adolph Aims had been the telegraph operator since it was first brought here to Denver. He was excited about this one, and it took a lot for old Adolph to get excited about a telegraph.

The deputy read it and looked down at the man standing there eagerly waiting. It seemed Adolph didn't know what to do with himself. First he crossed his arms, showing his impatience. Then he uncrossed them to put his hands in his pockets while loudly exhaling. Then the hands went behind his back and he started tapping his boot on the boardwalk. The deputy looked back at the telegraph and read it again. Then back at Adolph. "You can't say nuthin' to no one, you know that."

The deputy stared hard at the little old man, who pulled his shoulders back, stood himself as erect as he could, and very indignantly reported that he never revealed the contents of any telegraph, not like this, nor any other. He reminded the deputy that he was an officer of the telegraph company, and that he was bound by oath to not talk about what he saw.

The deputy never heard a word of it. He was already stepping off the boardwalk, and slowly walked down the street and around the corner to the jail, all the while reading the telegraph again.

***

"Sheriff, you need to see this." He handed the telegraph across the desk. The sheriff glanced up for a moment and then took the telegraph and set it on his desk. He was in the middle of writing out yet another report.

He hated paperwork. Felt like he was nothing more than a glorified secretary. His deputies got to do all the real work.

It took a couple of minutes for him to finish. It was his second report today. Once he was done, he followed it up with a big sigh, followed by a question, "What's this?" And without waiting for an answer, he picked up the note and started to lazily read it.

He immediately perked up and stared across the room at his deputy for a moment. The deputy was watching him, wanting to see his reaction just as old Adolph had been so intently watching him earlier.

The sheriff looked down at the telegraph again and reread the message; then his attention returned to his deputy. "You told Adolph not to talk about this?"

The deputy slid forward in his chair and nodded. "Yes sir, he got real indignant like he does, but I believe he won't this time—too dangerous."

The sheriff was reading it for the third time. He just grunted and answered, "Hope not. We don't need this story to get out. We'll have half the town out searchin' for these people, an' the other half demandin' we form a posse an' go find 'em right away."

The deputy couldn't wait any longer. "You believe it then?"

The sheriff never lifted his eyes from the paper in his hands. "Why not? It's from that major up at Fort Laramie. You don't think he's one to exaggerate."

"No, sir, didn't mean that. It's jist that it's comin' from that other major at Fort Casper, who tells this here major, who sends out this message. So who did it? Says the ground was full of rifle shells, from those Spencer repeaters. People jist don't have repeatin' rifles. An' there was a wagon train that gone through there after it happened, but in front of the one that sent word back to Fort Casper. He also said there was a wagon train that was in there just two or three days prior, that was full of ladies an' hardly no men. Made me think 'bout them fellers what was in here hollerin' 'bout some wagon train that was full of women an' no men."

"I was thinkin' 'bout them. You think them kidnappers mighta caught them, but got themselves shot up in the process? But what about that white flag? Surrender? Parlay? Who had that, the kidnappers? Ask 'em to come along with 'em peaceful?"

"Not hardly." The deputy chuckled.

"I agree. That's jist not sumpthin' you parlay."

The deputy was pondering that last statement when a thought came to him. "Meybe it's jist a way to get 'em to stop. People can't ignore a white flag no matter who's holdin' it. You're sorta stuck by honor."

The sheriff read the note a fourth time. "But if they parlay an' don't agree, what then? Shoot out? Then how do them men die right there, if they was holdin' a white flag? Says here it looks as if three men died while under the protection of a white flag, or they happened to fall right where one had fallen earlier, not a likely circumstance."

He looked up at the deputy. "Or they was surrenderin', an' got executed, under the flag?"

The deputy practically jumped to his feet. "No, sir. That's like a sacred thing. Durin' the war we met with the enemy several times; it's just not possible."

The sheriff was curious. "So how'd those three men get killed all in a row like that? An' who ran 'em over? An' why do that? I mean that seems pretty... I don't know. I never heard of anyone doin' sumpthin' like that. An' why would they just leave 'em there. Why not bury 'em? Or at least drag 'em away. What kind of people run over someone with wagons an' then just leave 'em there for ever'one else to find 'em."

The deputy's face was turning red. "They tromped 'em right into the dirt! They had to run the wagons over 'em on purpose! You don't do that kinda thing by accident. Said you could hardly tell they was men anymore. That ain't no accident." The deputy shook his head, trying to figure out how something so horrific could happen in modern times.

The sheriff watched him. "That white flag is the problem. What if it was a flag to parlay? I got nuthin' but questions."

Getting up, the sheriff moved over to his stove and poured himself a cup of coffee. He started walking around the office, moving his cup and gesturing as he talked.

"Okay, so let's say you came home from the war, an' found your wife run away, an' then find out she joined a whole bunch of other runaway wives—why they all did that, I don't know, but just say they did—would you tell anyone?"

"But why'd they run away?"

The sheriff paused and squinted at his deputy, thinking, then started pacing again. "Who knows? People that got nuthin', they do crazy things sometimes—maybe they was headin' back to family, I don't know, maybe to a new place to live."

The sheriff stopped again and looked at his deputy. "It could be someone convinced 'em they could make some money, become whores; it happens, since the Bible times. Meybe they figure they got no other options."

Now the sheriff glanced out the window at the people walking by. "They would need someone to guard 'em. Someone would need to show 'em where the men were. Make a fair profit doin' that."

He looked back at the deputy. "Suppose them husbands catch up to 'em, an' their leader convinces them ladies they got to shoot it out, for whatever reason. Meybe they was husbands who beat 'em, or meybe he's threatenin' their young'uns."

The sheriff resumed pacing, swinging his coffee cup as he went. "Anyway, the leader shoots the husbands all dead. He murders 'em right there an' takes ever'one outta there, no burial, no nuthin'."

The deputy stood next to the stove now, having poured himself a cup of coffee. "Them men that was in here? They was husbands? From the war? That would explain the shells from them repeatin' rifles, if they took 'em home when the war ended. They got murdered? You'd have to be the lowest kind of murderin' no-good to shoot their own husbands, especially while they're holdin' a white flag like that. You just can't do that! White flag means you gotta put all the guns away an' talk. It's a matter of honor. Even if yer a wife stealer. You gotta have a little bit of honor. I never heard of no one havin' none at all. If we can catch 'em, we need to hang him, no doubt 'bout that."

The sheriff regarded him. "I agree, but we'll need more proof other than what we got so far. Someone killed them men. Probably the leader has others with him, to keep the ladies in line. He an' his men killed the husbands. Did he kill 'em to keep the husbands from takin' their wives back? Did the ladies want to go back? We'll have to do some investigatin'. That major figures they'll head this way, or maybe up into the mountains to the miners' camps. Work 'em as whores. We'll hafta see what we can find out."

"You want me to let the others know or do you want to tell 'em?"

"Let me tell 'em. We'll have a meetin' tonight after supper. I'll send out some telegraphs back east askin' if they know anythin' 'bout an all-women wagon train. Or a group of whores formin' their own wagon train an' headin' out this way. I'll send some out west too. Let 'em know to start lookin' for 'em over the next couple of months. If he's headed up into the mountains it's gonna be mighty hard to find 'em, but if he's headed out to Oregon or California we got a fair chance of findin' him. Thanks, Charlie, we'll all get together an' talk tonight."

9
Hello

"Mr. Zebulon! Would you lead us out, please?" Walt shouted up to the young man in the first wagon.

Zeb smiled and glanced back at Walt, who was in the second wagon again. Zebulon stood up the way he thought a wagon master should and hollered out, "Okay, ever'body! Move 'em out!" He waved his hat.

The three other wagons got in line behind Zeb as he pulled out into the trail, and they all started to rumble off toward the east, again, returning toward Fort Casper, and then on to Fort Laramie.

Everyone was a little put off at having to go back again, but at least they had a solid plan now. They knew what they were doing. Soon enough they were all back to talking and laughing, and generally enjoying the morning.

***

The next day, morning once more, Billy was in the lead wagon, and it was just after they had started up when he saw two riders coming their way. He nudged Zeb, who said he noticed them. He was sure Walt had seen them by now, so no need to holler back to get ready, to start asking questions.

It wasn't long before they reached each other and Billy saw they was just boys, probably local ranchers' boys, so he decided not to stop.

Billy gave them a wave and let them pass; besides, the boys didn't look too friendly. *These ranchers' boys are prob'ly tired of all the commotion from ever'one headin' out west. Been goin' on since before they was born.*

They eyeballed each other as they passed and kept heading in their own directions.

***

"Do you think we should head back an' warn Michael or Mr. Clem?" It was Eddie Hod asking Harry Hindle. Harry was the younger but Eddie had a lot less experience as an outrider, so he still deferred to the others when a situation came up that was new to him.

"Nah, don't think there's anythin' to worry 'bout with this bunch. They seem to have as many womenfolk as we do. But we'll ride up to the top of this hill an' watch from there, jist to be sure."

He pointed to the rise on their right, so they turned their ponies, crossed the stream, and headed up to a small flat spot halfway up the hill; now they could keep an eye on this new group as it approached their own wagons. It wouldn't be but a moment before they reached each other.

***

Michael was in front of the wagons as this new wagon train came within hailing distance. Michael raised his hand in a hello and Billy raised his in an answer back. They were both tired and didn't really want to stop, and it was immediately apparent each one was content to let the other go on by.

Billy noticed that the first wagon was driven by a woman who was probably near forty-something, hard to tell. She was cautious and obviously didn't want to talk, which was understandable; she wouldn't want to appear too friendly without her husband beside her.

The next wagon also had a woman driver, then a young man by himself, then another woman, and then another woman still, and yet another woman!

102

Billy sat up straighter and started wondering. He looked over at Zeb, who seemed puzzled himself.

Billy held up his hand to stop the other wagons behind him as the westward wagons kept filing by.

He turned to look back at Walt, who was staring at the wagons as they passed. Everyone in his group was staring at the wagons, and the ladies driving the westward wagons were staring back now.

Then two "mule skinners" came bringing up the last two wagons. They waved as they rode by and Billy raised a hand as they passed him.

He gaped at Zebulon, who had turned around and was looking back at the wagons. "Do you think...?" He never finished his sentence.

The two old skinners were followed by a small herd of mixed animals, cows with a couple of larger calves and then quite a few more mules and several horses, followed by four young men driving them all as if they had been born herd drivers. The young men halfheartedly waved as they moved past. They were obviously suspicious of the folks sitting there watching them go by, as if they were some kind of circus.

Those boys were followed by still two more young men who had evidently been out on the trail for some time now. They were dusty, dirty, and looking as tough as fifteen-year-old men can be.

They were just as unfriendly as the previous group. They also eyeballed the little wagon train sitting by the side watching and kept their eyes on them as they passed, even continuing to peer back as if trying to determine if they were going to be pursued or not.

They were the last ones to finally disappear over the little rise behind them.

Billy didn't say a word. His mind was reeling. *Could it really be them?* He turned to look at Walt, who was turned around and staring at the hill where the wagon train had disappeared.

Walt swept his eyes back to Harvey, who was in the wagon following him. He was looking up toward both Walt and Billy obviously confused, waiting on one of them to say something or do something because he was at a complete loss.

It was Sergio who broke the silence by hollering at his team to bring his wagon up next to Walt's.

Jodi Mesto jumped down from the back of his wagon and ran to Walt's. Everyone started scrambling out of the wagons and talking to each other at once as they all gathered around Walt's wagon.

"Well, what do you think, Amigo?" Sergio practically shouted over the noise.

"It's got to be them! Whatta ya think?" Walt looked down at Billy.

"Could there be another wagon train with so many women drivers?"

Now Harvey spoke up. "Well, we ought to go back an' ask anyway, before they're gone an' we can't catch up till tonight. What'dya say?"

Jodi Mesto's glance hopped from one to another, waiting for them to make a decision. "I say someone better go find out, say hello, or ask if they seen another, an' you better hurry or we won't never know. Don't know what all the fuss is 'bout. Jist go an' ask if they're the ones we been huntin' fer."

Walt shook himself. "Come on, Billy, saddle up." He pointed at Harvey. "Y'all bring the wagons around. If we're wrong, no real harm done."

Jodi looked at them and then over at Emerald. "Leave it to the men to finally snap to after they been told what to do, then act as if it were their idea all along."

Walt and Billy quickly saddled up and untied their horses that trailed along behind. It didn't take long before they were on their way.

***

Michael informed Clem about the signal from the boys on the hill, telling him there were riders coming up behind them now. Clem signaled the wagons to pick up the pace and split into their square formation creating a corral for the animals, and he had the men bring in the herd.

The trailers brought them in easily, and now the two boys who were on that hillside dismounted and took a defensive position waiting for the wagons to approach. Finally, the last two wagons moved in behind the herd, enclosing them and forming a corral.

***

Walt and Billy crested the little rise and slowed to a stop when they saw that the whole wagon train had changed.

"Whoa. Walt, what happened?"

"I got no idea. Maybe there's trouble up ahead. Come on, they might need some help."

They gave their mounts a kick and started running hard up toward the wagon train, and that's when the wagons slowed dramatically and came to a sudden stop.

Then rifle fire exploded from the back wagons, shooting up the ground all around Walt's and Billy's horses.

Both riders pulled their horses to a dusty sliding stop about fifty yards away.

"Whatta they doin'?" Billy grabbed his pistol but didn't bring it all the way up to aim. He left it out to his side.

Walt held his hand out sideways to stop his friend. "Wait, they didn't try to shoot us, jist stop us fer some reason." Walt sat on his horse holding the reins with one hand while the other rested on his gun butt.

They sat there for a moment watching the back of the wagon train; they couldn't see anybody looking out or any of the rifles that shot at them.

"Hold on." Walt pulled out a white handkerchief, waved it back and forth, and nudged his horse to trot up a little closer when another round of bullets erupted all around his horse's hooves, scaring the horse.

It jumped straight up in the air, came down sideways, and reared up pawing at the air.

Caught completely by surprise, Walt tried to hold on with one hand and wave the handkerchief with the other, but fell off backward and hit the ground with a thud.

Billy thought they shot him. As he dismounted and aimed his pistol, Walt stuck both hands up in the air and yelled out, "Hold yer fire! Hold yer fire!" He waved his handkerchief back and forth again.

Billy slid next to him with his gun pointing at the wagons ready to defend his friend.

Walt saw the pistol and put his hand out again to stop Billy.

And that's when their four wagons came flying over the hill running as fast as they could, having heard the gunshots.

Jodi Mesto drove the lead wagon with Harvey sitting next to her, and when she saw Walt on the ground with Billy kneeling beside him, she yelled back to get ready to fire.

Walt spun around waving his arms. "Hold yer fire! Hold yer fire!"

Right then another round of gunfire made the dirt under Jodi's mules erupt, and they started jumping and bucking, and the whole wagon started to jump and buck right along with them.

Jodi was trying to hold on. Harvey was trying to hold on. The ladies in the back were trying to hold on. It was all they could do to stay in the buckboard. As they bounced up and banged down, Jodi started yelling, "Fire! Fire!"

Harvey jumped and went flying through the air, hitting the dirt hard but rolling out of the way of the wagon before pulling his pistol, ready to fight.

The ladies in the back of Jodi's wagon could be seen flying up and down and on top of each other with legs and boots and arms all flailing at once.

No one from either wagon train could do anything but sit and watch in horror as the mules jumped and bucked, in danger of turning the whole wagon over on top of the people in the back.

When they finally stopped, the wagon sat sideways in the trail, with the mules facing back toward their other three wagons, and Jodi, holding the reins, staring out toward the river.

The wagon was sitting still, but the mules were quivering, tense, ready to go again at the least little sound.

No one moved.

Then a hand came up from the back of the wagon box and grabbed the side, and then another came up over the edge of the wagon and waved. And then a lady's head peeked out over the edge with her hair in her face sticking out in every direction.

It was Rose Krepser. She found herself looking at the Ladies Wagon Train. She turned and glared up at Jodi, who hadn't moved at all yet.

"Don't you move a muscle, Jodi Mesto, or so help me, I'll shoot you first."

Jodi blinked and looked around at the other wagons in her group. They were all staring at her in alarm. Then, turning to the other wagon train, she saw that people had come out now and were looking at her and Rose.

She lowered her eyes to Harvey. He had been lying on the side of the road, pistol pointing at the wagons in front of him, but now he had holstered it, slowly, begrudgingly got up on all fours, and stood. Then he eased toward the mules, who seemed to be getting ready to jump again, so he held up his hands and as soothingly as possible started in with "Whoa there!"

The mules stared at him, still wild-eyed, tight as bowstrings, and ready to let go again at the slightest noise.

Jodi noticed the mules were ready to take off. "Whoa," she said very softly. "Whoa now." They were quivering, they wanted to jump. She slowly leaned over the side of the buckboard and slowly pulled back on the brake. "Whoa now, you two, we're all fine, you jist whoa there."

She looked back at the Ladies Wagon Train and held up one

107

hand. "Don't shoot! We're friends! We're here to help y'all!"

Everyone, from both wagon trains, waited for someone else to do something.

Billy looked over at Walt, who sat up now. "Don't wave that flag."

Walt stared at the ladies who were now surrounding the back wagons in front of him. "Oh, believe me, I won't. Put yer gun away."

"Huh?" Billy holstered his pistol.

Walt laid the handkerchief behind him and got to his feet, followed by Billy. Holding his hands up and out, he turned back toward his own wagons. "Everybody, climb on out now, real slow. No weapons. Bring the young'uns with you; we'll gather up over here. Jodi, you stay there an' hold them mules. The rest of y'all, let's all gather over here."

***

Clem was sitting on Cherry at the outside of his group, next to Rachel La Fayette's wagon. He got back there just as the shooting started again and he stopped it by yelling at everyone. He sat there feeling helpless as Jodi's buckboard jumped and danced around.

He thought someone was going to die for sure. But they finally got the mules stopped and everyone somehow stayed inside, except for that one old feller who jumped for his life and finally put his pistol away. He was holding the mules now.

Clem watched as a man, about thirty-something, started to gather his group together. There was one younger man and two older gents about his own age and a bunch of women. *Great, I ain't had enough women round me already.*

The leader of the new group turned and slowly walked toward him and his wagons, keeping his hands out in front where everyone could see them.

"Hello! Don't shoot! We mean no harm!" He stopped about forty feet away and raised his hands up higher. "Hello, we're friends, we're supposed to be. We've actually been lookin' fer you."

Clem wore a painful expression. He knew it! They were looking for his ladies, or himself! He knew this wasn't going to be good. "Put yer hands down, mister, but keep 'em away from yer gun."

"Oh yeah, shoulda taken it off; don't mean to worry nobody." The new man lowered his arms. "My name's Walt, Evans." He touched the front of his hat brim.

Then, not knowing what to do with his arms, he tried to find a safe place to put them before finally folding them across his chest. "We been lookin' fer you. Fer a while now. We heard 'bout you havin' no men along, an' thought you might need a little help goin' out to California an' all."

Clem, sitting on Cherry, said nothing. Cherry was antsy and kept shifting her weight and bobbing her head until Clem leaned over and said something to her, patting her neck to calm her down.

He hollered back at the new man, "Why you figure we need help? We don't need no help, we're jist fine."

"Yeah, I can see that now."

"How'd you hear 'bout us anyway?"

"Some men back in Denver, in a saloon. They was drinkin' too much, an' talkin' 'bout comin' out to take y'all an', well, you can imagine. Anyway, our friends"—he unfolded his arms and jerked his thumb back over his shoulder—"overheard 'em an' tried to git the sheriff to help out, but he jist thought it was none of his bisness, er sumpthin', so when they bumped inta my friend an' me, we met up an', well, we prayed 'bout it—"

"Wait, you prayed? 'Bout what?"

"'Bout this." Walt waved his arms around, encompassing both groups. "I mean, not this, not havin' a shootout with you; we was s'posed to be helpin'...anyway, that's why we're here." He hooked his thumbs inside his gun belt but quickly pulled them out again and folded them across his chest. "So, that's why we're here, to help."

Clem was so tired of this. "Well, thanks, but don't need no help. 'Preciate the trouble you went through, but we're jist fine. We'll let you go on yer way now."

Walt didn't know what to say to that. "Yeah, I can see that yer okay."

"Good, it's settled then. No one got hurt. Yer not hurt, are you?"

"Me? No, I'm fine."

"Good, then we'll be on our way, an' y'all can go 'bout yers."

"Oh well, wait, hold on jist a minute. Look, we came a long way to git here. We been shot at, been shot...look, can we jist stop here fer the night an' talk a bit? We come a long way to meet up with y'all."

"We didn't ask ya."

"I'm sure we could all stop for the night, couldn't we?" This was a new voice, from down on Clem's side. "Clem? Would it hurt so much?"

He looked down and Walt looked over at a new lady who had walked up during their conversation.

Leah was giving Clem a pleasant smile, as best she could do, hoping it was hiding her real thoughts toward the ornery, old, no-good...

He leaned down to talk to her as quietly as he could, something just short of a whisper. "I'll not argue in front of some stranger. We don't need to entertain ever'one who wants to meet us."

She started to protest, so he quickly cut her off. "Okay, I guess I don't see no harm in restin' here." He tried not to show how much he wanted to turn Cherry's rump right into her nosy ol' face...

Clem turned back to the new stranger. "Mister?"

"Walt."

"Yeah, well, I can't keep you from campin' wherever you like."

Leah hit him in his leg while still smiling at Walt.

Clem kept looking at him. "I guess my client is askin' me to stop fer the night, an' I try to be accommodatin', so maybe she'll actually comply with a request later, without the usual argument, an' needin' to have ever'thin' explained, before she agrees." He looked down again and gave her a very big smarmy smile.

110

She returned it. "Oh, I'm sure I would be most happy to, if ever you did actually ask anything."

She turned to Walt. "Sir, I hope your group will join us for supper tonight? It's been a long time since we entertained, what with being pushed...I mean having to go so long, and so hard. We would be delighted if you would join us, please? We have plenty to share." She walked toward Walt and stuck her hand out to shake his.

Walt stood there surprised to see her approach; then he strode forward to meet her and took her hand to shake gently. "I'm sure I can speak fer the rest of my little group an' accept yer kind invitation."

"Wonderful. As soon as y'all can make your camp, we'll have supper ready, and you can tell us about why, and how, you found us."

"It will be quite a story, ma'am. I believe you will enjoy the hearin' of it."

Leah turned and looked up at Clem, who was starting to think, *These two are deliberately tryin' to git my goat.*

When she addressed him it shook him out of his thoughts of revenge against her.

"Clem? Please? You will join us tonight? Perhaps bring a bottle; a little sip might do us all some good this evening."

He glowered at her, ready to say something back, when he realized she was asking him to bring a bottle! "What? Well yeah, okay, I guess I'll show up. But first I got to make sure the camp is secure."

"Clem, Michael can take care of the camp very well, thank you, don't you think? They might have vital information for us. Please?"

"Well yeah, okay, all right." He looked at Walt. "Tonight then, but mind you tomorrow we go our separate ways."

The new man tried not to smile too broadly. "Tonight then."

Touching the tip of his hat and nodding to the lady, Walt turned and walked away before the old man got any angrier at the woman. He was thinking as he returned to his group, *Married folk can cause some hard times to each other when they want to.*

10
A Very Kind Invitation

The two groups from the different wagon trains sat all together around a campfire that was kept going but not allowed to get too big, so as to allow everyone to be able to see over it. Some were sitting on kegs, some on boxes, some on actual chairs, but everyone made themselves as comfortable as they could.

Supper was over, and Walt had just finished telling their story to the group. Everyone had listened with rapt attention during the meal. Now they were all quiet. "Well, that certainly is some story, Mr. Evans. You did that for us?"

Walt looked at Mary Williams for a moment. He didn't know what to say. He shrugged. "Please call me Walt."

"Walt, why did you do this?" Her voice trembled a little. "I know what you told us, but it doesn't really explain why. You didn't even know us. You all could have been killed, several different times."

Walt pursed his lips but didn't say anything.

Mary glanced over at Clem, who was sitting across from her about halfway between her and Leah. "Clem? I'm ready for a sip of that whiskey if you don't mind."

"Yes ma'am." He picked up the bottle from near his boot where he had it stuck in the sand. Pulling the cork, he started to hand the bottle to Fritzy but stopped, turned, and handed it to Mrs. McKinnis, who was on his left.

Fritzy grimaced and shook his head. Hugh would have been the next man after Fritzy, so he shook his head also and muttered something about hoping it made it back to him with something still in it. Clem heard him and had to smile.

Mrs. McKinnis poured a small amount into her cup, about a finger width, and handed it to Mrs. Chase, who was on her left. She poured about a finger width and passed it to Mrs. Hafin, on her left; she did the same and handed it to Mrs. Hollingsworth, and so it went around the group.

When it came to Hugh, he took the bottle and gave himself a very generous portion. Clem leaned forward a little and gave him a dark look.

Handing the bottle to Fritzy, Hugh leaned over to whisper to his friend, "Careful, he don't want you to git the back of yer teeth wet."

Fritzy suppressed a grin and poured himself a finger width, and hesitated with the bottle hanging over the lip of his cup. He held it there for a split second before returning the bottle to Clem, who poured himself about twice as much as he felt Hugh had given himself. He looked over toward Leah, who was frowning at him, and raised his cup to her in a salute.

Just then Hugh stood up and cleared his throat. "Ehhmm, uh, may I ask us all to remember Mrs. Saddenwasser, who died tryin' to protect our young ladies." He sat down and started to take a drink with several people murmuring their agreement, and him having to acknowledge each of them while trying to get the cup to his lips, when Mrs. Hollingsworth stood up and with a strong, clear voice said,

"And my Timmy."

Several more people nodded their heads and raised their cups along with Hugh, who tried again to take his drink when Mrs. Hindle rose up. "And my Oscar." She said this with great emotion in her voice. Everyone joined in, and Hugh was forced yet again to wait before he could finally get his drink when Mrs. Hod stood up.

"And my Tom, who died trying to save us from the Indians."

"Yes, yes, Mr. Hod," was heard around the group.

Then Clem got to his feet and cleared his throat.

Hugh had to suppress a moan.

"Folks, I believe we have many people to thank, not jist those that died tryin' to help us." He fixed Hugh with a sour look. "Thank you, Hugh, fer startin' this." Hugh was looking up at him with a pained face, and then his gaze fell away and he shook his head ever so slowly.

Clem was still holding the bottle in his right hand and with his left he raised his cup. "To all of them that's helped us git here tonight." He took a drink, as did everyone else in the group.

Hugh bent toward Fritzy again and whispered, "Thought I was gonna die of thirst."

Clem gave him another glare. So did Leah from across the fire. Hugh saw her and could not figure out how she heard him.

Sitting down, Clem looked over at Walt and raised his cup again. "An' to Mr. uh..."

"Walt."

"Yeah, Mr. Walt, an' his bunch, fer stayin' the course an' comin' all this way to rescue us. Walt, sir. May I call you Walt?"

Walt gave him a cautious eye, wondering what was coming next. "Yeah, sure."

Clem had taken another sip from his cup and was pouring again when he looked over at Hugh and raised the bottle as if in a salute, and then with a bit of flair dug it into the ground next to him.

Walt waited patiently for the next insult he knew was coming.

Clem took a sip, letting everyone wait. Then he raised his cup, causing everyone else to raise theirs, but lowered his again, leaving some with their cups still up and others not knowing what to do. They all eventually brought theirs back down and watched Clem. "Mr. Walt, I hope you an' the rest of yer group will consider stayin' with us fer the rest of the journey, even though we don't need no help, but seein' as how you came this far, an' fought what..."

He thought for a second. "Four, or five battles against fierce miners, pert near got killed yerself, jist to help us poor wanderers. I want to extend the invitation, formally, in front of ever'one here, so there can be no doubt as to my sincerity, in askin' you to come along keepin' us safe."

He waved his cup somewhat during his little speech and gave it a high wave at the end, emphasizing his tenderheartedness.

He started up again after sending Leah a smirk of satisfaction, and in return received a stern look back from her. He swept his eyes to Walt again. "An' after all, as you will see if you choose to remain with us, that I, as wagon master, have little or no say at all in who comes, or who stays, or which way this wagon train will go next. So, knowin' that I will have to face these many lovely ladies in an unendin' argument if I was to do what I know is right, I would rather ask you to stay, 'cause already I know which way the wind blows, an' they'll want you to stay, an' I already have enough to worry 'bout with Indians, an' kidnappers, an' such of a lesser problem to me."

He grinned at Walt. "Not the most endearin' request you will ever receive, I don't doubt, but it stands"—then looking over at Leah and with a flat voice—"an' my word is my bond, as these ladies can attest." He gave Walt one of his smarmy smiles.

Walt tried to mimic Clem's smarmy smile with one of his own. "Well now, I believe I can speak fer us all when I say I humbly accept yer very kind invitation."

Clem actually liked him; this new man had enough sand to not back down. He raised his cup to him in a salute. "Good, then I git to make a decision without havin' ever'one attackin' me. Peace in the home is a good thing."

Walt smiled. "You are correct. Peace in the home is always a good thing." He lifted his own cup in a salute back at Clem and finished it off.

Clem waited for him to lower his cup. "Care fer another tip?"

"No, sir, I'm fine jist here."

Hugh coughed and cleared his throat again. Clem glanced in his direction and coughed himself and then turned back to Walt. "You sure? There's enough fer the both of us."

Walt looked over at Hugh, who seemed resigned to the news. "No, sir, I am fine, but there might be another you could share with."

"Nah! I'll jist finish it meself I reckon." Walt watched Hugh shake his head slowly and Fritzy chuckle.

Clem made a big show of pouring himself another drink. There were actually about three or four more still in the bottle when he set it down next to his leg.

Hugh nudged Fritzy and nodded toward the bottle. Fritzy looked aghast at his friend, got up, and walked away shaking his head. Clem picked up the bottle and moved it outside his opposite leg.

Hugh got up now and sauntered off muttering to himself.

Walt couldn't hear much, but he did hear "Bible" and "stingy," and by then Hugh was out of range.

Standing up, Walt touched the edge of his hat and nodded toward Clem, who hadn't moved but was still watching him and everyone else who was starting to leave.

"I better say goodnight. I guess I will see you in the mornin'. What time do y'all git started around here?"

"Four sharp, movin' out by five." Clem took another sip.

"Oh, well, that's good, we'll be ready then. I really do need to git to sleep then—not you yet?"

"Me? No. I got my men. They're up all night, and they'll git things goin'. Someone will come git me in time, an' help me up on my horse an' point me in the right direction."

"Yeah, well goodnight then." Walt turned and followed everyone else already leaving.

"Goodnight." Clem raised his cup in a final salute and finished it

116

off.

He watched the new man leave, thinking that he should let him know he was just joshin' him about leaving tomorrow. He told himself he should get up and go tell him. *Well, meybe before I go to bed. If I don't fergit.*

He smiled to himself thinking they might be pretty mad in the morning if he forgot to tell them. *An' them gittin' up at four to boot.* Clem smiled again, very contented.

***

He was interrupted from his humor when Leah Knott came over and stood next to him with arms crossed, glaring down at him.

He looked up and gave her a weak smile. "Good evenin', Mrs. Knott; nice night."

"Clem, I need to speak to you."

"Sure, what now?"

"You call yourself a Christian."

"No, you call me that."

"Never mind, we need to talk about you being so rude to our new guest."

He stared at her, not wanting to do this. "Fine, take a seat. I'm not standin' up, an' I'm not havin' you stand there while you berate me."

She sat down in a huff. "So why do you treat people so ugly?"

"I didn't ask no one to come an' join us, an' we don't even know these folks, an' here yer ready to let 'em join right in, as if you grew up with 'em er sumpthin'."

She actually tried to reason with him. "But Clem, you needn't be so rude to people. You're a Christian, sort of. You believe in Jesus."

"Not His name, fer meybe the hundredth time."

She rolled her eyes, looking up at the night sky. "And why must you drink so much?"

"Tonight, someone else asked me to bring it out."

Then he got real sober-looking, and she knew she was in for it.

"Look here, Mrs. Leah Knott, you still owe me one fer that first meetin' when you stuck this whole business on me, so you can jist listen. I try to love my neighbor, but I happen to love God more. So who loves who?"

"I have no idea what you're talking about, as usual."

"You Christians are always willin' to do fer a perfect stranger, or yer neighbor, or jist 'bout anybody, an' you think that's showin' God's love. Well, I'm gonna do fer God first, an' if my neighbor or my family can't make time, I'm still puttin' God first! You Christians ought to try it."

"It is showing God's love. That's what Jesus showed everyone to do. He healed everyone they brought to Him, and He never asked them a question that needed qualifying, not that I remember. And we try, every day, and it's you that has no idea what it means to show God's love. Look at the way you were acting tonight."

"I'm talkin' 'bout showin' God yer love, fer Him. First by livin' yer life the way yer Savior told you to. That's what I try to do. Eat only the food He said we could eat, worship on the day He said to, an' celebrate the holy days He said to do. You say you love Him, an' I know that you b'lieve it, but you won't do not one thing He said He wanted you to do, 'cept love yer neighbor. Big fat deal; try livin' yer life the way God said to. Yeshua even said He don't do nuthin' but what His Father told Him to do, an' so did ever'one else back then, even after He died, but you Christians won't do none of it, so who really loves who? Y'all do fer yerself an' tell Jesus it's fer Him. He's prob'ly thinkin' 'thanks fer nuthin'.' An' while I'm gittin' mad, what was the very first commandment? Love yer neighbor? I don't b'lieve so."

"Love God with all your heart, soul, and strength."

"So put God first, then do fer yer neighbor. An' it's the laws of God that shows us how to do both, but you say they're done away with. Don't make sense."

"Clem, Jesus fulfilled the law; they were nailed to the cross, we don't have to do them. You should know that; Jesus Himself said so."

"I think Paul said that. But I follow God's laws 'cause I want to, 'cause God asked me to, an' He died fer me, not 'cause I have to. An' I don't want to be released from 'em; they're good, not evil. Jist think. If they was nailed to the cross an' done away with, then why didn't none of His followers stop doin' 'em? Peter didn't. Remember when that sheet came down. Three times God told Peter to kill an' eat! An' Peter said no! He told God no! He knew better than to go agin God's law, an' remember God said He'd test us. That time Peter passed that test.

"Even James, the livin' brother of Jesus, told them gentiles who were first learnin' 'bout Yeshua to go an' learn Moses. It's right there in the book of Acts; read it yerself. I'm sorry fer gitten mad but you came over here, gripin' 'bout lovin' yer neighbor...whatta 'bout obedience is better'n sacrifice?"

"What about 'if I do all things and have no love, it's like clanging brass'— means nothing?"

"Well, I do try to love my fellows, the way God told us to in His book. An' that's different than the Christian way, different than the Jew way too. Both groups made up their own religion an' tell ever'one it's God's way. Well, I'm not listenen' to no rabbi or no preacher tell me sumpthin' what ain't in the Bible, an' I see the Savior tellin' people that God never changes, so either He doesn't change or Jesus is a liar."

She was about as mad at him as she had ever been since they left. "God doesn't lie."

"I agree. It's them teachers an' preachers who are liars, or they're jist ignerent, I b'lieve the book says they been taught lies. The people were lied to back then by them Pharisees, an' we're all bein' lied to today, by anybody tellin' you to do sumpthin' the Bible don't say to do."

She got to her feet and looked down at him. She was done for this night. "I don't think you got any idea what you're talking about, and I don't think Jesus cares much about—"

She stopped and let out a big sigh. "We'll never agree, so I'm going to bed, but I wish you'd think again about leaving in the morning. Don't you think it would have been a good idea to let the new people learn how we do things? Or are you just going to let them trail behind and eat dust?"

"We're not leavin', an' we do need to teach 'em how to move with us an' not drag us down."

She was caught off guard again. "What? You just lectured me about telling the truth and you were lying to them? Were you planning on telling them before they all go to bed?"

He gave her another one of his big smarmy smiles. "Yeah, but seein's how yer so all fired ready to tell yer neighbor how much you love 'em, meybe you can let 'em know fer me. Let me know what yer new friend says when you come back."

She paused for a moment because she really had to suppress what she wanted to say. "I'm sure he won't say anything. He's just trying to help us, save our lives, is all. And I'm sure he's just trying to live his life like a true Christian. Not like you! The others, they'll just have to learn what kind of person you really are, so goodnight to you."

She smoothed out her dress, turned, and marched out of their camp and into the other camp to inform them of the change.

***

Clem was still sitting in the same place when she returned. She shot him a scowl but otherwise ignored him.

Michael came over to discuss the next day and Clem's plans for working with the new group. He wanted to know who would take on what duties, and such things. They discussed it for a while before Michael excused himself and went about securing the camp for the night.

***

The four men from Walt's group told everyone else the change in plans, and then waited until the ladies got over almost being the object of a

120

cruel joke and went off to make their beds before they started to discuss the news.

Billy was the first to speak up. "I bet a dollar he wasn't gonna tell us. I say the lady came over here to tell us to ruin his joke. He was goin' to let us git up an' then figure it out. That was a pretty sneaky thing to do." He surveyed the others.

Harvey nodded. "Yeah, would of got us too, if that nice young lady hadn't come over to warn us."

All three looked at him, questioning his sincerity.

He returned their stare. "What? She was very nice to do that. I'll be sure an' thank her again tomorrow."

Walt grinned. "I'm sure you will. An' yes she was very nice, an' rather lovely too, don't you think, Sergio?"

Sergio kept smiling at Harvey. "Oh yes, very nice looking, and very polite."

Harvey could tell they were goading him. "She was jist very nice is all, that's all." He started acting all ruffled.

"Well, when you think 'bout it, it woulda been pretty funny if he got us."

Now they all looked at Billy again.

"What? I never said it wouldn't of been funny." He grinned openly.

Sergio sported a big smile, and when they all returned their attention to Harvey he got defensive all over again.

"What? I thought it was funny. Jist didn't say nuthin' to her. It was funny, so what."

The other three tried not to let even bigger smiles break out.

Billy started up again talking to no one in particular. "Yes sir, you know she is a fine-lookin' woman. Shame her husband ain't here to help her on her way. Wonder what happened to him anyway? Whatta you think there, Sergio?"

"Me? I have no idea, but it is a shame that such a wonderful-looking woman, and one who is so caring, would have to be out here all alone in the world. Do you not agree, Harvey?"

Harvey glowered at his friend, then at the other two, and got up and stalked out into the night grumbling to himself.

The three friends watched him leave and exchanged broad smiles as they turned to make up their own beds for the night.

***

The next morning the two groups began to integrate. Clem had Michael put their wagons through the routines to show the newcomers what the different signals meant and how to get in line or circle up, depending on which signal was given. The new folks were impressed.

Then all the wagons from both groups practiced together. It was quite an eye-opener for the ladies of the main group to see how far they had come, watching the new people struggle to get in line or move whichever way when needed. There were many smiles, some laughter on all sides and lots of apologies, and words of encouragement.

Many times it got so bungled up all they could do was stop, regroup, and start all over again.

Michael called a halt to the exercises just before dinnertime. He wanted to have a meeting with everyone who was not detailed to be an outrider.

Clem made it clear to the whole group that Michael kept his position of trail boss. He explained that the new men would stay near the wagon train at all times, keeping two on each side. They would be allowed to move up and down at their discretion, and that would be their main job.

Fritzy and Hugh would remain as the final two wagons in line as before. They made sure everyone knew they didn't mind choking on all that dust, all the time.

Afterwards Leah gathered all the women, from both groups, and had another meeting. She felt it was important to explain what they had learned as women living out on the trail, especially with Clem Bentone along.

She didn't want to be harsh but felt it would serve the new people better if they knew a little of what to expect before they had to witness it firsthand.

11
Independence, Missouri

Jed's new plan was well on its way when he finally found himself back in Independence, Missouri, where this whole thing started. It took just over a week and a half to get there.

He had taken the stagecoach, and even though the cost of a hundred and eighty dollars seemed outrageous, especially considering he still had to buy his own meals, and worry about Indians who were increasingly angrier about stagecoaches crossing back and forth, it was the going rate, so pay up or saddle up as the man said, and he knew how long that would take.

It was a long ten days. Mostly day and night. Stopping to change teams, and sometimes drivers. The jostling in the coach took a great deal of getting used to. He even had to ride almost half the way with a sheriff from Abilene. He thought that was pretty funny.

The trip should have taken eight days, but just before their arrival at the station in Riley, Kansas, Indians had killed the people and their stock was stolen.

He was pretty upset about having to bury these perfect strangers. He didn't bother to bury Dickson, and here he was helping to bury someone he never even knew.

There was no arguing though—they had to spend the night to rest the animals, and even then it was slow going until they reached the next station house.

But he made it home. He only had to be there for a couple of days and then back out to Denver before he could finally make that old man pay for causing him so much trouble.

***

The first thing now that he was back was to go see old Beamer and rent a horse—least he wouldn't be asking questions—then get out to the ranch to get his money.

He entered Beamer's livery but didn't see Otis anywhere. He walked out back to the corral and there was some new kid exercising a horse.

"Hello! Lookin' fer Otis!"

The young man turned around. "He's not here. I'd be glad to help."

"When will he be back?"

"Hard to say."

"Where'd he go?"

"Don't know, he moved." The boy had a big smart-aleck grin on his face.

After what Jed had just come through, he wanted to drag the little...but then he grinned; he decided he liked this kid.

"I need a horse, fer a couple of days. I'll pay up front."

"Yes sir! Ridin' or pullin' kind?"

"Ridin'."

"Got three in their stalls right now. I got a form that needs yer name, an' to know where yer takin' it. Can you read an' write?"

"Enough fer yer form."

The kid grinned at Jed. "Okay, I'll git one saddled up. Need saddlebags or sleepin' gear fer yerself?"

"No. You ask a lot a questions. I said I'd pay up front."

"Yes sir, 'preciate that, but if yer takin' our horse somewhere, I need to know where, an' why."

Jed stared at the kid. He still looked friendly, but not smiling like the smart aleck anymore; he wasn't going to be intimidated.

Jed gave him a big smile. "Now, you don't own this place, do ya?" He chuckled out loud. "Name's Clive, Wilton. An' I don't know where I'm takin' it 'cause I don't know where I'm goin'. I'm out here lookin' to buy a place, call it my own."

He rubbed his chin. "I bet a man like you would know of a good deal fer a poor man."

The kid was trying to figure out if he was for real or a liar. He relaxed again and got his big smile back on. "Follow me, Mr...."

"Wilton, call me Clive."

"Can't call you jist Clive; my pa would have me fer that, not showin' proper respect. But if you come in here an' have a seat an' fill out this form, I'll think while I'm gitten yer horse ready."

Jed finished up his form. It wanted a dollar a day rent and ten dollar deposit for each day. *Seems fair enough; these days folks can't be too careful.* He laid the money on the desk.

He walked out to the barn where the kid had brought out a large bay mare. She was a good-looking horse, seemed strong and wasn't shy.

"She looks fine, she'll do good. Now I git the deposit back when I return the horse?"

"Ever' penny, we're nuthin' if we ain't trustworthy."

Jed smiled at the kid. "Good, where do I git some grub fer a couple of days? I got my own sleepin' gear."

The conversation went on for a little longer. Finally, he mounted up to leave, and that's when the kid asked the question he was waiting for.

"Mister? You came in here lookin' fer the old owner. How'd you know him?"

"I don't. I was told he was the man who owned the livery. I was told he was a hard man to deal with; I 'preciate you not bein' him. Stranger don't know who they can trust in a new town. Now I do need you to keep quiet 'bout me bein' here. Folks know yer new here an' lookin', an' the price always goes up. I'll let ever'one know once I'm ready."

"Yes sir, I'm not talkin'."

"Thank you, Mr....?"

"Jethro, Kerr. You can call me Jeth, ever'one else does."

"I'll call you Mr. Kerr if you don't mind, till I feel I know you anyways."

Jethro couldn't help but smile at that.

Jed touched the tip of his hat brim and walked the horse out of the barn. The kid told him of a couple of places he might look at.

He headed out to Dickson's ranch.

***

A little over an hour later he sauntered into the front yard and stopped to look around. It was a fine place indeed. The help had been keeping it up. *Good, don't need shiftless no-goods takin' a person's money and doin' nuthin' fer it.*

He rode up to the house and dismounted, then tied the horse to the post and walked inside.

"Hello! Anybody home?"

He heard people in the back running toward him, and then an elderly couple came into the front room and stopped dead.

The old man was medium height, skinny, and balding. The lady was just about five feet tall, slender, and worried.

The old man stood up straight and took half a step forward. "Hello! What...can I help you?" He was obviously agitated at this cowboy barging into Mr. Ross's home like this, but he had to keep his temper in check or he would hear it later from the missus.

Jed raised his hand. "No problem; Jed Hansen. I work fer Mr. Ross. I know you remember me."

They both broke into big smiles. Jed noticed the old man was not smiling quite the same as his wife, but at least he seemed more relaxed.

Then the old woman exclaimed, "Oh yes, Mr. Hansen. Yes, we remember, how are you?"

"Good. I'm here on business. Dickson needs money an' he can't git here, that's why I'm here. I know where the money is an' the combination, so you two can go 'bout whatever you were doin'. I'll take care of this."

They both dropped the smiles and got really worried looking.

He put on his friendly face again. "It's okay, I won't be here long."

He turned and went into Dickson's study, leaving them standing there staring after him.

He looked over at the rifle cabinet; it was empty. He could see through the glass doors with those etchings of the roses. That shotgun was gone.

He froze. *What is this? They stole the money! They must have known the combination to Dickson's safe was in the butt. Those two old thieves! I'll kill 'em both!*

He stormed back into the front room to find them, and they were still standing there waiting for him. That took him by surprise, but he recovered quickly.

"What's goin' on here? Where's those rifles? Where's that fancy shotgun?" He was fuming, and now they were really scared. The old woman moved halfway behind her husband and took his arm in both of hers. He moved his arm to draw her even further behind him. Jed realized he needed to calm down to get his information before he scared them to death.

"They're in the bank." The old man's voice was hard, flat. He was not going to let this cowboy buffalo him, not here in Mr. Ross's own house. "That's where Mr. Ross wanted us to keep his rifles while he was gone. I thought he would of told you if you needed them."

Jed stuck his finger out at them. "Don't tell me what he shoulda done."

128

Then he caught himself, heaved a big sigh, and straightened up. He realized this old man was just going to be harder to deal with the more he tried to push him. *The bank? Dickson Ross, you didn't even trust yer friend?*

"Okay, they're in the bank? Why the bank?"

The old man stared at Jed for a moment. "Don't know; that was just the way he always had us do things."

Jed looked down and pondered this. "Okay, too late to go into town today. You'll have to go first thing in the mornin'."

He thought for a moment and then smiled sadly. "I need a drink."

Exchanging glances, they crossed to the far wall and stood there waiting on Jed.

He poured himself a whiskey from the cabinet and motioned for them to sit down. They didn't move.

"Take a seat."

They shook their heads. The old man asked, "Where's Mr. Ross?"

He shrugged and sat on the edge of the sofa. "Okay, here it is. Dickson, I mean Mr. Ross, is in danger of never comin' home agin." He let that hit them, hopefully setting them off balance a little.

"We was waylaid by some squatters on one of the ranches we was out lookin' at. They killed one man an' shot Dickson in the head, but he didn't die; he's one tough hombre. I got wounded on the way out but managed to git us outta there. Then it took another day to git him back to Denver an' a doc. Well, the doc got him restin' an' said he'd be okay if we can git the bullet outta his head. The doc said he can't do it, too dangerous fer him; we need this special doc from down in Houston to come up an' do the cuttin'."

Jed was trying to figure out if they were buying the story. He saw the old woman wanted to believe him; the old man wasn't buyin' yet.

"Anyway, he telegraphed the doc, who said he'd come, but he wants fifty dollars an' stagecoach fare fer both ways before he comes up an' does any cuttin'. Can you imagine? That's most of five hunnerd dollars! Jist to cut somebody open an' sew 'em back up! Anyways, it's pay up or Dickson's dead. So I'm here to git the money an' git right back, so that Denver doc will git that other doc to come up."

Jed rose, walked over, and poured himself another glass of that good whiskey Dickson had.

The old man obviously still wasn't buying the story. "I don't understand what the rifles got to do with Mr. Ross's money."

Jed wasn't going to put up with much from this old codger. "An' you don't need to know. Jist do what yer told, I do what I'm told, an' he told me a long time ago not to talk 'bout them rifles if I needed to git 'em. So, I'm not talkin' 'bout why I need 'em."

The old man took on a casual attitude. "I see. Well, I guess you'll have to go to the bank yerself, Mr. Hansen. I gave Mr. Ross my word I wouldn't give them to no one without his note or the password."

Jed gave him a hard look. "Well, I think you don't unnerstand. That bank ain't gonna give me nuthin' without some proof of what I jist told you. I got none, an' I don't know how to git none. I prob'ly could telegraph that doc out there, or the one in Houston, but then how does the bank know they are who they say they are? No sir, you got to git them rifles an' git back here as soon as possible. It's the only way."

The old man stood a little more upright. "I'm sorry, but I won't be able to do that. I gave Mr. Ross my word."

"But then what if he dies waitin' on you?"

"Then the bank will notify his kin, an' they'll have to take over from there."

Jed could see he was not willing to budge against his vow to ol' dead Dickson. The old woman was getting more fidgety.

Jed tried to figure out the easiest way to git this old man to quit being so stubborn, without having to hurt the old guy. *He's jist standin' up fer his dead boss, shouldn't git mad 'bout that.*

Jed let out a big sigh and rubbed his face. "Well, we can't do

130

nuthin' till tomorrow anyway. How 'bout sumpthin' to eat?"

The old man lightened up a bit and the woman seemed downright relieved to be able to do something that was near normal, in spite of the stranger and the news he just brought.

The woman stepped out from behind her man. "Oh yessir, would you like a bath too? An' I could warsh up them clothes fer you while yer eatin' yer dinner, an' we can turn down a bed, an' go get 'em first thing, like you said."

"Sounds fine, let's do that."

The old man turned to his wife, who hurried off, and he motioned toward the bathroom. "It's right through here, Mr. Harvey."

Jed noticed the name change this time. He was getting irritated with this old man. "Name's Hansen, not Harvey."

"Oh right. I'll try to remember that. Mr Ross's bathroom is right this way."

Jed remembered it now. It was so impressive. Big brass tub, cabinet right there with a water pitcher and shaving kit, big window looking out over the pasture. He was going to have a bathroom right in his house, jist like ol' Dickson had, but better.

He was still admiring it when there was a kick at the door with the old woman asking if she could come in. She was carrying two big copper kettles, both steaming away. She set them down and left. The old man had been pumping a bucket full of cold water from the pump next to the cabinet. Water right in the bathroom! Jed shook his head at the luxury.

The old man arranged some towels on the cabinet and got out a brand-new bar of soap.

"Would you like me to help get the tub ready, Mr. Hansen?" The old man put extra emphasis on the name.

"What? Uh, no, I'll take it from here. Look, can you git me some clothes before I give these up? I hate the idea of havin' to wait around in my drawers while they git cleaned."

"Yeah, I guess; you and Mr. Ross seem to be about the same size. I'll be right back."

"Good, bring me some clean drawers if he gots some too."

"Okay, he has plenty."

Jed smiled to himself. *Even plenty of extra drawers. I'm gonna live like a king.*

***

That night the two old folks were lying in bed. "Adam, what do you think he'll do next?"

"Sweetheart, I'm afraid we'll have to wait till mornin' to find out. But I can't go against my word to Mr. Ross."

"What if he gets real mad? Do you think he knew we had guns?"

"Clair honey, he thinks we're just a couple of worn-out old folks. If he tries anythin', though, he'll find out we ain't so worn out as he thinks."

She didn't say anything more.

He was snoring away before she could finish praying. Her man was still one tough hombre, but she didn't need him to be quite so tough anymore. She knew he wouldn't back down. It was going to be a long night.

***

Jed was all smiles as he came into the kitchen. "Good mornin', folks, sleep okay last night? Ma'am, may I git some of whatever it is I smell?"

He sat at the table. They had obviously already eaten and were having a cup of coffee while waiting on him. It appeared like the old man slept okay, the old woman, not so much. *Good, I thought it would go this way.*

Adam took his plate to the sink, then turned and leaned against the wall before realizing he would have to have his back open to be able to grab his pistol. He moved over and leaned sideways against another cabinet while his wife tried to relax and make up a plate for the guest.

She set it down and moved to stand next to her husband. She was really getting worried. Jed smiled up at them as he started in. The food was wonderful.

Then Jed pulled out his pistol and pointed it at Adam.

Still chewing his food and smiling, he waved his pistol for them to come sit down. They froze for a moment and then the old man gently took his wife by her arm and led her to the table.

"Thank you, ma'am, this really is great." He kept right on eating away while pointing his pistol in their direction. "Pa, I need you to keep both yer hands folded together, right here on top of the table where I can see 'em."

The old man did as he was told.

"Thank you very much. Dickson has it real nice out here." He took his time eating. "Ma'am? May I please git another cup of coffee?"

She got up and walked over to the stove. Jed stood and pushed his cup clear across the table, to keep her from getting any ideas like pouring it on him. She didn't try it and went back to stand next to her husband.

Jed watched her carefully, making sure she didn't try anything foolish. "Thank you, I really 'preciate this. Home cookin' is sumpthin' I didn't git when I was home."

Finished, he put his fork on his plate and slid it out of the way. "That was really good, thank you, an' now we can git started on the things we got to git done so I can git back there an' save Dickson."

Looking disapprovingly at Adam, Jed shook his head. "People like you, who'll let their friends die jist 'cause they gave their word. An' when they need you, you won't budge; let 'em jist die fer yer honor." He shook his head at the old gent again.

The man was defiant. "He told me not to, under no circumstances."

"Well too bad. He didn't tell me that; 'course he can't talk now, can he? Not with that bullet in his head. An' I ain't got time to argue, old man, so here's what we're gonna do."

He pointed his pistol directly at the old woman. "Yer gonna go to the bank. You'll fetch them rifles back out here, an' you better hope nobody decides to talk to you or come back with you, 'cause I will shoot Pa here, in order to save my friend."

She was frantic, what with not sleeping, then Jed dressing down her husband; and she would never admit it, but Jed suspected she agreed with him over her husband's honor. "Please, no, I'll do whatever you want. Don't shoot him."

"Oh, don't worry too much, Ma, I won't try to kill him, jist shoot him up real good. Make him pay fer interferin' in this rescue attempt."

She stepped forward a little. "I can't go myself."

Jed's eyes narrowed. He just knew Ma was trying to play a trick on him to get Pa away. "Oh, sure you can, you'll be fine."

"No she can't," the old man interrupted. "Mr. Ross made sure we have to go together. The bank won't release nuthin' to her by herself."

Jed stared at the old man. He pointed his pistol at him and cocked the hammer all the way.

The old woman just about fainted. "Oh please, no! He's telling you the truth! I can't, the bank won't, not without him, please, please."

He glanced over at her. She was trembling; she looked a little like his own ma. *The witch.* He released the hammer slowly but kept pointing it at Adam. "Stand up."

The old man obeyed slowly.

"Turn around an' raise yer vest up."

The old man did as he was told without hesitation. The pistol grip was sticking out of the top of his pants. He looked down at his wife as if to say he was sorry.

Jed let out a big sigh and said, "Ma'am, would you please take the gun out of yer husband's pants an' set it down on the table, very slowly. An' would you please take yer own gun out?"

She pulled her pistol out of her boot and laid it on the table, then pulled the gun out of her husband's pants and laid it down next to hers.

The old man stood there, hands in the air.

Jed shook his head slowly. "I am not happy. Y'all don't trust me, an' I never done nuthin' but try to save my friend an' protect myself from Pa here tryin' to kill me. Okay, both of you sit down. How does this work, exactly?"

Adam hesitated, then decided to tell the whole truth. "We have to go in together an' sign the paper together; then we can have the rifles, or money."

"What money? How much?"

"Not that much. We're allowed twenty dollars a month for whatever we need, but we have most ever'thin' we need, so we don't—"

"Yeah, okay, got it, so you sign it an' git out, an' come home."

"Well, we usually shop while we're—"

"Yeah got it, prob'ly not shoppin' this time. What'dya think?"

The man didn't say anything. He glowered at Jed, but the old woman just looked down and occasionally up at her husband, and nudged him to stop glaring.

Jed stood. "Okay, so this is what we gonna do. We all go in together, you sign what you need to. I'm along to do the liftin', an' we ride back out here. No shoppin' this time. No conversations with yer friends. No stoppin' fer a picnic or a sarsaparilla, got it?"

She looked up and nodded right away, then eyed her husband and gave him an elbow. "Agree, Adam." She looked at Jed again. "We agree."

The old man loved his wife. "Yeah, we agree."

Jed was all smiles again. He stepped around and gathered up the two pistols. "Great, let's git goin' an' git back here as soon as possible. An' no more guns, Pa. I don't need to be shootin' people yer age, but I won't hesitate to kill you, if you make me."

"I know. So tell us the truth, now that we know why you're really here. Mr. Dickson, is he alive? Where is he?"

Jed put on a sad face. "He's in the doctor's office. I still hope he's alive, waitin' fer you not to kill 'em, so let's git goin'."

***

The couple was in the buckboard with Adam driving and Clair next to him. Jed rode his horse alongside.

"Let's pick up the pace, old-timer; we'll slow down when we git closer."

They made it into town and pulled up beside the bank. Just then Jethro from the livery stepped around the corner and smiled at the old couple in the wagon before noticing the man he knew as Mr. Wilton.

Seeing him, Jed quickly held his finger to his lips and shook his head. Jethro thought he must be doing some business deal, so he was going to keep quiet for business's sake.

As the couple started to go into the bank, Jed gently grabbed each by an elbow and stopped them. "Now remember, I'm gonna save my friend, even if he hates me the rest of his life. That means if you try to stop this from happenin', I'll start shootin' an' be gone, before anyone even knows who I am or where I went."

The old man was steady. "There won't be no problem, mister, we'll be in an' out."

They were in and out and heading back to the ranch with the rifles when Jed had them stop.

He opened the butt end of the shotgun, pulled out the note, and put it in his pocket, then had them drive on back to the ranch. It all went without a hitch, just as it should have.

***

They pulled into the yard and stopped at the house. Jed dismounted and had the woman get out of the wagon and told Adam to put the buckboard away.

He took Clair by the arm. "You come with me."

After leading her into the study, he had her sit across from the desk. Then he walked around to the chair and sat down at the desk facing Clair. Giving her a big smile, he reached down on his left and

136

pulled out the bottom drawer, all the way out just like he saw Dickson do it back at the beginning of their planning. At the time it was obvious Dickson was just being braggadocious, but thankfully he was, or Jed would never have known there was a safe at all, let alone that it was hidden under the floor, under that desk drawer.

He took the paper he had extracted from the butt of the shotgun and carefully read the combination printed on it. He ran the dial first one way, then slowly back the other way, then even more slowly back again. He pulled the handle. Nothing.

He yanked on it now, still nothing. He ran the combination again and turned the handle, nothing.

He started to get mad but then told himself to relax, so he sat back studying the woman. She was worried. A thought crossed his mind. "Did you two change the combination?"

She near panicked. "What? Oh my no, I swear, mister, we never open that drawer! We never open any drawers in this desk. I never even knew anythin' was there. As God is my witness, please."

"Yeah okay, hush up." He tried it again, real slow, glancing from paper to tumbler wheel and back again with each number. He ran them real slow to make sure he did it just right, and this time when he pulled the handle, nothing.

He looked up at her again. He was mad and she was scared. "Dickson changed it." Then he smiled all of a sudden and became real relaxed, which scared her all the more. "Well, we can fix that. You got dynamite out here?"

"Dynamite? Well...Yes, we do. I'm not sure where it is, but I know he keeps some somewhere. Adam will know where it is."

"Good, let's go find Pa." He stood up and motioned for her to lead the way.

They were just heading out the front door when Adam came into the room through the kitchen entrance. He heard the front door close as they stepped outside, and he ran to it and threw it open. Jed whirled around and stuck his pistol in Adam's face.

Adam froze. The woman screamed. Jed stood there for a moment. Adam never moved; his wife was frozen with fear. Jed was breathing steadily and then finally, slowly released the hammer and lifted his pistol away. Giving the man a hard look, he waved it at Adam to move in front of them before holstering it. "Pa, raise up the back of yer vest."

There was nothing there.

"If you git yerself shot it'll be yer fault."

Adam slowly lowered his vest. "No, it won't."

Jed was growing tired of everyone wanting to fight him. "Yer wife says you got dynamite, where is it?"

Adam sent a look at Clair, who returned it defiantly.

"He needs it; please show him where it is."

"It's this way."

Adam led them to the barn, and once inside, over to a smaller side shed. Lighting a match, he put it to the wick of a lantern and opened the door, then walked across and held the lantern up before a tall cabinet.

Jed had Clair go in front of him. Adam opened the cabinet door and there on a shelf was a small case. He stood back and pointed to it.

"Grab four sticks an' let's go." Jed stepped back and gestured for them to lead the way again.

Clair protested as they walked across the yard. "Mr. Jed, you can't blow up the safe in the room. It will destroy the room. It's so beautiful."

"Hush. We'll see if we can haul it out from the floor. Come on, let's go."

He motioned for them to get going and followed them across the yard.

Back in the room again he told Adam to lay the dynamite on the desk.

138

"Good, now stick out yer hands."

Adam held them out, and Jed took a piece of rope he grabbed from the barn and wrapped it around the man's wrists, tying his hands together.

His wife got still more upset. "That's not necessary."

He looked over at her. "An' it wasn't necessary fer you two to start plannin' on how to shoot me neither."

"We never were!"

"Yeah, I'll believe that when I'm back in Denver. Now let's git outside."

He led them across the yard to a bench under a big oak tree and sat them down.

"Ma, I need you to give me yer word that you won't release him till you see me agin."

"I won't, I promise." Adam glared at her, then softened his expression and smiled, and she smiled back.

"I'll be back in a few minutes." He went inside the house. Then came out and went to the barn. Then came out again carrying a pick and a shovel and went back into the house.

They could hear him attacking the floor.

The woman dropped her head into her hands.

Jed reemerged and this time he got his horse, brought it over to a window of Dickson's office, and tied it there. Going back inside, he opened the window next to his horse and crawled out with a rope in hand. He tied it around the horse's neck, turned her away from the house, and urged her to pull.

She walked about five feet and stopped. He urged her on. She strained and strained but couldn't move any further. He tried to coax her, then spanked her flank, then tugged on the rope with her, but the horse just couldn't budge that safe.

Jed took the rope off and led her back to the corral and then returned to the house.

A few minutes later he ran out of the house and was pushed off the porch by a huge explosion! Smoke and dust and bits of debris blew out of broken windows and the front door.

The wall that used to be the outside part of the office had broken loose from the main house and shook before leaning and falling to the ground, leaving a gaping hole and a sagging roof where there used to stand a beautiful yellow climbing rose bush clinging to the home.

Smoke billowed out from the office, the front room windows, and the front door.

Jed had been thrown to the ground with the blast, but now he stood back up and staggered a little. When he turned to look back at the house he was a bit woozy. Then he turned toward the old couple with a big grin on his face before heading through the front door and disappearing into the smoke.

Adam just stared at the house. Clair burst into tears and held her apron up to her eyes.

Jed was inside perhaps five minutes before he came out again. He was holding his saddlebags and that beautiful shotgun in a gun bag Dickson kept with his rifles. He was completely covered in dust. He walked over to them and, coughing, tried to talk.

His voice came out hoarse but cleared as he talked. "Like I said, he can hate me fer the rest of his life, but right now I got to save his. So I hope y'all won't go tellin' the sheriff what happened here. He might not want to let me git all the way back to Denver, an' I ain't got time to be 'splainin' to ever'one what I'm up to. I'll send you a telegram when the special doc's done whatever he's gonna do. If you care 'bout Dickson, you'll let me git back there to save him. Sorry 'bout the room, I couldn't git the safe out."

He trotted over to his horse, which was still nervous from the blast. After taking his time saddling her up, he mounted up and rode out and down the lane and was gone.

***

140

It didn't take long before Jed found himself back in town. It was suppertime and the place seemed abandoned. He made his way back to the livery and found it empty, so he took the saddle off his horse, put her in a stall, and gave her some hay. He still had another day left on his contract but figured he was happy to get back without having to talk to the kid again.

He didn't need to return for the deposit, not anymore, not with the saddlebags bulging with Dickson's cash and coins. Let the kid have it to start up a little side business.

Grabbing his saddlebags and Dickson's silver-plated shotgun, he headed down to the hotel. He checked in under the name of Abers, a good name that no one would remember.

At the front desk he checked to see when the stage would be in. He wanted to be notified of its arrival and gave the clerk two bits for taking the time to do so.

The clerk assured him he could wait in his room and relax; he'd know the minute it was here and not have to worry. Then Jed asked if it was possible to get a meal brought up to his room in the morning? The clerk assured him he would get it for him.

Jed gave him three dollars and told him to remember the coffee and add a slice a pie to it and he could keep the change. The man's eyes lit up thinking it was only gonna cost about two and a half dollars for breakfast with a steak, even with the pie.

The clerk told this Mr. Abers to think no more about it, he'd have his meal up there first thing in the morning and with the newspaper to boot, no charge.

Jed thanked him and headed up to his room. All done, no one saw him, and he didn't need to go out again until he got on the stagecoach.

12
South Pass

This climb was the worst one yet. The mules really struggled. The herd lagged behind and the men driving them really had to work hard to keep them close to the wagons. It was only when they looked back that they got a real perspective of just how high they were. Finally, when they stopped at the top Clem let them know where they were. South Pass, Rocky Mountains.

No one even realized they were crossing the dreaded Rocky Mountains. They were expecting something much more dramatic with narrow canyons full of raging rivers, with towering cliffs and giant pines leaning over them menacingly. But there was nothing here. Just scrubby grass, and the never-ending climb. And now the ladies noticed that several of the children were feeling poorly for no reason. Clem told them it happened to a lot of folks although he had no idea why. He felt it was due to the strain of the long climb.

They made camp for the rest of the day. That next morning after they were loaded up and ready to move out, Clem gave them the news he had waited on. South Pass was halfway. It was so disappointing to everyone. They had been through so much and they were only halfway.

Clem had the new wagon train, as he liked to call it, up and over the South Pass easily, but he got no pleasure out of that—he was already spending a lot of his time thinking about how he would get past all those towns ahead. He was sure the word must be going around about the killings.

His hope was to find a way to skirt past the towns without being seen. They surely were a recognizable group, but he didn't dare split them up, not even with the new men along. He had to figure out something, and he had just a couple of days until he would be tested for the first time.

They would be coming to the Green River where they would have to wait to ferry across, then on to Fort Bridger, where they could very well meet some kind of authority—probably the Army—then on to Salt Lake. No doubt about a sheriff being there. They had a real city growing and plenty of law enforcement to go with it. That could certainly be trouble.

The idea of sheriffs, or military officers now that the war was over, out searching for them was really starting to worry him.

He had all but stopped drinking his whiskey, and all the ladies were delighted about that, but they also wondered why he was more somber than usual.

It didn't take long to realize the problem was modern technology—the telegraph.

It could be used to track them down, and at least get a lot of questions asked about what happened and why no one sought the law when it did happen. It didn't look good.

***

Jed's men back in Denver were running out of patience. Even Yancy was growing tired of waiting, and he was the patient one.

Fred and Horse had stopped jawing at each other by order of Yancy, who had been left in charge.

Willy and Bill were on the mend and telling everyone they were going to be ready when Jed got back.

Ralph kept speculating that Jed wasn't coming back at all.

In fact, Jed considered it at one point. He already had more money than he ever could have imagined before, but he wanted revenge, and he also wanted more money. The boys would never know how much he took from Dickson's house, but they would be satisfied with their take once this was over. And he would be really, really rich.

He knew that Old Leather would be watching for them again, but this time, they wouldn't give him notice they were there. He'd figure that out when the shooting started.

The men stayed out of town to avoid the sheriff, and Yancy insisted at the point of his gun that they avoid the saloons.

They all knew the doctor told the sheriff about two shot-up cowboys coming in, so Yancy made it a point to visit him and tell him they were ambushed by Old Leather, and Yancy, Bill, and Willy were the only survivors.

The sheriff asked if they were the husbands of the ladies on the wagon train, and he quickly agreed to that and told him they were too embarrassed to say so because of how it looked losing their wives.

The sheriff said he would keep it quiet and didn't ask for any details, although he did say he would need to later for the trial when they caught the man. And he promised they would do what was necessary at the time.

The sheriff had gotten that telegraph from Fort Laramie already, so it didn't take much to convince him now about Clem's guilt. He had sent telegrams west to the towns that the wagon train should be coming into next.

He wanted those sheriffs to be on the lookout for any unusual wagon trains matching their description and to be very careful with them, even warning them not to think twice about shooting the ringleader on sight rather than trying to take him alive.

Yancy told the sheriff he was camping just outside of town due to the circumstances of their arrival and as soon as Bill and Willy were well enough to travel, they would ride out again after the wagon train, using much more caution this time, and hoping the sheriffs ahead of them would have captured them by that time.

In fact, they were worried one of the sheriffs actually would capture them, and then they would have a whole different set of problems to deal with.

And Jed was still at least a week away.

***

The wagon train reached the Green River late in the afternoon on the second day out from South Pass. Clem had been pushing them hard to get there, but he decided to wait until the next morning to cross the river. The reputation of the ferrymen drinking up all the money they made was legendary.

It would be safer to wait and cross in the morning, when they had a much better chance of the ferrymen being sober.

They made camp up and away from the river's edge, close enough that they could be down at the river ready to go by sunrise.

The riverbank was very steep, but the road down to it had been cut out and smoothed to allow the wagons to descend without any real danger; that is, if you had your animals under control.

In the past, many wagons had been pulled over that edge and plummeted straight into the river because the animals stampeded and the men from those wagon trains couldn't control them, all because they had just come forty miles with no water and hadn't prepared for it.

That was yet another reason Clem used mules. They covered that distance in two days, and he made sure they had enough water with them before they left the Big Sandy River and headed west.

It was two long days for everyone, and real dry too, because the mules and the rest of the herd got most of that water. He didn't want a stampede once those animals smelled water again. Too many people were killed that way.

They were safe from that now. He had half the boys take the animals down in small groups to water them, while the other half brought water back up for the rest of the group.

***

Walt decided now was the time to take another shot at trying to befriend the old wagon master. He waited until everyone was busy and the old man was standing just outside the wagons, looking out over the river.

Walt walked up next to him and saw that he was watching a wagon going across on the ferry.

Walt stood beside him for a moment, never getting any acknowledgement from Clem that he was even there. Finally, while watching the ferry himself, he started the conversation. "Afternoon."

Clem gave him his customary sour look. He turned back to watch the wagon on the ferry and answered, "Howdy, what can I do fer ya?"

Walt never moved. "Nuthin', jist thought I'd come over an' meet you agin. We've all been in a bit of a hurry since the first time; thought we got a little breathin' space fer a bit."

Clem stayed silent watching the scene on the river. Walt was ready to try again when Clem finally spoke up. "Yeah, meybe. What's up ahead got me worried. You know they'll be lookin' fer us, an' I'm not sure if I'll git a chance to explain before they shoot me."

Walt kept his eyes on the ferryman taking the wagon across. "You mean the law? They might not be lookin' fer us. They don't know who killed them men."

Clem turned to Walt. He wasn't mad or anything, just matter of fact. "We left 'em right there where they died. I presume their friends didn't bother to bury 'em. I don't think they're the helpful kind. So I think the next group of wagons got an eyeful. They woulda been three, four days behind us. So I think they musta sent word back to Fort Casper, tellin' 'em what they saw. An' them in the fort knew of us, an' I believe you were there earlier talkin' to 'em 'bout us? Am I right?"

Walt kept his eyes on the river. "Yeah, I see yer point. An' them others are still out there somewheres. They ain't gone home."

Clem was looking back at the river again. "Yeah. So you got any

146

ideas how we avoid 'em? The law first. I figure our boys won't try nuthin' till the Sierra Nevadas. They could agin goin' across Nevada—they got mines all over that place—but I'm bettin' it's those mountains. Then they can take 'em an' git rid of 'em quick."

"That's my thought, an' my friends agree. We feel we're in good shape till then. So, I do have a option fer t'other problem."

"Yeah, shoot—whoa, not that—go ahead." Clem chuckled at his inadvertent choice of words.

Walt smiled but never glanced over. "We could go to Oregon. We'd have to explain ever'thin' to the ladies. I mean they wouldn't know we done it till it was too late, but that wouldn't be right."

"Yeah, but the less we have to tell 'em the better, trust me."

"Yeah, but we both know we can't do that. I'm told yer an honest man, an' a Bible man."

"Yeah, not that anyone round here would testify to my spirituality." He chuckled again.

The raft on the river below was looking perilous—turning and starting to tilt in a very bad way. The people on both sides of the river were raising their arms and running back and forth.

The ferryman worked hard poling against the current. The man with him pulled on the ropes attached to the other shore while the ferrymen on the shore pulled ropes to bring the raft in. It looked real bad but then somehow they got the raft turned back straight and moving across again, but much further down from the landing where it was supposed to come in.

Clem never showed any emotion, just watched the whole thing play out in front of them. "Drunks, should be horsewhipped. That's why we wait till mornin'."

Clem had to think for a moment. "Where were we? Oh yeah. These here lawmen will prob'ly want to kill me rather than bring me in; easier that way. I don't really care to find out. So, how do we git around 'em?"

Walt still never looked at Clem, just kept gazing at the river. "Well, we got to go through them towns, no way around 'em really. We'd draw more attention tryin' to bypass 'em."

"So far you haven't said anything that helps. Ain't got all night."

"I'm jist statin' the facts."

Both men kept looking at the river.

Walt smiled to himself. He really did like this old cowboy. "We need to send some of us men into the towns an' see what the news is on us, if there is any. We'd tell 'em we saw this very wagon train, say two weeks back. It wouldn't be a lie, 'cause we did see y'all all two weeks back. If they asked where you were now, we'd say we don't know; not a lie, I got no idea where we are, never been out here. Then we'd tell 'em you mentioned headin' towards Oregon. Which we did talk 'bout it. So if they was to infer that y'all was headed up that way, an' if they head on out that way, that's on them fer not investigatin' more."

Clem glanced over at him now. "That's yer plan?" He looked back at the river.

Walt never turned. "I didn't say it was a great one. I ain't got nuthin' else right now, an' we'll be in Fort Bridger in 'bout four days. We got time to think of sumpthin' else. Meybe they don't even have law there."

"Oh, they prob'ly got Army there now that the war's over." He sighed again. "I guess we'll keep thinkin' till we git there; hopefully we come up with sumpthin' better...shouldn't be hard."

Now Walt gave him a sour look. Clem was smiling. Noticing it, Walt couldn't help grinning himself.

Just then a group of ladies approached.

Jodi Mesto spoke up first. "Gentlemen, we would like to have a talk with the two of you, seein's how yer both sort of the leaders of this wagon train."

Walt held up his hand. "Jodi, Clem here's the leader; I'm followin' along jist like ever'one else."

"Oh, all means the same. Can we talk, please, without havin' to clarify ever'thin' we say?"

Walt nodded at Clem. "As long as we all unnerstand, he's the one that takes the blame."

Clem stood there with his customary sour look directed at her now. "Miss, uhh, May-esto, please say what you got to say."

"Thank you. First, it's Mesto, not May-esto."

"Sure, got it, Mayesto."

She pinched her lips at that but decided not to pursue it. "Second, we got a plan 'bout what we're supposed to do with these towns comin' up an' the lawmen prob'ly lookin' fer us. An' those others are still out there somewhere, or soon will be anyway. We still have to deal with 'em."

Clem and Walt glanced at each other. Then Clem spoke up. "Well, you've stated the obvious, so now what?"

She ignored him. "We think the only thing to do is to break up into small groups, one man with three or four wagons. We have eight men countin' those two old smelly sheepdogs you've got. We draw straws an' those that git the short straw have to go with 'em. We head out in two or three groups. We can pretend we're those Mormons with several wives, or those that have to go with those two can claim 'em as their fathers or sumpthin'. No one should suspect anythin' with us being such small groups, especially in this part of the country. Once we git past Salt Lake Town, we can regroup an' we'll figure out that part at that time. So whatta you two think?"

Walt spoke up this time. "Jodi, that's fine; now we need to let Clem think 'bout it."

Clem glanced at Walt and then back to Jodi. "I'll think 'bout it. An' I'll talk it over with Walt an' Michael. Then we'll talk it over with yer committee, then we can hold a vote, an' then we can submit it fer review. Then—"

"Oh hush up!" It was Leah. She gave him her usual disapproving look. "Clem, we're trying to help. You can at least listen to us and give us an honest opinion. No one is stepping into your position. We have the same thing at stake as you do, even more. We had to pay you to take us."

"No need to go back to that first meetin' agin."

"No we don't, and I thought we were even now, so there is no need for you to bring it up anymore. Just the same, you should consider what we have to say. If we're the ones who are being targeted out here, then you could give us a little respect and let us be heard."

Clem nodded toward his new friend next to him. "I was jist talkin' with Walt here, 'bout who's gonna be a target. But, yer right, an' I apologize, an' I mean it. I will think 'bout it, an' we will talk, after we cross the river in the mornin'. If they don't drown us in the process."

He held up both hands to stop their reaction. "Don't worry, we'll be fine; they'll be sober in the mornin' or I won't take us across."

"Fine then, thank you." Leah turned to the other ladies. "I suggest we all go and tend to our things now. We'll want to be ready extra early. These crossings are never fun—I fear for my life every time—but I trust Clem and he says he'll not let us go if he's worried, and, well, I trust him."

Clem was a little surprised. "Thank you. Ladies? Is there anythin' else?"

They all shook their heads uniformly.

"Well then, if you don't mind I would like to talk to Mrs. Knott fer a moment."

Leah was surprised now and then immediately got worried. She smiled weakly to the others. "I guess I'll catch up to you in a little bit, if he doesn't throw me over the cliff."

Clem gave her his smarmy smile at that.

Walt and the ladies all nodded and returned to the circle of wagons.

Clem looked back out over the river. The wagon had just pulled away a small distance from the bank, and the group of people on that side had obviously been yelling at the ferryman, because he was using his push pole to defend his position on the raft.

Clem kept his gaze that way. She was looking at him and finally gave up on him looking at her, so she stared across at the people at the river and waited for him to say whatever it was he had to get off his chest.

It took him a moment to begin. "Mrs. Knott, I'm worried 'bout what's up ahead. I don't think we can git past Salt Lake, an' perhaps not even Fort Bridger. The law will be lookin' fer us, if fer no other reason than to ask us what happened. I'm worried they won't agree with my reason fer what I did. I am guilty, I admit that, but I'd do it agin in similar circumstances."

He quickly held up his hand again to stop her from whatever she was going to say. "But they won't care if I felt I was right. It might not even git that far. Anyway, so now's the time to say I'm sorry."

He swallowed hard but kept his eyes straight ahead. "I am sorry I've been such a drunk out here. It's not my nature."

He started to get choked up and had to wait a second before he could speak again.

"I'm not like that at home. I loved my Veda an' I tried to do right by her, an' she would not approve of my actions, but they are what's happened an' I'm sorry. I'm sorry I've been so hard out here, but it's what I felt I got to do to keep people alive. You've noticed the wagon pieces along the way. That's from people goin' too soft on t'others an' they git their wagon broke down, or attacked by Indians, or they plummet over the riverbank 'cause the animals break free an' the nice people can't control 'em, an' they end up dead. I'm not like this at home. I'm friendly, I'm a nice person; I can't be that way out here."

She was looking at him but didn't know what to say. Finally she said, "I'm sorry."

"Thank you. I'm scared, an' I don't scare. I may worry, but I don't scare, till now. They're out there somewhere an' they'll come fer us again. They won't be fooled this next time neither, an' we have t'others now, but that's only four men, an' two of 'em are as old as I am. So, if I can keep y'all alive somehow an' keep you away from 'em, I want you to help Emmie. Help her come out to California, an' of course that means Henry an' hopefully that young woman he fancied."

He looked down now and stood there silent for a moment. Leah waited knowing he wasn't done.

"When y'all git there, I want you to take my money, an' after you git Emmie out there, you give her half, an' split up the rest amongst t'others, an' Michael gits a equal share, same as ever'one."

"No! That's your money. You will be there and you can spend it however you want."

She stopped. He was staring at her with a look that said to hush up. He turned away again.

"It's mine, so I want ever'one to git an equal portion, after my—I mean Emmie got her half. I also have other money of my own. I want Emmie to git half of that too, an' then give the rest to Michael."

"We won't need it. It's yours! We can have forty acres free." She stopped again. He was smiling at her this time.

"Those forty acre parcels are all gone. The good ones are anyway. You'll have to ride two days out of town to git one worth livin' on. You'll all have to buy land to git a decent piece. Even at that, some will have to group together."

She started to say something but he stopped her by shaking his head. "Don't argue, please. If I live I'll do what I thinks best then. But if I don't, I'll need you to help me do this. So that's it. Now I'm not gonna change between here an' the end of the trip. I'll most likely have a few too many drinks now an' agin, so save yer looks. Then if I make it, great, I'll go back to bein' the man my Veda knew. If I don't, you know what to do. Will you help me with this?"

She stood there looking at him. He was looking down at her now.

152

She certainly didn't want to agree to this. He finally frowned at her and asked again, "Do you agree, Mrs. Knott?"

She made a face. "Yes, I agree, and I...never mind, I agree and that's that."

She pivoted and walked away briskly.

***

It was the next morning, around three thirty, when Michael had Tom Williams come from his night watch and wake him. Michael took a minute to get himself together, and then he and Tom went through the camp waking everyone else up.

When Michael had the camp awake, everyone got the children ready for the day. They all washed faces and combed hair with the customary yowls and protests.

By daybreak Clem had the first team down at the water's edge waiting for the ferryman to bring his raft across. The sun hadn't risen over the horizon yet when the ferryman showed up on his side. It took about a half hour for him to get himself ready and the raft over to Clem's side of the river. The sun would be showing itself soon.

The man pulled the raft up to the dock in front of Lucy Master's wagon. She had Jodi Mesto, Lizzy Keehn, and Lizzy's Zeb and Annie. Zeb wanted to be on the first raft going over, so Clem allowed him that, and he liked the idea of the ferryman taking some of the smaller wagons first until he was wide awake and knew how the river would be acting today.

The man stepped off the raft and reached out to shake Clem's hand.

"Howdy, mister, you must be the wagon master of that big train I've been watchin' up on the hill."

Clem hesitated, then said hello and told the man his name was Smith.

The ferryman looked at him and smiled. "Okay with me. How many wagons you got?" They talked about the wagons and taking them across.

"I saw you up on the bank yesterday an' wondered what you were doin'. Smart to wait. Jeff can't hold his liquor an' near killed them people last night. We fired him again fer causin' trouble, but we need someone who can drive these rafts, so after he dries out we'll hire him back. Always do; hafta have someone who can do it, drunk er no."

The ferryman sized Clem up. "Well, we better git to loadin', but first, I'm gitten twelve dollars a wagon, paid in advance, an' I'll have you all over in no time."

Clem grimaced. "Well, I say ten dollars sounds fair."

The ferryman shook his head. "What? Ten?" He started laughing. "Well, I say no, not ten, but I'll go eleven if we got no more barginin'." He stuck out his hand again and Clem grabbed it, and they shook hands. "Good deal fer both of us, best kind of deal, I say."

Clem was ready to get away from there. He stepped out of the way and motioned to Lucy to prepare to drive onto the raft. The mules were a little nervous, but Lucy seemed to be a lot nervous.

Clem had the most experienced mules hooked up to the first wagons because he didn't want any problems. But Lucy might not have known that, and she sure hadn't forded a river this big before.

Noticing this, Clem turned and winked at the ferryman. "Meybe I better bring 'em onto the raft then?"

"Sounds right to me, mister!" He had a big smile on his face.

Clem gestured for Lucy and Jodi to climb in the back and asked Zeb to come sit up front with him. Lucy was delighted; Jodi not so much. She scowled but said nothing as she climbed over the seat.

Clem climbed up and took the reins, and once everyone was situated he leaned over and looked at the boy. "Now you pay attention, you'll be bringin' one on yerself before we're done."

Zeb was wide-eyed and grinning. "Yes sir, I'll pay good attention, no worries 'bout me."

Clem slowly drove the mules onto the raft as it swayed deeply and sank with the weight. The mules were very much at attention, but they had done this several times already; they knew what was coming.

The ferryman got them across, and Clem and Zebulon steered the wagon up and away from the river and parked it. Then they unhooked the animals and brought them back onto the raft to take to the other side again.

The man asked Clem if ferrying both ways was included in the price.

Clem was leery, unsure if the man was serious or not. He said yes, and the ferryman laughed and went about his work getting them back.

Another wagon was waiting when they pulled up. Clem and Zeb led the mules off and handed them over to the boys who were waiting. The next wagon was another one from Walt's group. Emerald Trask was driving. Emerald was not quite as nervous looking as Lucy, but Clem asked her anyway if she would rather he take the reins. She agreed and climbed into the back.

Clem and Zeb climbed aboard and Clem looked at the young man. "Think you can bring 'em on?"

"Me? Already? Well, yes sir! I can do it!"

"Okay then, nice an' slow, no rush but don't let 'em stop neither."

"Yes sir, I got it. Hyuup there! Git on up." He gently slapped the backs of the mules with their reins. They lifted their heads and then just walked out onto the raft as if they had done this every day of the trip, no worries.

Zeb was almost surprised by the nonchalance of the mules. He looked at Clem with a big grin and shining eyes. Clem looked back and gave him a big smile.

Brennen and Tom brought two more mules onboard next to the wagon. Clem smiled at Zeb. "Real good, son, real fine. Now let's allow Mr. Ferryman here to take us over."

Once the group was ready the ferryman took over and got the raft ready to go. Then the whole party went across and unloaded. Tom and Brennen went first and stayed there to unhitch the wagon that just came over and re-hitch the waiting wagon with the extra mules they brought.

Clem and Zeb returned with the experienced mules and repeated the process over and over and over again, twenty-three times.

Tom and Brennen stayed on the far side and added men as more wagons came across.

Zebulon ended up driving four teams on. Clem drove eight. Walt, Billy, and Harvey each brought one, Hugh brought his, and Fritzy, his. Michael brought his mother's on and several of the older boys brought their own. By the end of the day the ferryman was plumb tuckered out.

He had to stop three times to rest up and once to take his afternoon dinner. But he was a very happy man, and much richer for the day.

***

Now that Clem had made it past that hurdle, he started thinking about the next problem up ahead: Fort Bridger, and the Army, which meant the law, which meant going to jail, or getting hung or shot or both, for shooting men under a white flag of truce.

Shooting men under a white flag wouldn't be understood by anyone, Clem knew that, and those lawyers wouldn't care about circumstances; they wanted to be the one to get his name in the papers for convicting the killers.

***

Jed and his men were camping just outside of Salt Lake City that same night. They had made hard riding ever since he got back and now were out in front of the wagon train again.

They also had added three new men. Yancy met an old friend named Dillon while in Denver, and he had two friends, Wallace and Stacy.

Jed and everyone else agreed those three made up for the loss of the original five, and they didn't need any more.

***

Clem called a meeting later that evening for just the adults again. They were in a semicircle and he took a position in the center.

"I b'lieve those men who attacked us last time are still after us, an' they're prob'ly out in front agin by now. An' I b'lieve the law is prob'ly after us, at least to find out what part we had in that fight. I b'lieve they won't care why I shot them men; the fact I did it under a white flag will be all they care 'bout. Y'all should be different. You were defending yerselves, so they shouldn't be mad at you. They'll jist be madder at me fer causin' the fight in the first place."

He sighed. "We're safe from them killers fer now, an' we should remain safe, till we git to the Sierra Nevada Mountains. Here we're too close to Fort Bridger an' Salt Lake City, an' the law, an' there are no places around here they could easily sell you off to."

The group started whispering and exchanging glances.

He looked around and began again. "I think they'll come after us closer to the camps an' small towns in Nevada an' California. So fer now, I want y'all to relax, 'cause we still have a long way to go, an' it's gonna be hard till we hit Carson City, where you can rest agin. Then we'll figure out which route we take up an' over. They got meybe ten different ways. I'm positive that's where they'll try fer us. It's the only place."

"Why don't we tell the law the truth, before they come out after us!" It was Verlie Hamilton.

"Tell 'em what? These men want to take you an' sell you off to whoever wants to buy you?"

Seeming perplexed, she looked around at the other ladies. "Well, yes! Exactly that!"

"Ma'am, I unnerstand. But what can the sheriff do? Look fer 'em? Where? We don't even know who they are. Jist some men. We don't know how many, we got no idea where they are, what they look like.

They look like pretty much every other cowboy out here. If they don't arrest me, all they could really do would be to make us stay in town. You ready to quit?"

"But! There ought to be something we can do!"

"Fer right now, all we can do is relax, an' not scare the young'uns, an' take it easy goin' across the desert. Then we decide which way we go over the mountains. It'll take us 'bout a week to git over, if we don't catch snow. That's why we push so hard now till we reach there."

"Maybe we shouldn't have stopped all those days of yours." This was Wheaton Lindy. She was standing stock straight with her head held high. Not proud, or angry, she felt it was a bad decision on his part and it needed to be acknowledged.

He looked over at her. "I do what I feel is right. Love God, with all yer heart, soul, an' strength—it's what I read in the Bible an' I make no excuses, an' we'll continue to stop on Sabbath day till we git to Sacramento. We've discussed this before an' I'm not changin' my ways now."

She was undeterred. "I'm not about to start arguing the point either. I'm putting forth the question because I didn't agree with the idea then, and I still don't. You put us in jeopardy with you taking all those days off for no other reason than you think the Bible says so. We could have been at least at the mountains by now, maybe; close if not there."

"Meybe. I'm sorry you feel that way." Then looking at the rest of the group, "So is there any others who have a question or a statement they wish to make? Please, feel free. I know in the past I closed such things down, but I've come a long way with you ladies, an' you certainly deserve to be heard if you feel you have sumpthin' to say." No one seemed to want to say anything for the moment.

Then a voice off to his right.

"Can we have more target practice between here and the mountains?"

158

He turned to Mary Williams. "Yes we can. I b'lieve we'll try to practice more shootin' from the wagons as we're movin', point an' shoot."

He looked all around again. "Any other questions? I don't mind. Nuthin'? Okay then. Remember: do not be afraid, the young'uns will notice. We still have a month before Carson City, an' then we git to rest, then git ready fer 'em to come agin."

He looked at them all one more time. He really liked them, and he was very impressed with them. He never saw that coming.

13
Fort Bridger

It would be four more days before the wagon train reached Fort Bridger. Though it was a trading post more than anything else, the soldiers were there again, so this would be their first chance to test Clem's theory. If they could get past there they had just six more days until Salt Lake City.

They made camp that night later than usual. They let the herd graze outside the wagons because Clem stopped keeping them corralled inside. There was much less danger of Indians, and the kidnappers were not going to make an appearance anytime soon, so he tried to make life as easy as he could for everyone.

It was the new normal. Clem wanted to keep them moving as far each day as he could, getting them to the desert as fast as possible, going longer into each night as long as they could see. But rest stops in between were longer also, anything to help out with the growing tension.

Everyone was tired and wanted some time alone if possible. Except for Harvey Elkenberry—he seemed to be enjoying the company of all the ladies, especially Mrs. Leah Knott. He was found near her wagon more and more these days.

She had taken to asking some of the others what she could do to dissuade him, but no one seemed to have an answer that worked. She even spoke with Clem, who offered to tell him to stay away. She refused that as being too harsh, seeing as how they were all forced to live in such a confined environment for still another two months.

Harvey had grown bolder in showing his fondness for Leah. She was not amused, and Michael did nothing to help. Even when he could be there, rather than shrink away, Harvey welcomed the young man into whatever conversation he was trying to hold with his mother. And Harvey was always ready, able, and willing to help with getting water and seeing to it that her mules were readied each morning. Finally, she felt she had to confront the situation head on and let the consequences be what they may.

As usual Harvey found himself at her wagon after making his own rounds, stopping by to visit with whoever would talk with him.

"Good evenin', Leah."

"Good evening, Mr. Elkenberry."

She stood up, regarding him and his amused bearded face. "I would prefer Mrs. Knott, please, Mr. Elkenberry. I've spoken of this before."

Seeing her refusal to shake his hand, he offered her his best smile. "Yes ma'am, you have, an' as before I have chosen to deny yer request. I have asked you to call me Harvey, an' yet you refuse to do so. An'—wait!"

He held up his hand to stop her interjecting. "I'm speakin'. Thank you."

The impertinence! She was going to tell him exactly what she thought of his refusals. Her mouth was still open in surprise.

Harvey motioned for her to close it by bringing his fingers together in front of his own open mouth and closing them together along with his lips.

She was flat-out angry now and did not try to hide it. He assumed a look of kind tolerance like one gives a willful child. "Leah, no." He held up his hand again. "I'm not goin' to start this over-formal routine with us, jist as I'm not goin' to go around here referrin' to ever'one by Mrs. This or Mrs. That, an' please, may we sit down?"

She stood there glaring at him, obviously mad. But gaining control of herself, she glanced down at where she would sit and plopped onto a stool, still showing him how angry she was.

He kept his kind countenance in the face of her anger and chose a keg opposite her. "I'm glad you brought this subject up, as a matter of fact. I am a rather shy man."

She rolled her eyes and rolled her head in amplified exasperation to his comment.

He ignored it. "I've been wantin' to talk to you almost since the day I first met you, but circumstances, an' polite company, would not allow such things. Not to mention proper conduct amongst adults."

Now her expression changed; she got concerned.

"I know yer husband is gone, an' yer a single woman, an' I am a single man a little older than yerself. I have a small inheritance that I have chose not to rely on, but I'm a man that would be able to provide fer his wife. I have remained a bachelor up until now, an' Leah, I think yer wonderful—"

"Stop!" She stood up. "Stop and do not say another thing."

"Agin, I have to refuse. I'm sorry, but yer—"

"No! You stop right now!"

"No, I will not."

"Mr. Elkenberry—"

"Harvey."

"Okay, Harvey, you must stop!"

"No."

"What do you mean 'no'? How dare you!" She stomped her foot into the dirt.

He sat there peering up at her. "Oh, I dare all right. I'm not waitin' till somebody else comes along—"

"Stop right now!" She got a little louder that time and others in the camp looked over to see if she was all right. Seeing that Harvey was over there, and knowing how he was wearing on her patience, they all decided she must have had enough and was letting him know about it.

She started to pace but then decided against it and faced him again. "I will not sit here and listen to this."

"Then I will leave." He stood. "I'll not make myself a problem to you. You can relax. Please enjoy the rest of yer evenin'. I'll speak to you tomorrow."

He started to walk away.

"Mr. Elkenberry."

He turned and held up his index finger, wiggling it back and forth in the familiar way.

She spoke in a very loud whisper now. "Harvey, you cannot come back tomorrow. You cannot speak to me on this matter."

"May I sit down again, please?"

"No."

He turned and she spoke up again. "Okay. Sit down, but you cannot speak about such things. I mean, we have to get this straight between us. I cannot listen to such talk. It's not proper. I'm a...well, ah—"

"Widow, yer not married anymore."

"You hush!" She still spoke in her loud whisper. "I don't even know you. And it wouldn't matter. I'm, well, I'm too old for one thing, and, well..."

Harvey stood there quietly, smiling very slightly and being attentive. "Well? Yer what? Too old, you say? Oh not at all, I say."

"Be quiet. I'm trying to talk."

He shook his head. "Yer not as old as I am, an' yer very lovely, an' I agree that I am a little forward with you, but it's still true."

She pursed her lips. "Thank you, but it's not for me. I have my son to look out for."

"I believe he has a young lady ready to look out fer his future.

Whatta 'bout yer future?"

"I'll not discuss my future with you. That's final, thank you. I would really appreciate it if you left me alone."

She turned slightly away from him signaling for him to go.

"As you wish, Leah."

She visibly bristled at the mention of her name.

He waited a moment to see if he could get her to start up again. Realizing she was done, he said, "Goodnight then, until tomorrow."

She turned back to him with fire in her eyes, but she didn't say anything.

He made his way over to his wagon and his friends. Billy saw him coming and was waiting for him as he arrived.

"Evenin', Harvey, how'd it go this evenin'?"

"This evenin'?"

"Yeah, with Mrs. Knott."

"She's a lovely woman." He was all smiles.

Billy beamed up at him. "What was you talkin' 'bout tonight?"

"Nuthin' I want to talk to you 'bout." He gave Billy a big smile. "I'll see you later. I'm goin' to patrol the perimeter fer a while."

"Yeah, you do that. Watch out now. Don't want to git in trouble with any of them widders."

Harvey gave him a hard look. Billy grinned from ear to ear.

Harvey broke out into another big smile. "No chance of that happenin'."

"Good, a person might git the wrong impression from watchin' you."

"Jist you keep watchin' out fer Billy. I'll look out fer me." He walked out into the night.

Just then Walt came over to where Billy was sitting next to his wagon.

"Evenin', Billy, how's things?"

"Good. Givin' Harvey a hard time 'bout that Mrs. Knott."

164

Walt chuckled. "Yeah, he's gitten' bolder. Next thing you know he'll come right out an' say sumpthin' to her."

"Yeah, sooner or later."

Walt looked across the camp, leaning against the wagon. Billy was sitting on a keg next to him and his eyes followed Walt's. There was that Christine lady with the little boy and his younger sister. *Cute kids, Ma is pretty too.* Billy glanced up at Walt and laughed.

Walt came out of his trance and looked down at Billy. "What?"

"What? What? Didn't mean to wake you." Billy said it with a large smile.

Walt stared at him as confused as he had ever been. "What are you talkin' 'bout?"

Billy made a big deal about looking back across the camp again, over at Christine. "I seem to be losin' two friends."

Walt followed his gaze and realized his friend was looking at that pretty Christine lady. He glanced down and then back over at Billy. "Ain't like that."

"Yeah, I can see it ain't. Jist looks like that, but a'course, it's not."

"Shut up." Walt straightened up and stalked away toward Fritzy and Hugh, hoping he could get some peace over there. He left Billy chuckling.

He was thinking that those two might be a little hard to be around because of their reluctance to bathe, but at least they didn't go around poking their noses into other people's business.

"Evenin'."

Fritzy nodded at the new company. "Evenin', Walt, what you up to this fine evenin'?"

"Nuthin', jist killin' time till I hit the sack."

Hugh never lifted his eyes but kept his gaze at the wagon directly opposite them. "You ought to go over there to kill yer time with that Miss Christine, 'stead of two old grungy freighters like us."

Walt gave him a sour look.

Fritzy leaned toward his friend and nudged him with his elbow. "I thought he woulda by now." Then he looked up. "So what's keepin' ya?"

Walt sent him that same sour grimace he gave Hugh. "Y'all worse'n women gitten' in other people's business."

Now Hugh squinted up at Walt with a puzzled look and scratched his head, then turned to his friend. "What's with him, Fritz?"

"Not sure, never had no hankerin' to git married meself. Don't know what he's goin' through."

Walt got all indignant. "Married? Where did you git that? Whoever said anythin' 'bout...anythin'!" He turned and walked toward Sergio's wagon but then veered sharply away and strode between two other wagons out into the night.

"What's eating him, do you suppose?" Cassandra McKinnis came up to Christine to get her children who had been playing there.

"I wouldn't know—could be anything." She was glad it was dark; she could feel her cheeks warming. She wouldn't want anyone to get the wrong idea.

Cassandra smiled. She noticed they were talking about the same man when it could have been anyone with all the activity going on.

***

The wagons were lined up in their customary two rows about a half day outside of Fort Bridger, keeping out of sight just behind a small hill.

Clem had decided to go along with a combination of ideas he had been listening to.

He was sending in two wagons with a man and a woman in each pretending to be couples from the wagon train, to see if they could find out any news about themselves or the kidnappers.

He chose Walt to go with Christine, said they made a nice couple. That made both of them turn a little pink. Everyone else tried to keep their smiles at a minimum.

The other couple was Harvey and Leah. He chose them as

166

payback for Leah. He knew Harvey was sweet on her and she did not care for his advances.

She was mad as a hornet and tried quietly to get Clem to change his mind, but he wouldn't take no for an answer. He finally had to remind her that he was the wagon master and she was the one who hired him.

That stopped her cold and she climbed aboard her wagon without further comment. Harvey took the reins and she tried to grab them away from him, but he pulled them out of her reach.

She glared at him. "It's my wagon! I've driven it all the way here."

"My dear, it is my place as the pretend husband to drive the wagon."

"I don't need you to try and pretend anything! I can do it!"

"The town folk don't know that, my dear."

"Stop saying that. I'm Mrs. Knott."

"Once we git back, you may be whomever you wish to be, my dear, but until then, I'll be polite, but it won't do fer me to be callin' you Mrs. Knott. Not if we wish to continue our trip all the way to California. Yes?"

"Fine." She looked away and never did glance his way again until they actually rode into Fort Bridger.

***

Walt and Christine got along famously after a few moments of very awkward silence. At first they didn't pass a word between them as they rode along uncomfortably close, until he finally got up the nerve to ask her how she came to be part of the wagon train.

She told him about meeting Leah back in Independence, Missouri. It was actually Leah who asked her to join after learning of her circumstances—being a presumed widow and not having any real way to sustain herself. And it was Leah who outfitted her wagon and made arrangements with Clem to bring her along.

She knew most of the story now about how Walt and the rest

came to be searching for them, but not all the details because she missed that big meeting when they first joined up. So she asked him if he could fill in fact from fiction.

When the two wagons finally came into Fort Bridger, there was a lot more there than they expected to find. There was a fort, but overall it was more like a little town with a trading post, a sawmill, a gristmill, and even a school! The first one in the whole territory, they were to learn.

The fort itself consisted of large, thick adobe walls that were somewhat battle scarred, but the other buildings were all fairly new, replacing the ones that had been burned to the ground by the Mormons during the "Utah War" in 1858—a fact they learned from the man in the trading post. He liked to brag about it to anyone coming in.

The military occupants of the fort were the newly formed Eighteenth Infantry. Their barracks consisted of two long buildings built out of logs; the officers' quarters were two small log cabins. There was even a small building for a jail. A fact the two couples took special note of.

They left about two hours after they arrived, having bought a few provisions and finding out what information they felt they could safely gather without drawing any suspicion.

They generally felt good about things overall. The post commander offered no word about the gun battle, or the kidnappers, or anything other than pleasant conversation, just asking about where they were headed to and where they were coming from. It was a perfectly normal meeting all in all and they left very happy with the mission.

Upon returning they gave the details of their reconnaissance, and everyone agreed that they seemed to be safe, at least as far as bypassing Fort Bridger and the Army contingent stationed there.

That's when Lester came riding in from his watch.

"Excuse me, Mr. Clem, but the Army's ridin' in."

14
Post Commander

Clem stood up, followed by everyone else. Coming up from the direction of Fort Bridger was a company of soldiers, about thirty men on horseback.

They stopped a hundred yards out, and then four of them rode in from there: two officers, a sergeant, and another soldier carrying the company banner.

Clem stood there looking up at them and then walked over to meet them.

"Afternoon, major, what can we do fer you?"

The first officer touched the brim of his hat. "Major Andrew Burt, post commander, Fort Bridger. I brought my doctor out to meet you all. He likes to meet with the folks driving through, to see if he can be of any assistance. You never know who might need some help; sometimes folks don't even know they need it."

He finished with a smile that told Clem he was going to be friendly only as long as he needed to be.

Clem smiled up at the major and touched the brim of his own hat. He tried not to let his growing fear show. "Well, thank you, sir, but we really don't need any help; we're all as healthy as can be."

"Good, that's good, glad to hear it." The major dismounted and was immediately followed in this by the other officer and the sergeant.

The last soldier, holding the company flag, stayed mounted.

They all stood next to their horses smiling at Clem. He was struggling now, trying not to look nervous.

"As long as we're out here, I'm sure you wouldn't mind the doctor walking around and checking on everyone. I appreciate that."

The major turned to the sergeant and held out his reins. The man came and took them and also the reins from the other officer. The two officers then stepped forward and Major Burt reached out to shake Clem's hand.

He smiled again and Clem, smiling back, gave him a firm handshake.

Clem could see the man was not going to be denied. The major stared at him with a very serious look and a forced smile. Clem met his gaze and tried to be calm, hoping he wouldn't start sweating. Then he felt a little bead run down the side of his face.

The major noticed it. He already knew this man was nervous. "Hot today, going to be a hot summer."

Clem wanted to run. "Yeah, I s'pose. Got to make our way across the desert, during the worst time a year, but we got to deal with it. Headed to California an' want to make the Sierra Nevadas before October."

"October? Well, you're on good time then. Hope we don't hold you up."

Without saying anything, the doctor walked past them now toward the camp. Everyone there was still standing stock still watching the conversation between the two.

Stopping at the group that had been having the meeting, the doctor said hello to one of the ladies and started to talk to the others standing there.

At first they seemed nervous and were trying to act very calm, but after a couple of awkward minutes they realized they would just make things worse unless they relaxed. So they began to show him around the camp, introducing him to the children and the other ladies who hadn't joined the meeting.

Walt, Billy, Sergio, and Harvey all came over to join Clem and the major. Michael joined them too, and they all kept a genial conversation going about how the trail had been so far while they watched the doctor wander from wagon to wagon and child to child.

When the doctor approached Willa O'Hara's wagon, Willa was standing there, so the doctor talked to her while at the same time peering in the back of the wagon.

Clem knew he was looking at Maddy with her leg up in a sling. She had been healing nicely, but now that doctor would want to look at it, and surely ask questions. He watched as the doctor climbed into the back of the wagon and disappeared.

Clem said to himself, *This is the end.*

Major Burt was asking questions about Indians now, if they had seen any, traded with them, had any problems, or if they had seen anything else unusual along the way. He appeared to be simply keeping up a pleasant, general conversation.

Then he just as casually asked Clem if he knew about some men who were supposedly murdered under a flag of truce. He was gazing directly at Clem, no smile now.

Returning his look, Clem didn't know what to say. He had to come up with something. "Yeah, don't have any particular information to give you."

"You heard about it then? Did you see them by any chance? The wagon train that might have been involved."

"To be perfectly honest, as soon as we saw the dead men, I got us outta there fast as possible. Didn't want to wait around with these ladies an' find out what was gonna happen next."

Major Burt was looking at him sharply. He was about to ask Clem another question when the doctor came back toward them, so he waited and turned his attention to the doctor.

The doctor saluted and it was returned by the major. The doctor stated, "Sir, they're all as healthy as the man said."

Ignoring everyone, he reported directly to the major as if they were all alone. "They even got a young girl that got shot in the leg. Someone did a fine job of patching it up and keeping it clean so as to keep the infection out. She'll probably keep a limp, and a little crook in her leg, but I think it's better to leave it alone now than breaking it again and trying to do better. Sometimes you just got to live with it."

The major took in all the information without any reaction. Then he turned to Clem and asked him, "How'd the poor thing get shot?"

"Accident, never shoulda happened. Things like that do sometimes, though."

The major nodded slightly in recognition of Clem's statement, then turned back toward the doctor. "So no other people hurt or infections or disease, nothing to worry about here?"

"No, sir, they're as healthy as we can ask for."

"Good. Mr. Hastings, would you take the corporal on back to the men and have them make camp where we are. Do them some good to sleep outdoors. I have a couple more questions to ask Mr. Bentone here."

The doctor saluted, it was returned, and then he took the reins from the sergeant and mounted up. Followed by the soldier holding the company banner, he rode back out to the soldiers who had dismounted and were waiting.

Now the major faced Clem again. "There're Indians in the area, and they've been causing trouble lately. I can't blame them; they believe this is their land, but it's my job now to keep the peace, their land or not."

Clem nodded soberly. "Major, we can take care of ourselves if needed. No need fer protection, haven't had any trouble out here."

The officer regarded Clem. "I have no doubt you can. But we will stay the night just the same. Will you walk with me? I hate just standing around making conversation. Feels like I'm standing at attention."

Holding his arm out, he turned away from everyone else without any acknowledgement, and Clem naturally followed his polite command. The others let them walk off without them.

"This should just take a moment." He had that unfriendly smile again.

The major pointed in the direction of a large rock sticking up out of the ground. Long, like a bench, it would make a nice place for them to sit, and it would be out of earshot from everyone.

Clem didn't say anything but walked over to the rock with the major, and they sat down next to each other facing the wagons.

The major put both his hands on his knees, rubbing them. Then he spoke up, looking at the wagons and the ladies trying not to look at them.

"Thank you, sir, I appreciate your willingness to speak with me for a while longer. It's hard out here, harder on my Elizabeth, but then she loves me and wanted to accompany me, even knowing what she was in for." He waited for Clem to respond but when he didn't get any, he turned and pulled his leg up to sit sideways on the rock to look at Clem more directly.

"So tell me what you know about that murder, if it was one. What can you tell me about it? What happened?"

Clem turned his head to look the major in the eye, then turned back to the camp.

"All I can do is tell you what I think happened, an' you'll have to figure out the rest fer yerself."

"Okay, let's start with that. What happened? You think."

Clem kept staring toward the wagons. "I know there was this wagon master who was hired by these ladies to take 'em out to California, jist like we're doin' here." He glanced at the major.

The man nodded he understood. "Yeah, okay."

Clem looked back to his wagons and saw everyone trying to act normal. "Well, it seems there were these others, these men who learned 'bout the wagon train, an' they must of decided they was gonna kidnap the women an' sell 'em off to whoever would buy 'em."

He looked over at the major again. The man was calmly listening, staring at Clem; he didn't seem upset about anything.

Clem continued. "So this here wagon train was on the trail travelin' along an' they find these men blockin' the road. So the old man knows he's got nowhere else to go an' figures they're already behind him anyway, so better go see what they want. Anyway he comes out, an' they send these three men out with this white flag. They're all puffed up an' grinnin' 'cause they know they got 'em, an', well, he knows it too, so anyway they tell the old man jist what their plan is. Take the women, an' the boys, an' supposedly they'll let him go with whatever he has in his saddlebags. They also give him the option of goin' back an' fightin' it out with 'em, but then they'd kill him an' the boys as punishment."

He shot another glance at the major, who hadn't moved a muscle, no sign of anything, just listening.

"So he, a'course, he don't know what to do. He knows they gonna kill him anyways leave or stay, so he's tryin' to think of sumpthin' when he tells 'em that the cavalry from Fort Casper knew 'bout 'em, an' they was right behind him, so they better git while they can. A'course they don't believe him. Then he looks up at this hill off to the side wonderin' what he can say next, when he decides to try an old child's trick. It's all he's got. So he starts to say sumpthin', then stops an' gits this big stupid grin on his face, an', an' he don't look back at the men, he jist keeps lookin' up at the hill, hopin' an' prayin' they'll look, an' they actually do! He can't believe it."

Clem lowered his gaze to the ground and shook his head remembering.

"So, when they do, he—he pulls out his pistol an' shoots 'em, right in the chest, one, two, three, then back agin, one, two, three. He's so scared he jist 'bout faints right there on his horse. But he turns round an' takes off back fer the wagons, which was chargin' hard right at 'em by then, not sure why, but awful glad they was."

Clem looked up at the wagons—it was kind of a loving look—then over at the major, who was still staring at him, no emotion of any kind, just the same cold, unassuming stare.

Clem didn't know what to make of that but continued after a big sigh. "So anyways he made it back into the wagons an' he rode straight into the herd, an' straight out the back before he could stop. Those men, the ones that were lined up behind the first three, they came chargin' after him, an' the wagons, an' both them an' the wagons started shootin' it out with each other, point-blank. Two boys were killed; one was sixteen, an' one was jist seven years old."

Clem paused for a long moment.

"A woman was shot, an' two more men, boys, but they'll be fine. All 'cause these men felt they could take these women by force, an' do what they wanted with 'em, an' then sell 'em off, jist 'cause they was big enough an' hard enough to do it. Two young boys dead."

Major Burt spoke now. "And one young girl shot in the leg."

Clem stared at the ground. "Yeah, one young girl almost lost her leg, an' mighta got the gangrene an' died." He finished speaking real softly.

"Just like that young girl you got with you, that was wounded by accident."

"What?" Clem looked up at him. At first he didn't realize what the man was saying; then when he did, he looked him right in the eye. "Yeah, jist like our Maddy."

Clem was staring at the officer this time. The man didn't flinch.

Then the major fixed his attention on the wagons. "How many ladies you got with you?"

"'Bout forty now. One woman was killed 'bout two months back, Irma Saddenwasser. That was a different kidnappin' attempt. They was jist some cowboys that happened to come up on us while the girls were bathin'. I guess they saw an opportunity, an', well, it ended badly fer 'em."

The major noticed that Clem had dropped the pretense of just knowing about the story. He decided not to mention it.

Clem looked back at the wagons and all the ladies. "I give these ladies credit; they been through hell an' come out t'other side."

Clem turned back to the major. "So what's next?" He wasn't nervous anymore. That's when another thought came into his mind. "You ever take a drink a whiskey?"

That actually startled the major, and it took him a second to recover. He gave Clem a grin. "Do summers get hot?"

They both chuckled at that.

Clem nodded toward the wagons. "I got a bottle of some real good drinkin' whiskey."

The major looked over at the wagons thinking for a moment, then turned back to Clem. "Would you care to join me for dinner, at my tent tonight? Say about an hour from now? The food's no good, but there's plenty of it. I'm sure you eat much better here, but I'm not sure I could talk freely amongst all the women; wouldn't feel comfortable."

This surprised Clem, but he recovered just as fast. "Can I bring a couple of the men? I'd want 'em to hear anythin' you got to tell us."

"Yeah, bring 'em. We got plenty if they're brave enough to join us. See you in about an hour."

"Okay then."

They both stood and walked back to the horses with the sergeant, who came to attention as the major approached. Taking the reins without another word, Major Burt mounted up, followed by his sergeant, and they rode off.

Clem watched him for a second and then turned toward the wagons and froze. Everyone was standing stock still staring at him.

Oh great. He dropped his head and walked into his inquisition.

***

176

The food at the major's tent was bad, and burnt, but not enough they didn't notice it was really bad. And they had gotten used to better cooking with the ladies.

They all felt obligated to eat the plateful they were handed, but no one wanted seconds. Once they were done, they sat around while the enlisted men cleaned up.

Once the orderlies were gone the major told them that when the couples came in, he knew something wasn't right. They just didn't seem very comfortable with each other, something forced, so he asked the doctor if he wanted to go out and meet the wagon train, and the doctor was more than agreeable to get out of the fort.

Doc Hastings was with them for the meal, and he asked about Maddy's leg. He had his suspicions but didn't care to ask outright without the major giving him permission first. The major got his full report upon returning and hadn't decided yet what to do with the information.

After dinner Walt talked about the campaign in the Rockies. The major thought the best part of that story was the running fight with the wagons and everyone's inability to shoot anyone else while racing across the meadow.

They talked about the war. That's where Doc Hastings first joined up with Major Burt, then Lieutenant Burt, under General George Henry Thomas, the Rock of Chickamauga. They were part of Sherman's Atlanta Campaign.

It went long into the evening and it was Clem who noticed the bottle wasn't even half empty, yet everyone was still feeling fine, including Michael, who was there at the insistence of both Walt and Clem. Michael's going had been adamantly opposed by his mother until he reminded her that he was a man now, and the trail boss, and it wouldn't seem appropriate to leave the trail boss behind on such an important meeting.

Finally, at the end of the evening the major asked Clem if he might stay at Fort Bridger tomorrow, and then they could leave for Salt Lake on Saturday. His wife would be very grateful to have the company of so many women, and he was sure she would want to throw a party on Friday night.

Clem started to object, worried that the major, as friendly as he was, was still trying to get them to stay until he could further investigate Clem's version of what happened. Clem thought he was going to start sweating again.

He had to try to get away. "Well sir, as much as I would truly love to stay, an' I can imagine how much the ladies would want to stay, I still have to decline yer generous offer. I am sorry, I truly am."

The major shook his head and waved his hand. "Clem, I must insist. I still need to think about your story that you gave me. I got a lot more information that I need to consider, and knowing my wife, if I didn't bring you in and invite you to a party, I'd be the ox before the cart."

Clem pursed his lips and slightly shook his head in exasperation. Michael looked on, wondering how Clem was going to get out of this.

The major could see Clem was really feeling caught in a trap, and he felt sorry for the man. "Come on now, you know everyone here wants to take a day off, and you'll enjoy the rest yourself, and your ladies will think you're wonderful for it. So we leave tomorrow morning at nine sharp, agreed?"

Clem had nothing he could come up with. "Well okay, I guess we stay."

"Good, it's settled then, and we can have that party Friday night."

Again Clem found something else to worry him. "Well, now, I'll not be able to attend yer party, not that I'm not appreciative."

"Okay, what now?"

Clem was relieved to notice the man was smiling. "I don't go to no parties on a Friday night."

The major turned curious again. "Never?"

"Never."

"Why not?"

"How 'bout I explain that on Saturday. I'm sure ever'one else will be delighted to attend the party, an' I don't mean no insult, but you'll jist have to trust me on this one."

"I'll not have to post a guard to watch you?" The major was smiling.

"No sir, I'll be there in the mornin', promise. I'm not leavin' without the ladies; I jist won't be at a dance party Friday night."

The major scratched his head. "Okay then, you'll not be there and I'll find out why on Saturday. Well, if there's nothing else, I'm going to call it a night, and I'll follow you all into the fort tomorrow."

**

They returned to the wagons and were caught completely off guard by the ferocity of the attack.

The ladies all turned on Clem as one furiously wronged woman, multiplied by thirty.

He was truly shocked. He actually thought he had done something nice, and that they would be happy, but when they learned he had agreed on their behalf to attend the post commander's wife's party for the very next night, some suggested they shoot him dead and go on to California by themselves.

Now, because of him, they had to drive these stinky, smelly old wagons into Fort Bridger, tomorrow, which would take them until somewhere around noon to get there! And then they would have about half a day to clean themselves up and clean and press a dress that would be somewhat acceptable for a party at a post commander's house!

And he didn't even have any idea if they were supposed to bring something with them or not! The suggestion to shoot him dead came up again.

After much heated debate amongst themselves, they finally

calmed down enough to make plans, which started with getting everything ready to move out even earlier than normal and how they had to feed the children without stopping on the way to the fort, to buy more time.

Michael then stepped up and made the unpardonable error of reminding them that they would have plenty of time to feed the children when they stopped to change the mules out.

Now they turned on him. Even his own mother mumbled under her breath something about a witless imbecile. He retreated in haste, embarrassed and thankful to be alive.

***

The main wagon train pulled into the fort a little after ten that morning. The mules were sweating profusely, lathered up terribly, and never in the last four months since they left Missouri had they been in such need of rest.

The trailing herd and the two wagons driven by Fritzy and Hugh were still over an hour behind them, but it was impossible to keep them going at the pace set by the women for more than thirty minutes at a time.

Clem and most of the other men, along with the cavalry, stayed with the herd and the two freighters. They kept the wagons in sight for as long as was needed to make sure they arrived safely, although at the pace they were running no Indians, or anyone else for that matter, could have caught them.

***

The ladies and the young gentlemen from the wagon train made it to the party that evening right on time, with several dishes in hand.

It was held in the fort's barn, which had a wonderful wood floor in the large main room. The soldiers had moved all the stock outside to the corrals and temporary holding pens early that morning, and the floor had been cleaned thoroughly, twice, per the major's wife's instructions.

This had all been accomplished in good order because the major had judiciously sent word back to his wife of a planned party.

He actually sent in four riders prior to his dinner meeting with the men of the wagon train, having witnessed an attack early in his career on a superior officer for failing to notify his wife of a similar situation. He never forgot that lesson.

They all had a wonderful time and stayed long after midnight, when they finally said their goodnights and left to go back to their wagons, which had been moved to just outside the main fort itself.

Everyone was all smiles and of good cheer, with tired feet from dancing, and many, many stories of the wonderful Mrs. Burt, her husband the post commander, the other soldiers, and all the other people who lived around the fort.

There were several stories, not spoken of so openly, of Walt and Christine dancing together quite a bit more than with others. There were also several stories about Leah having to politely dance with Harvey on a few occasions, although he did not press her courtesy too much.

Michael and the other young men showed themselves to be proper escorts for the otherwise unaccompanied ladies.

And when several of the town folk asked about the absence of the wagon master, there were still those who, in spite of the good time they had, and the much anticipated rest, held out for shooting him and moving on, but that group was dwindling.

***

The next day came bright and early, but most of the people from the wagon train were still resting with blankets, hats, or scarves draped over their faces to keep the sun at bay.

Clem was up and about, but he let everyone else sleep in as much as they wanted to on Saturdays, with never any complaint from them.

He quietly made himself something to eat and walked about the fort until he saw the major stretching on his front porch. He waved and the major beckoned him over to his house.

This turned into the beginning of a very long and enjoyable Bible study for the two men that lasted most of the day. It was joined off and on by several others and interrupted only by dinner, then ended with supper.

They both agreed they learned something from the other and from others who would drop in for a while, and all in all it was a most enjoyable day, one never forgotten by either man until their last days.

The next day, Sunday, all the people of the wagon train and most of the town's residents held a right proper church service right back there in the barn again, which was not unusual. It seemed that the only people absent from the wagon train were Fritzy and Hugh, and Clem, and none of them were missed.

Clem did not attend the Sunday luncheon either, although Fritzy and Hugh were able to make it to that.

The major managed to wander off during the luncheon to talk with Clem further about different subjects on the Bible, and it turned into another good Bible study that was ultimately interrupted by the major's wife sending word that he should not neglect his guests who were actually in attendance at their Sunday service.

They all eventually had to say their goodbyes as Clem insisted they had to move out, much later than he wanted to and much earlier than the ladies felt was needed.

Clem was standing beside Cherry when Major Burt came up and handed him a letter. A final gift of safe passage. He said, "It should help if you get stopped again."

When Clem questioned him about the telegram that he was sure the post commander must have received, asking to keep them under his custody, the officer smiled. "The way I understand that telegram, I was to be on the lookout for a wagon train of women, with possibly several men, true killers. You don't fit that description."

They shook hands and Major Burt bid them safe travels.

It seemed like the entire trading post came out with fond farewells, and once again the ladies were off, without one smile to be seen.

15
Salt Lake City

They made their first camp after driving long into the night. Clem felt it would be better overall to get the party and the church service and the whole atmosphere out of them as soon as possible, and get them back into a survival attitude.

Clem also wanted to reach Salt Lake City as soon as possible because if they could get past it, then they would have a free run from there to Carson City and the Sierra Nevadas and finally California, the end of this very long, hard trail.

The wagon train headed west and south from Fort Bridger looking for the Wasatch Mountains, with the City of Salt Lake on the other side.

They would cross over and through a pass and then down into the valley. The road would bring them south of the city, and with any luck, they would be able to skirt on past without being stopped by anyone.

They were starting earlier now than before because the days were becoming longer and hotter. They would take much longer breaks in the middle part of the day to rest the animals and then drive far into the night while they had a bright moon.

On the fourth day they reached the mountains and the pass they were seeking. The next morning found them already moving through the mountains, and they made it relatively easily. It was hard on the mules, but they were still in good shape, and everyone heard repeatedly from Clem that he attributed it to the regular weekly stops he insisted on.

They made the valley floor around noon and were able to see the city off in the distance as they descended, but even though they had a longing to go see a real city again, the first one since leaving Independence, they knew it could mean trouble. They already had more than their share of it up to this point.

Just up ahead the road split, where travelers must decide to head straight west into the desert and on to California or turn north into the city.

And right there at the intersection were two men sitting in chairs in the shade of a large tree, their horses tied up behind them.

They seemed to be waiting for someone.

Once they saw the wagons coming, they never moved until the two front outriders reached them. Then they rose and talked to the boys as the wagons got closer. Finally, Clem and Michael came riding over to meet them and see what this was all about.

Carl Roch and Joseph Copher were sitting on their horses beside the two men; they didn't look happy.

The two men were deputy sheriffs from Salt Lake City. They were looking for a wagon train full of women wanted in connection with a murder outside of Fort Casper, in the Dakota Territories. They felt this particular wagon train seemed to fit the description very snugly, as they put it, and they had refused to let the boys ride back to warn the others of their presence.

Now that the wagons were here the two deputies wanted the entire wagon train to accompany them back up to the city to have a meeting with the sheriff.

Clem refused. "I have a letter of safe passage from the post commander Major Andrew Burt of Fort Bridger. He knows us an' knows of the incident you spoke 'bout, an' that we're not the people you lookin' fer. It says so right there in my letter."

"You got a letter? Well, let me see it." It was the first deputy; he seemed to be the one in charge.

Clem asked Michael if he would go get it. Michael turned Cloud around and rode back into the wagon train, ignoring all questions that came at him as he passed the wagons.

He returned with the letter and handed it over to Clem, who took it, looked at the deputy, and then handed it to the second one, the one who hadn't talked yet.

The first one noticed the jibe but didn't say anything. The second man took the letter and had to remind himself it would be impolite to break out in a grin just then.

He read it and glanced up at Clem, then over at the first man. "It seems to be authentic, but it could be from anywhere really."

Clem's blood began to simmer and his face turned dark. "Look at it. It's written on Army paper. It has his stamp at the bottom. How could I do all that?"

"You can accompany us back to see the sheriff and explain it all to him." The first deputy appeared to be agreeable, but Clem could tell he wasn't going to budge on the matter.

Clem got real vocal. "We won't move two feet in the direction of that city. You can go git yer sheriff an' bring him out here to us. That's the best I can offer you, deputy."

The first one seemed a little unsure of what to do now, so Clem pressed the issue, sensing victory and the ability to leave here as quickly as possible. "Well? What are we goin' to do, deputy, dance in the road? Leave us be or go git yer sheriff."

The second one spoke up again. "Not so fast. You can calm down or we will drag you into town. We are ready, and you ain't gonna run with all these wagons."

He stared at Clem. He wasn't angry, but he wasn't looking so compassionate either. He was telling this cranky old cowboy that he was in charge and wasn't going to be buffaloed by him.

Clem relaxed a bit. He knew they had the right, and he wouldn't fight them. He was trying to bluff them down but that obviously didn't work. It seemed like nothing worked how he wanted it to, ever since that first meeting with Leah Knott.

"Okay, what's yer plan?" Clem reminded himself to be polite, until they really did something wrong.

The second one answered, "You all will follow us inta town and talk to the sheriff, an' he'll tell us what the plan is, but I 'speck he'll send a telegraph back to Fort Bridger an' verify that you are who you say you are."

"You ain't takin' my letter, I'm keepin' it. Jist send a telegram yerselves."

"I want the sheriff to see it. So you ready?"

Clem realized he had no other option. *Father, please save me again.*

The first deputy was smiling broadly again. Clem considered that they must have been out here a long time and thus weren't happy about some old codger trying to dictate to them.

He thought of another idea. "Okay, I'll go with you an' keep my letter. My wagons stay here waitin' on us. You can telegraph that major, an' he'll verify it. Then I come back out here, an' we leave. How 'bout that? Fair?"

The two thought about it, then exchanged glances to make sure the other was in agreement. The first deputy nodded. "Okay, mister, you got a deal. Let's get goin'. The sooner we get this done, the better."

Clem turned to Michael. "I'll be right back."

Michael told the boys to follow him. Then he looked at the deputies, and the second one smiled and nodded his consent. Clem kept his eyes on the deputies as if there was nothing unusual at all about Michael calling his men.

That was not how he felt inside. When he heard Michael call the boys, he was worried this might be the last time he ever got to hear that.

He faced Michael. "You know what to do if I'm not back by nightfall."

**

Michael turned Cloud around and led the two boys back to the wagons, to a small group that had gathered at the front.

Michael talked to them while the others waited in their wagons. He told the two men to go around and tell everyone to relax and have the other men help take care of the animals.

If Clem didn't return, they would send Walt and Billy to find out what happened. This was not Clem's plan, but Michael would remind him later that he was in charge when Clem wasn't there.

Michael told everyone not to argue; he knew no one would leave without Clem, they just had to wait it out.

**

As soon as Michael and the boys left, Clem turned to the second deputy. "Let's go, gentlemen."

The first one sauntered over to his chair under the tree, sat down, and tilted it back against the trunk, smiling at Clem. The second one walked to his horse, gathered up the reins, and mounted up, then looked at Clem. "Let's go."

It took them a little over an hour at a gentle gallop to reach the middle of town, and Clem followed him as they rode up to the telegraph office. They dismounted and stepped onto the boardwalk.

Clem asked the deputy about the sheriff looking at his letter first.

"He'll get to see it. He'd ask me to do this anyway, so I might as well get it done first." He opened the door and Clem followed him inside.

"Hello, Oren, how's things goin' today? Do you have time to send off a telegram for me?"

Oren never looked up. "Nope, hafta come back tomorrow, sorry."

188

He was hunched over his desk.

The deputy glanced at Clem, whose stomach was starting to get queasy.

He looked back at the man working away. "Sorry, but it's official business. I need you to stop whatever you're doin' and do this for me."

The telegraph operator made a big show of sighing and laid his pencil on the desk. He talked as he straightened up his desk. "Sure, I always got time for official business. I got no time of my own, as a matter of fact; I'm always doin' something official for somebody round here."

He turned around then and, noticing Clem standing there, looked suspicious. "This got somethin' to do with your friend?"

"Yes sir, it does."

The operator brightened up. "Well then, that's not official, is it? Favors ain't official accordin' to the National Telegraphic Union, says so in the code book."

Oren looked over at Clem. "Sorry, mister, come back tomorrow. Late morning would be better." Smiling, he turned around again, picked up his pencil, and went back to work.

The deputy was a little embarrassed now and cleared his throat. "Oren, it is official business, an' it concerns this particular gentleman, an' I need you to tend to it now. I am sorry." He said that last part with less sentimentality than normally accompanies an apology.

Oren noticed. He stopped again but made no big show this time. "Fine."

Laying his pencil down, he rose and walked over to his telegraph desk and sat down, picking up another pencil. "Okay, what do you need?"

The deputy pointed to a chair in the corner and ordered Clem, "Take a seat." Then he leaned over near Oren and directed him what to write while Clem did as he was told.

The operator spoke to the deputy. "It might be a while before they get back to me. You don't know if anyone's there or not. You want me to come find you when it comes in?"

"Nope, we'll wait right here."

Oren grimaced at the deputy. "You know it could be hours before they get back to me. They don't always answer right back."

"I know, just send it and we'll wait, thank you."

The deputy strolled over to the operator's desk and sat in his chair. He surveyed what the man had been working on. "Your house?"

Oren was apparently studying the message. "Hope so, someday."

The deputy's attention shifted to Clem.

Legs straight out into the room and hands folded together on his chest, he was staring at the two of them. He just wanted to get back on the trail and it showed.

The operator began typing out the telegram and turned around when he finished. "Well now, I guess we wait."

The deputy never said anything. His gaze drifted to the operator and back to Clem, and then out the windowpane in the front of the office.

Twenty minutes went by; it seemed like hours. The deputy and the operator were talking about life in the city when the machine started clacking away.

When it first started up the operator just about jumped. He whirled around and wrote down the message, then brought it over to the deputy.

The deputy read it and looked at Clem. "Jist not your day, mister. Seems this major fella is gone. Left the fort headed east. They don't know when he'll be back; they sent a telegram ahead to notify him, but no tellin' when he'll hear about it. Guess we can go wait in the sheriff's office now."

Clem never said a word. He drew his legs in and stood up.

As they headed out the door with Clem leading the way, the machine started clacking away again. They were ready to mount up on

190

their horses when Oren called out the open door, "Hold on, deputy, I might have somethin' for you."

They both stopped and looked at each other, then at the doorway. The operator hollered out again, "Come on back in, this is for you."

The deputy climbed the steps and started to reenter but stopped and turned to Clem, who hadn't moved. "Come on back in, you don't know the way to the sheriff's office." He stood there watching him. Then he waved his hand, as if to invite a guest in.

Clem led the deputy back into the office and sat down.

The deputy followed him and walked to the desk. He took the message and after reading it looked over at Clem. "Did you know a Dr. Hastings there at the fort?"

Clem's face wrinkled up in worry. "Yeah, I mean, I don't know; jist some doc, looked at all the ladies an' young'uns. He remembers me? Good then, we'll be goin'."

"Hold on. He ain't answered none of my questions. We'll leave only when he has, if he can." Facing the operator, the deputy bent and spoke to him real low. Then the operator got to work on his telegraph.

When Oren was done he turned around and looked up at the deputy. "Shouldn't be too long if he knows the gent."

Almost ten minutes went by with them all very uncomfortable and trying not to stare at each other; then the telegraph began clacking away and the operator started writing.

The machine went quiet for a full minute. The deputy eyed Oren, who was reading the message. He returned the deputy's look and held up a finger and shook his head no. That set the deputy pacing, but when it started up again, he stopped and stared at Oren.

When the operator was finished he handed two notes over his shoulder to the deputy, who was hovering over him trying to read what he was writing.

The deputy took them. He read the first note and looked at Clem, and then read the second before giving Clem his full attention.

The deputy wore a puzzled expression on his face and twisted up his mouth. "Okay, he answered my questions, but really it could be anybody."

Clem felt like he got punched in the gut again.

The deputy glanced at his telegram, then back to Clem. "But he gave me a couple questions of his own. So, how often did you stop to rest your wagon train and the animals?"

Confusion swept over Clem's face. "What?"

"You heard me. What's your answer?"

Clem stared warily at the deputy. "Ever' Saturday, ever' week." He worried this was not what the doctor remembered.

The deputy gave Clem a strange look, offering no indication of what he was thinking. Oren was doing the same.

Clem got frustrated. "Well, send it back an' let's see what he has to say. Whatta ya waitin' fer?"

The deputy pursed his lips. "No need." He held up the second note. "Got the answer right here, an' you answered it perfectly. He gave us the question, then sent us the answer, at least what he thought you'd say."

The deputy smiled all of a sudden. "I guess we can let you get on your way. I hope you understand, we got to be careful. You could be a kidnappin' murderer an' still be as friendly as a clergyman. You just never know."

Clem just about fainted with relief but quickly gathered himself so as to not let on. "Yeah." He let that grumble out. He was standing up now. "Well, if there's nuthin' else, I'd like to git back to my wagons before they leave me." He wasn't about to be happy in front of the deputy.

The deputy for his part just let his smile grow bigger. "Yeah sure, let's get goin'."

Back on their horses, they headed out toward the wagons. They were silent for a long time and then finally the deputy asked Clem, "Why ever' Saturday?"

"Sabbath, it's in the Bible." Clem kept his eyes straight ahead.

The deputy grinned at the old codger. "You never heard of the Sunday Sabbath?"

"Yeah, heard of it." Clem still didn't look over at the deputy or add anything else to the conversation.

The deputy waited for a moment before deciding the old man wasn't going to talk. He was in no mood himself to try and start a Bible study with the old "wood knot," so he'd just let him be. They rode the rest of the way in silence.

They had just got within sight of the wagons when several saw them coming, and word began to spread throughout the wagon train. Just about everybody came forward to see what the news would be.

Clem stood up in his stirrups and gave them the signal to move out.

Everyone erupted in hearty waves and hurrahs, many with both arms in the air. The deputy leaned over and spoke to Clem. "Nice to be loved."

Clem never looked at him. "Yeah."

Michael gave orders to get things going and everyone started in immediately.

Clem and the deputy soon approached the first deputy, who was standing by his horse. The second one dismounted and spoke to him, and the man took a deep breath and sighed. "Guess we're still sittin' out here, for a while anyway."

The deputy tied his horse to the tree alongside the other one, then walked to their chairs where they both sat down and watched the commotion.

*****

The wagons were ready to go in short order. Clem sat on Cherry during the whole scene and watched. He looked over at the two men leaning back in their chairs.

"Thank you fer bein' fair, 'preciate that."

The second deputy glanced up at Clem. "Well, we got to do our job." He pitched his chair back forward, stood up, and strode over to Clem while reaching in his shirt pocket and handed up the two telegrams. "You might want these, jist in case you get stopped again. Might help save you some time."

Then he took them back. "Wait." He wrote something down and gave them back to Clem.

Clem took them and read them for the first time.

The deputy had added his name to both telegrams. "In case they want to ask me, as a witness."

"Thank you, 'preciate that." Clem looked over at the first deputy and touched the brim of his hat.

The deputy gave him a wave back with a friendly smile now. "Well, y'all take care."

Michael watched them, then turned around in his saddle and gave the signal to move out.

The mules started pulling, and the wagons started moving, and once again they were on their way.

16
The Sierra Nevadas

The desert was actually the most pleasant part of the entire trip, and it was the part Clem was most worried about. They still had to awake extra early to get going, but they also stopped early and didn't start up again until what would have been suppertime.

Then they went far into the night, long after the sun set, as long as they had enough light for Clem to see the surroundings and the others to see the wagon in front of them.

They found all the springs full of water and weren't harassed by anybody during the entire trip across.

They saw Indians a couple of times, and they did have one small band of warriors come in at one watering hole, but Clem had the wagons circled up long before they arrived.

The braves demanded horses for passage. Clem was going to refuse and have everyone get ready for a fight, when the new unofficial women's committee asked him to give them one of the calves.

The ladies were amazed at how fit the men were, seeing as how there appeared to be absolutely no forage of any kind or animals to hunt anywhere that could be seen, but yet these men were obviously healthy. Still they worried what the rest of the tribe must look like and pleaded with Clem.

He felt it was too much, but they prevailed on him and he

relented, so he gave them one of the older cows.

The braves seemed satisfied with the bargain and took their prize and left.

***

It took them twenty-six days to cross the desert.

They arrived at Carson City, Nevada, on October tenth, just three weeks behind schedule, which had Clem very happy considering all they had been through getting there.

They made camp just east of town on Wednesday night, and Clem told everyone they were staying until Sunday because the next day was God's High Holy Day of Tabernacles.

Most still had no idea what he was talking about, but they were happy to get the rest, so no one offered any objection.

Then while several of the ladies were in town, they found out there had been snow flurries in the mountain passes already. When they returned they wanted Clem to get them going right away. He wouldn't budge and wouldn't discuss the matter, in spite of many objections now.

Sunday arrived with several ladies very worried, but he was in no mood to hurry in spite of the protest.

Then the sheriff of Carson City came out later to meet the wagon train. He had been notified of their arrival after returning to town, so he felt he should go out to make sure they weren't the wagon train he was supposed to be looking for.

The sheriff told Clem he was mighty suspicious of him and didn't give a hoot about his letter or telegrams. He could have paid anyone to make them up.

And he wasn't obligated to confirm there was a post commander or deputies, or anything else Clem told him about. "The only good news I got fer you is the judge ain't here today and won't be back till Monday afternoon, and I ain't got enough evidence right now to keep you. But if I come out here tomorrow and you ain't moved on, I'm gonna bring you in anyways and keep you till the judge decides what to do with you."

Clem assured him they would be gone. And as soon as the sheriff left, Clem told Michael they had to be ready to go in one hour.

***

The Ladies Wagon Train had several people from town coming out to see them, and to make their own determination of whether or not they were in fact the ones the sheriff had been talking about. One particular group of men who had the most interest in them were keeping their distance.

Jed and his men had been watching since they arrived in town, having arrived themselves about two weeks earlier. They were definitely in favor of the sheriff letting them go.

"Which way you think they gonna go, Jed?"

Jed looked over at Willy. "Not sure, but we'll know soon enough."

"How we s'posed to git by 'em when there ain't nuthin' but trails, an' we got to ride right past 'em?"

Jed laughed. "We'll figure that out once we know exactly which way they're headed."

***

Clem decided to use the Dutch Flat toll road into the Henness Pass. It cost fifteen dollars just to go one way, which everyone felt was criminal, but it was a much better and much safer road compared to most, and Clem wanted to take the easiest way over. So they left and headed north to the little town of Lake's Crossing, and from there they turned west and started the climb into the mountains.

***

Jed and the rest of the men had been watching by sending various members out of town as if they themselves were heading up one of the many roads over the mountains. They would ride up a piece, and once they felt they had gone far enough, and no one was around to notice, they would turn around and come back down.

"Okay, they're takin' that Henness toll road," Jed told his men.

"So the basic plan is the same as the last time, 'cept this time we don't use no stupid flag of truce. We jist kill all the men outright before they even know we're there, an' anyone else who puts up a fight, then grab whoever's left alive, an' all the wagons an' such, an' off we go to the camps."

He looked all around. They were ready for the next meeting.

"This should happen day after tomorrow, I 'spect. They'll be movin' out agin early tomorrow, an' those mules should prob'ly be tired by the time they reach us."

Willy spoke up. "Okay, so how we gonna stop 'em from runnin' on past us like before, an' whatta 'bout traffic? These roads seem pretty busy since we been here."

"You got guns, an' we'll chop down trees or drag one across the middle of the road to stop anyone from comin' in. Most of the traffic is jist freight wagons anyway, an' I 'spect they won't come into no shootin' war they hear. They might go fetch the sheriff to protect 'em, but while they doin' that, we'll be killin' Ol' Leather an' t'others, an' gitten the ladies what's left, an' the wagons, an' be gone. Think that might work?"

"Better'n last time."

"Good, we're all settled then? You happy? I want ever'one to be happy."

***

Clem had the wagons pulling up into the mountains. They stopped early to rest and eat because he told them they were going to be hard at it for the rest of the day. It would be long, hard pulls and very narrow roads, many times with a steep cliff on one side and a steep wooded mountain on the other.

He didn't mention the many places for an ambush. He didn't need to; they all realized it as soon as they entered the canyon leading to the pass. They all knew it was only about seventy miles up and over. That would be three to four days under normal circumstances, but this time it meant a whole week because of the steep road.

Clem had decided that for the mountain portion the only men on horseback would be himself and Michael, and the four new men. Everyone else was in a wagon with rifles ready.

Harvey and Sergio would share duties with Walt and Billy leading and following the train. Clem and Michael would stay around the wagons moving up and back as needed to help.

***

Clem had them make camp at the first station house they came to. It was only a little after four in the afternoon, but the animals were spent. The ladies and everyone else were exhausted themselves, just getting used to the steep grade and having to make the mules pull harder than they ever had to before.

They didn't have enough animals to make the long trains the freighters used, and they didn't have the expertise anyway, so it would just have to be a long, slow pull.

They didn't want to whip them all the way up either, so they were trying to urge them by hollering more than usual, and that alone tired everyone out.

In a small clearing in front of the station house, Clem had them circle the wagons, forming the corral for the herd. Everyone decided to just lie around and do nothing after taking care of the animals, before going to bed.

They didn't want to overwhelm the folks at the station house, so they made sure they went over in small groups or just stayed with the wagons.

The folks at the house were very much used to the people traveling to California, even though the main flow had slowed down a lot, so they were friendly but busy with the freighters that composed most of their business these days. They didn't have much time to spend with another wagon train coming through.

Clem and others were inquiring, but no one recalled any unusual men stopping by, and they were sure no one had stopped in, asking about some all-woman wagon train. The station folks were starting to wonder just who these people were, asking all these odd questions, but then they had to rush off to work and forgot all that was asked of them.

They would remember all the questions later.

***

Jed and the rest of his men pulled up to the second station house they came to and dismounted.

"Come on, boys, I b'lieve I found our spot. Let's go in an' make ourselves to home an' see who's here. Then we'll wait till the mornin' an' take 'em all down."

They stepped into a large open room. It was mostly kitchen, with a very large cook stove and the pantry right next to it. The place was built to feed and sleep a lot of men—hard-working, uncaring men.

Tables and chairs stood along the outside walls under the windows to catch the mountain air, but the room was dominated by two huge tables in its center that were laid out for eating.

Across the big room on the far side was a bar with four small tables nearby and a piano next to the bar. There was a door leading to the owner's bedroom, and in the middle of that bedroom wall was a large fireplace, with a nice fire going. In the back of the main room was a staircase leading to rooms upstairs. That was all there was; it was all that was needed.

Jed saw the bar and held up his hand. "We're too close. One more day, then we take what we want."

***

The man working the bar was the owner and hollered across the room. He smiled at his new customers. "Howdy, gents, what can we do for you today?"

They sauntered across the floor. "Need a couple of rooms fer tonight an' somethin' to eat."

"You bet, how 'bout a drink?"

"No, no, not fer us, thank you. Jist the food an' a place to sleep is all we need." Jed was smiling. He could be at home with people like this. He surveyed the big room. "Anybody else here tonight?"

All the men were grumbling as they sat at one of the big tables.

The owner smiled at his guest. "No, sir. Not right now anyway. You got your pick of the rooms, not that they're any different. Each one sleeps twelve, so you'll fit just fine."

"Great, who's cookin' tonight?"

"That's me. The missus is in town to get supplies and visit with her sister, so she won't be back till tomorrow afternoon. Might be here to make dinner if you want to stay a bit longer. I can cook beef steak and taters, and she got beans done for us already, so if you're not too picky I can fill you up."

"Steak an' taters sounds perfect. We'll jist go fix the horses an' then find a room."

Jed led the men outdoors to get their horses unsaddled, fed, and put up in a small corral. "This'll be perfect. Hopefully no one else shows up. We'll kill the old man after breakfast. Hopefully the wife don't show up. I'm sure she's too old to help any. Then we'll git ready fer Ol' Leather an' our ladies. Time we got this over an' got paid."

The next morning they were all up before dawn and went downstairs, ready to eat. Mr. Gildenfor the owner was already frying bacon and potatoes and had the coffee going. "Help yourselves, gentlemen, the coffee's hot and I'll be throwing eggs in the pan in two minutes. No biscuits this morning—I don't know how—so we got plain bread and butter, but plenty of blackberry jam to go with it."

***

Breakfast was over and Jed was relaxed, ready for the day to come. He lounged around until about eight, then rose and stretched and hollered up the stairs and outside. The men all poured in, including Mr. Gildenfor, who was back in the pantry when he heard Jed hollering. "What's all the hubbub?"

Jed smiled at the man. "Mr. Gildenfor, we're takin' over. It's gonna be a robbery."

"What? You can't do that! I won't allow it!" The old man took a step toward Jed, then stopped as if reconsidering what he should do. Pausing, he got a new look of determination, whirled around, and leaped on top of the bar and fell down the back side with a thud. He popped up holding a shotgun.

"Don't move!" Jed held his hand out. The old man ignored the warning and started to bring up the shotgun. Jed casually drew his pistol and shot him square in the chest.

Mr. Gildenfor stumbled and hit his face on the bar but kept holding on to the shotgun. He tried to swing it around and Jed shot him again. The poor old man slid off the bar and down onto the floor.

"Oh, well, tried to stop him." He smirked as he walked over to the bar and shot him one more time. "Jist to make sure."

***

The ambush site was perfect in Jed's mind. The station sat in a little open clearing and was down lower than the road. A small cliff of barren rock on the edge of this side of the road would keep the wagons from turning into the yard in front of the house and circling up, and the hill on the other side was steep and wooded.

Horse and Jack were in place down the road before the station house, back in the trees waiting. They were to wait for the wagons to come by and then follow them up, shooting whoever they could from behind and stopping anyone from running back.

Willy and Bill were in the trees at the top of the road, ready to shoot straight into the lead wagons as they came up.

Fred was behind the station house, with Jed and Yancy in the house.

The three new men, Wallace, Stacy, and Dillon, were on the mountain ready to shoot down into the wagons as they would be stopped with no place to go.

And finally they had drug a few trees across the road above Willy and Bill to keep anyone in a wagon from coming down into the fight, just in case someone felt brave.

Now they just had to wait.

17
Henness Pass

Horse and Jack hadn't been there too long when they spotted two old men riding up the road. Then came a wagon pulled by mules right behind them with a lady driving it, and she was followed by other wagons, all driven by women.

***

Clem was about three wagons back when they rounded the bend and saw a station house. It was in a little, flat clearing at the bottom of a small rocky slope with a lane at the far end leading down to the house.

Clem was looking for the next station to stop at because the mules were tiring fast.

Harvey and Sergio were at the front of the wagons this afternoon when they saw the station house, so Harvey hollered back at Clem that he would go down and see about staying there for the night.

The wagons halted in the road across from the station house. The two men rode past the edge of the rocky cliff and down the lane to the house.

Harvey dismounted to walk in but Sergio spoke up. "Harvey, hold on a minute." Harvey stopped and turned to look at his friend.

Sergio lifted his left leg over the saddle and slid off, dismounting on the opposite side of his horse, away from the house. He stepped up to the horse's neck and rested his hand on the butt of his gun. Holding the reins in his other hand, he nodded for Harvey to go ahead.

Harvey watched him, smiling a big smile, and nodded in remembrance.

"The mining camp up in the Rockies." He chuckled. "You worried agin?" Sergio shrugged. Harvey opened the door to walk in.

Immediately shots were fired. Harvey stumbled back, arms flailing at his sides, and the whole countryside erupted in gunfire!

It burst from the woods above the wagons on their left. The woods in front of them. From the station doorway. The window in the house. Shots were flying from everywhere.

The man named Dillon had Clem dead in his sights. He pulled the trigger and Clem shuddered in pain. He never got to finish his prayer.

Michael sat on Cloud frozen with fear, watching Harvey stumbling back and then Clem getting shot.

Now two men strode out from the woods in front of everyone, rifles raised and aiming right at Mary Williams in the first wagon.

Leah was watching Harvey and saw him stagger backwards and fall flat on his back, arms straight out to his sides. All she could do was scream.

Sergio pulled his pistol and fired into the doorway. His horse stumbled sideways and started to fall on him, but he kept firing and had to step back out of the way as it fell. Then, doubling over from a bullet to his middle, he fell and fired the last bullet from his own pistol.

He lay there beside his horse in pain and fear and began to reload.

As Clem fell off Cherry, she jumped out from under him. He hit the side of the hill and rolled down to the road.

Tom Williams had just gotten off his mother's wagon and was walking toward the back when the shooting broke out. He looked up at the woods to his right and was raising his rifle when he lurched forward, staggered, and fell flat on the road.

All the wagons started taking gunfire. Splinters erupted everywhere. The ladies in the backs of the wagons grabbed children and lay on top of them.

Walt and Billy leaped off their horses and ran to the hillside. They shot up into the trees as they climbed, crawled, and slid their way up into cover, bullets kicking up dirt all around them.

The few animals not hitched to wagons—the cattle, horses, and mules—tried to run in every direction at once, but they were hemmed in by Hugh and Fritzy, who blocked the road with the last two wagons.

All the mules hitched to every wagon danced back and forth, trying to move away from each other and the wagons. The drivers screamed at them to whoa, struggling to hold them in place.

Fritzy was aiming for a shot up into the hillside when Hugh stood up and looked at him, then tumbled over the edge onto the wagon tongue and to the ground, causing his mules to try to jump forward and gain safety in the herd.

Fritzy saw he had been shot in the back and turned to see two men strolling up the road and casually firing rifles. He slumped down, calmly took aim, and fired at the bigger of the two men. He hit him square and the man stopped and staggered, but then kept coming.

Fritzy took aim again, at the smaller one this time, and fired. This man spun, his arms flying up, and fell sideways onto the road.

Mary Williams in the first wagon stared at the two men in front of her, their rifles pointing right at her.

She knew they were trapped unless she could lead them out. She slapped the reins on the backs of her mules. "Hyaaahhh!"

The mules were prancing and shaking from all the gunshots, but now they both jumped forward. The wagon took off from under her. She cracked the reins again. "Hyaaah!"

The men fired.

She got cut in the shoulder but grabbed her whip, reared back, and cracked it across the rump of her mule Jessie. "Hyaaah! Mule!

Move!" She reared back again but there were shots and she fell backward into the wagon bed, with nothing but her boots sticking out over the top of the seat.

Her mules were pulling now, trying to escape, with the wagon lurching and rumbling forward.

Leah saw Mary's wagon take off, and at the same time her mules started pulling, following the wagon in front, looking for a way out.

She didn't know what to do, but she stood up and cracked the reins on the backs of her mules. "Hyaaahhh! Hyaaahh!"

Her wagon jumped and her mules ran into the back of Mary's wagon.

Mary's three girls were screaming as they tried to grab and hold their mama.

With her mules practically pushing Mary's wagon, Leah cracked her reins again and again. "Hyaaah, Hyaaahh!" Then shots again and Leah flew out of her wagon and over the cliff.

Michael was running Cloud up alongside the wagons, yelling at everyone to get them moving.

All the ladies were snapping reins now and cracking whips. The wagons were moving and picking up speed. Straight at Willy and Bill.

Now the rifles emerged from the wagons and fired into the station house and up the hillside.

As Michael passed his mother's wagon, he looked but she wasn't there. He checked in the back and saw Jodi Mesto bouncing around trying to shoot, but his mother wasn't there!

He had to keep going and said a prayer for her.

He was coming alongside Mary's wagon when her mule on the right side staggered and stepped over the edge of the cliff.

The wagon tipped noticeably and Michael had to pull away, but he kept trying to reach for the lead mule.

When the first mule slipped, Jessie tried to pull it back up on the road, but the first one slipped again and the front wheel ran completely off the cliff edge, the rear wheel following.

The whole wagon tipped and slid sideways, dragging both mules with it. It rolled over onto its side, pulling both mules off their feet and flipping them up into the air as they screamed in horror.

Michael watched the mules lift and then disappear over the edge and slam down, one onto the rocks and the other on top of the first.

The wagon had rolled onto its top, crushing the tarp roof, then over again onto its other side, then flipped back up on its wheels. He could see Mary and her daughters flying around in the back. The wagon somersaulted, tossing both mules up and over and slamming them into each other and onto the rocks a second time.

Michael had slowed, and as his mother's wagon caught up to him he reached out and grabbed the reins of those mules. Just then he felt his shoulder explode in pain, but he fought to keep himself up on Cloud.

He looked ahead to see two men running in opposite directions into the woods and firing pistols at him. The pain was terrible as he tugged on the reins. "Hyaaah! Hyaah!"

He pulled the mules, trying to drag the wagon up the hill. The other wagons were right behind him, bumping into still other wagons and practically pushing them all along.

Shots still flashed from everywhere.

Fred was down behind the station house peering around the corner. He saw Old Leather was down. He saw that kid in the middle of the road starting to get up after he shot him in the back.

The boy was on his knees attempting to stand up. His back was leaking blood. Fred got mad 'cause the kid didn't die. He watched the boy stand up, and then he took careful aim again and pulled the trigger. The boy went flying forward and hit the dirt face first.

Fred laughed to himself as he quickly reloaded his rifle and aimed at the woman driving the next wagon passing by. *Pretty,* he thought and put his finger on the trigger.

He felt kicked as a bullet hit him in the chest. He staggered and fell back against the wall.

Even madder now, he gathered himself together and stepped out to shoot at the next wagon when another bullet hit him in the throat.

He stood there shaking and then bent over, not knowing what to do. He couldn't think straight, he couldn't lift his rifle, he couldn't... He fell face first into the mud.

Dillon was the highest one up on the hill and had been shot badly in the leg. Now he decided to get out of there before he bled to death; he knew none of the others would help him, so he had to go now or he might not make it at all. He started climbing away, dragging his leg.

Down just below him Wallace and Stacy were shooting it out with Walt and Billy.

Walt told Billy to cover him; he was going to climb higher and get the advantage on them. He picked his way through the trees, gunshots splintering wood all around him.

Wallace stopped to reload his pistol again and asked how Stacy was doing. He got no answer. He yelled at him this time, but still nothing, so he crawled down to him.

Bullets flew at him from everywhere. He grabbed his friend and pulled him back. Stacy stared up at him with dead eyes, his chest soaked in blood. Wallace dropped him and started firing.

He could see one cowboy was climbing up over him, so he knew he had to go. He turned and, firing behind him, looked for Dillon and made his way to their horses tethered a little further up.

Willy and Bill were fighting for their lives now. They had been chased back into the woods and couldn't stop the wagons from going by, and it seemed that each wagon had rifles sticking out, firing right at them as they went.

Both suffered from wounds already, so they couldn't move very fast.

Just then Willy took a bullet in his chest and fell back against a tree. He sat there with his back against the trunk, watching everyone rush by and shoot at him.

Bill kept trying to shoot and move further back into the woods when a bullet from one of the last wagons hit him in the stomach and he curled up in a ball. He was done.

At the other end of the fight, Jack was lying in the middle of the road dead. Horse was running straight at the old man in the wagon. Horse had been shot once by the old codger, and he was going to kill that old man for shooting him.

The wagon was moving now, following the others up the road. When he reached the back edge of it, the old guy popped up and shot him again. Horse was furious but he hung on to the wagon.

He was going to jump into that box and strangle him with his bare hands! He kept running alongside hanging on to the wagon, trying to climb up, when the old man leaned over, leveled his rifle in his face, and pulled the trigger.

Jed and Yancy were in the station house firing from two windows. They saw the wagons were getting away and the shooting was dying down.

Jed knew he'd lost again. He couldn't believe it! He knew the others were going to blame him for it and want Dickson's money, but he wasn't about to share.

Turning toward Yancy at the other window, he leveled his pistol at his friend's head and pulled the trigger. Yancy collapsed in a heap.

Jed took a quick look outside. The wagons were gone except for one of the old mule skinners trying to keep up. He aimed and fired one last shot. He missed.

Not seeing anyone else, Jed ducked out the door and ran along the front of the house, hugging the wall. Sergio sat up and shot at him, cutting him in the side slightly.

Jed fired back and Sergio ducked behind his horse, but he kept lifting his pistol and firing at the man fleeing.

Jed made it to the far edge of the house and turned the corner, Sergio firing away at him. He headed out to the horses tied in a thicket. Leaning against a tree, he reloaded his pistol and fired a couple of rounds toward the house and that man shooting at him and following him into the woods. Jed missed again. He ran over to the three horses and untied them all, tethering two of them in a line behind his. He mounted up and led them all away.

He would have to settle for more money than he ever had but not as much as he wanted. *Life jist isn't fair sometimes.*

***

Michael had the wagons running up the road away from the fight when he spotted even more men in the road up ahead, with a tree lying there blocking the way.

He didn't have a rifle, so he lay down on Cloud's neck and urged her on, pulling the mules.

The next wagon behind him saw the men and shot at them.

The men ducked and ran for the woods, jumping straight out into the trees, hitting the dirt and sliding in behind other fallen trees and rocks.

These men were freighters who had heard the shooting and were pulling the trees out of the way to get down to help whoever was under attack. They had just reached the last tree when they saw the wagons and came under fire. They dropped the tree and jumped out of the way as Leah's wagon stormed by, with Cloud carrying Michael streaming blood from his shoulder.

The horse leaped straight into the branches of the fallen tree and bounded through them and out the other side, with Michael doing all he could to hang on.

The wagon slammed into the small tree trunk and bounced into the air, throwing Jodi Mesto up practically through the canvas. She crashed back down and was immediately flying again as the rear wheels hit the tree.

The next wagon, driven by Millie Hafin, was right behind her and slammed into the little tree, tossing her and her boys into the air just as they were trying for another shot at the men running away.

Now Mrs. Hindle came through, and she and her children in the back were flying up and trying to grab anything as they plummeted down again just to feel the wagon hit the tree a second time and go up again.

Then it was Mrs. La Fayette. Then Mrs. McKinnis and then another and another, until finally Fritzy rushed through following the herd.

There was nothing left of the tree to even slow him down.

The freighters hid in the woods as the wagons went by shooting at them, wagon after wagon, apparently all driven by women cracking whips and screaming at their mules. And they all had rifles sticking out, bouncing around and firing away.

The last wagon passed, driven by a man who looked like them, but they didn't know if he was following or chasing, and they sure weren't going to stay around to find out.

They looked back up the road. Then down the other way to see if anyone else was coming. There was no noise other than wagons getting further away, so they ran to their own wagons that they'd parked in a wide spot as they were attempting to clear the road.

Climbing into the wagons, they cracked whips and got their own mules running, a little too fast for safety's sake, but they weren't sticking around.

As they came down to the scene of the battle, the first man saw bodies lying in the road. He cracked his whip again and hollered at his mules as he steered around all the dead and kept right on going.

The others followed and they never looked back, hoping they would not be caught by whoever was shooting everyone up.

They didn't stop again, riding all through the night until they were clear of the mountains and heading south to Carson City. They arrived in record time and went straight to the bar and got a drink, and then another, and then another.

Then they went looking for the sheriff.

18
Aftermath

Michael kept his wagons running hard long after he cleared the roadblock until he saw a small meadow. He yanked and pulled the mules into the clearing and signaled the others to circle up.

When the herd arrived and saw the circle forming, they knew exactly what to do. They ran right into the middle of the wagons with Fritzy behind them closing the corral.

Then rifles came out in every direction, forming a deadly defense against anyone who would dare to attempt another attack.

***

They waited almost an hour. No one had heard anything since the battle. Michael let Mrs. Lindy sew up his arm and put it in a sling before he was able to get free and give orders again.

The consensus was the killers were dead or gone, but either way they wouldn't be making another attempt today. Yet they didn't know when they would come again, so they had to act fast.

Michael selected a group from the men to return to look for any wounded and take care of the dead—Brent Hafin, Eddie Hod, and Jacob Wasterman. He put Mrs. Hafin in charge of the wagons. They were to shoot first and then shoot again.

The men mounted up and started down the road. He didn't think anyone would be approaching from the gang that attacked them, but he

214

had everyone spread out just the same and carry their rifles, loaded and ready, across their laps. He had them mostly at a gallop because he thought it would make them a harder target to hit.

They rode past the roadblock and then around the bend, and up ahead they could see bodies lying in the road. Over on the rocks was Mary Williams's wagon lying on its side. The mules were alive but not struggling.

They saw Tom Williams face down, Mr. Clem lying against the side of the hill, and the two others from the gang further down.

As they reached the edge of the battle site, Michael spied one of the gang members just inside the edge of the woods sitting against a tree staring at them. He whipped his rifle up ready to shoot but then noticed he was dead.

Then Brent saw one on the other side of the road, curled up in a ball.

Michael wanted to find his mother, but he was looking at Tom, so he dismounted and walked over to him. The others stayed far apart, wary that the gang could still be there waiting for another ambush.

Finally, they all decided they were alone, so Jacob, Brent, and Eddie quickly rode down to the station house, jumped off their horses at the back of the building, and started their reconnaissance there.

They found one of the gang members lying face down in some mud. Brent and Eddie crept cautiously along the back of the house and around the corner. Jacob moved out to the front corner.

He saw Harvey lying in the front yard.

He looked up and watched Michael rising from Tom and moving toward Mr. Clem and Cherry, who was standing over him.

Then he saw Michael's ma lying crumpled in the rocks just above the house, so he hollered up at Michael and pointed. Michael stopped, turned around, and hurried to the edge of the little cliff and the rocks.

Jacob looked over his shoulder and saw Brent and Eddie come from around their end of the house, making their way toward the front door.

They didn't see Sergio anywhere.

Jacob motioned to the others that he was going to look at Mrs. Williams's wagon. They nodded and proceeded down the front of the house. Brent popped up to quickly peer into an open window and ducked down again. He shook his head at Eddie.

They reached the front door, counted to three, and ran inside. Turning, they hunched down and slapped their backs up against a wall. As they tried to get their vision accustomed to the dark, they perceived one man dead under a window.

There was movement from the back of the room, in the corner behind a bench. They pointed their rifles at the bench and yelled out, "Come out or we'll shoot you dead!"

"No! Please don't! We'll come out." Slowly and carefully with their arms in the air, the three Williams girls rose up, Sharon, Willa, and Abby.

The boys stood up and dropped the barrels of their rifles, leaving them hanging from one hand only. The girls rushed across the room, grabbed the boys in a hug, and started crying.

Brent was almost knocked over. He had to take a step back with Abby hanging on as Sharon hugged Eddie and Willa tried to hug each one simultaneously.

Crying, the girls told them about their ma, and how they were left behind and thought everyone forgot about them, and they didn't know where the kidnappers were, all in one long lament.

The boys stood there with their arms at their sides, looking at each other, not knowing what to do. So they remained there until the girls were finished.

Once they recovered and stepped back from the boys, they smoothed their dresses and wiped their eyes before asking questions all at once, all talking at the same time again.

Eddie held up his hand. "Whoa, whoa, whoa!"

That stopped them.

"We jist got here. Is anyone upstairs?"

The girls exchanged glances and shrugged. Becoming scared again, they slipped behind the boys.

Brent held his arm out protectively. "Hold on, ya'll stay right here."

"No!" They grabbed them from behind their shoulders.

"Wait!" Eddie had to unravel himself from Sharon's and Willa's grip. "Okay, step outside. Jacob is out there with Michael; stay against the house until they call you up. Now go on, we got to look upstairs."

Huddled together, the three girls stepped outside and stayed huddled up against the wall of the house. As they glanced around they spotted Michael climbing down toward his mother.

They started to move toward him but he held out his hand to stop them. They didn't move another step. He motioned for them to stay right there, and they nodded their heads in agreement.

Michael looked over at Jacob, who was leaving the Williams wagon, and waved and pointed toward the girls, and then he called softly, "Mrs. Williams's girls. Go get them." Jacob was confused until Michael pointed down at them and motioned to them to come up to meet him.

Michael was with his ma now. She lay there crumpled up, head down, legs all akimbo, with her dress half up over on top of her. Tears welled in his eyes before he heard a shout behind him.

He dropped down, looking up toward the road, then crawled up to peek over the edge.

Jacob and the girls were crouched down but had no cover, so he had them quickly move behind the wagon.

Michael peered over the edge of the road, trying to lift his rifle up on the rocks and lay it there, struggling to hold it with one arm.

The voice hollered out again. "Don't shoot! It's Walt! I'm up here! I'm comin' out! Don't shoot!"

Michael watched Walt step out from behind a tree and wave. Michael waved back and then stood as Walt came sliding down the side of the hill.

Michael looked back at his ma. "Ma, I'm sorry. I'll be back." He clambered up and went to meet Walt.

"Michael, you got shot, you okay?"

"Yeah, I'll be fine, how 'bout you?"

"I'm fine." His eyes grew sad. "They got Billy." He hung his head for a moment, then looked up. "I see Jacob an' the girls. Who else is here?"

"Eddie an' Brent. My ma's over there in the rocks. I'm sure Mrs. Williams is in her wagon. There's Mr. Clem, an' here's Tom."

Jacob and the girls walked up the lane and over to them.

Walt looked around at the carnage everywhere. "They hit us really hard." He laid his hand on Michael's good shoulder. "I'm really sorry 'bout yer ma."

Jacob took a deep breath. "Mrs. Williams is dead in her wagon, and I'm going back down to look at Harvey."

Walt asked the girls, "Are any of you hurt?"

"We're fine. Mama's dead; she's still in the wagon. We didn't know how to get her out or what to do," Sharon said.

Abby and Willa knelt down next to Tom. "We're sorry, Tommy." They were crying. "We love you, Tommy. We'll miss you. They killed Mama too. We're so sorry."

Walt laid his hand on Abby's head. "We'll git yer ma out right away, honey." He glanced up at the sky and then to Michael. "It's gittin' dark. And colder. We'll need to hurry."

Then they all saw Jacob stand up next to Harvey and wave. "He's alive! Come help!"

At almost the same instant Brent stuck his head out the window upstairs. "We're clear in the house."

Jacob yelled up at him, "Harvey's alive, come down an' help!"

Walt gently grabbed Michael's good arm. "Come on, Michael, they'll git Harvey; let's git yer ma." He looked back at the girls. "Then we'll git yers. Y'all head over there an' git her ready fer us. Can you do that?"

"Yes sir. She's our ma. Abby, you stay here with Tommy, can you do that?" Sharon squeezed her youngest sister's hand.

Abby nodded and, sitting down fully in the road, put Tommy's head in her lap. "I'll stay here with you, Tommy, you won't be alone."

Sharon and Willa left for the wagon while Michael and Walt climbed down over the edge of the rocks to Leah. Brent and Eddie came out of the house and went to Harvey.

Walt called to Jacob they needed help with Michael's mom, and he started climbing the rocks to help them.

Michael placed her dress back down over her legs and lifted her head, and she moaned. Michael froze. "Ma, yer alive." He said it very softly.

Walt had moved around behind her and repositioned her legs so she was more sideways on the rocks than upside down. She groaned with the movement but didn't open her eyes.

Walt told Michael, "Wait here. After we git Harvey checked out we'll all move yer ma up onto the road."

"Yeah, go help 'em, we'll be fine." He smiled down at his ma. She wasn't moving and her breathing seemed very shallow, but she was alive and he would start from there.

Walt and Jacob gingerly climbed down the rocks.

Still, no one had seen Sergio anywhere. Jacob left the men with Harvey and traveled out along the wall of the house looking for him. He followed a blood trail into the woods and found Sergio slumped against a tree, unconscious and breathing unsteadily. He hollered up toward the house, "Sergio's over here. He's alive too, not doin' well!"

Brent jogged into the woods and found Jacob and Sergio.

The two of them returned hauling Sergio between them, each one holding an arm over his shoulder and dragging his feet behind them. Blood covered most of his side, and he was still unconscious, so they laid him next to Harvey.

Walt said to the boys, "We need to carefully bring 'em inside. Let's lift 'em gently."

They all four gripped hands under Harvey to form a litter, carried him inside, and laid him on one of the big tables in the room. Then they went back out and did the same for Sergio, laying him on the next table.

They all stepped back, not knowing what to do next, until Eddie asked Walt, "Whatta 'bout Michael's ma?"

"She's alive; she's hurt bad but doesn't appear to be as bad as these two. She's unconscious from hittin' the rocks, I s'pose; hopefully she'll make it out okay. We need to make a litter an' git her back to the wagons. I don't think we can move these two. I'm sorry."

"Well, let's help those we can." It was Brent. "We can git blankets from upstairs to make a litter."

"An' rope an' poles from the corral," Jacob said.

Walt smiled. "Good, let's go git her off them rocks an' up on the road, an' then we can tend to t'others in here. We won't have time to bury 'em. I'm sure they'd unnerstand. We have to git Michael's ma back; she needs help now, an' we need to take care of the livin' first." He regarded Harvey and Sergio again. "I'm sorry, compadres."

Brent and Eddie ran upstairs, and Jacob ran outside.

Walt laid his hand on Harvey and looked over at Sergio. "You boys saved them women. I'll make sure yer kin know it, but we got to leave you here. I'm sure you'd unnerstand."

He turned and walked outside with Brent and Eddie right behind him, clutching blankets. They pushed past him and climbed up the rocks to Michael and his mother.

Walt stood there for a moment gazing at them, and then up at the mountain where Billy was and shook his head sadly.

He said a prayer asking for mercy for his three friends, and that

220

their sacrifice would stand in good stead for them on Judgment Day.

"Better love has no man than to give his life for another, amen," he said quietly.

He watched the boys lifting Leah onto the blanket to carry her up. Michael was about to grab one corner, so Walt hollered out to wait up, and he climbed the rocks as quickly as he could to take Michael's corner.

It was a struggle to keep from scraping Leah against the rocks, but they did it and gently laid her in the road. Then they picked up Tom and carried him down the lane and into the house, where they settled him on the floor against the wall.

They looked at the other man still in a heap under the window.

"We can't leave him there like that, even though he was tryin' to kill us." Walt motioned at the one sticking out past the side of the bar. "Him neither."

They straightened out the first man where he lay and drug the other man over next to him.

"We can't git 'em all, we got to git goin'," Brent said to Walt, almost pleading.

"Yeah, someone else will have to git t'others."

They turned to look at their friends.

They walked over to Tom. Jacob was there gazing down at him and talking to him. "I'm sorry, Tom, an' I'm sorry 'bout yer ma." Then they all turned and left.

They climbed up to Mary Williams's wagon.

The mules had started thrashing around again when the girls came and were trying to get up, becoming real upset because they couldn't. Both had broken legs and many cuts. There was no help for them. Jacob and Eddie tried to calm them down, but that worked only slightly.

Eddie stayed with them while Jacob helped Brent and Walt move Mary Williams out from the wagon.

Her chest was covered in blood. They laid her on the rocks, then lifted her up again and made their way down the rocky slope and into the house, where they laid her next to her son, Tom. The girls smoothed her dress and fixed her hair while the men left to get Clem.

When they returned to where Michael was waiting with Leah, it started snowing, real heavy fat flakes. Michael looked up into the falling snow and said to no one in particular, "O God in Heaven, what's next?"

Walt walked over to Clem, who was lying against the hill on his side. Cherry was still right there with him, and Walt had to move her out of the way to reach him. His shirt was also full of blood.

Walt checked to make sure he didn't see any sign of life. He lightly grabbed Clem's wrist and waited, then put his fingers against Clem's throat where he had seen it done before. He looked over at the boys and shook his head no. Then to make sure, he put his ear against his lips. There was nothing.

They moved him away from the hill and laid him down, crossing his arms. Then gently lifting him up, they grabbed hands underneath to form the litter, and he moaned.

And they dropped him in the road with a thud.

They stood staring at him and back at each other. Walt knelt down and got real close to him. "Clem, are you alive?"

In a very soft whisper, "Not so much now you dropped me."

Walt glanced up at the boys. "I never was no good at that." He looked down at Clem. "Sorry ol' friend, my fault."

Clem groaned softly again, then in the same whisper, "Well, don't leave me here."

Walt smiled. "No, we won't. Come on, pick him up agin, real gentle."

They carried him bobbing and moaning as he went, with apologies from the boys all the way down into the house, and they placed him on the table in front of Sergio.

He was groaning louder now. Then he spoke again in his

whisper. "Who got shot? Who's dead?"

Michael's eyes went to Walt, who nodded, and he leaned close to Clem. "They killed Mrs. Williams, an' Tom, an' Hugh, an' Billy."

Clem winced as each name was mentioned, and tears leaked out his eyes.

"They shot Harvey, he's over here. An' Sergio, he's here jist in front of you. They won't make it through the night."

Clem stared at the ceiling blinking away tears while Michael kept speaking. The others stood around watching. "They shot my ma, but she should make it okay, an' they shot me, but I'll be fine."

Clem whispered again, "It's snowin'. You got to git outta here. You can't wait. Leave us be, we're done fer. Let my sons know. You can send a letter to the Hudsons; they'll pass it on. Give half my money to Emmie, Henry's ma, an' t'other half spread it out, yer ma knows." Then he passed out.

Michael laid his hand on his forehead. "Yes sir, you go to sleep."

Walt stepped over. "Michael, we gotta go. This snow might trap us if we don't git outta here. Someone will come an' bury 'em fer us."

Michael looked at him. He knew he was right. He squeezed Clem's hand; it was white as the snow.

Michael looked at the others. "Let's go." He glanced down at Clem again and turned and walked out.

They climbed the lane up to the road and over to Eddie, who was holding a blanket over Leah. He was covered in snow and shivering. Raising his eyes, he asked them, "How is he?"

"Not good, we got to git goin'. Can't git trapped by this snow." Michael gulped. "Mr. Clem said so."

"Yeah, he knows best."

"We got to git Hugh."

"Yeah, let's git him, then we got to git goin'."

They laid Hugh in front of Tom and headed back out to the horses tied to the corral. After leading them up to the road, they returned and broke out a couple of poles from the corral to make a litter for Leah.

On the way back to the road Brent took his rifle and put the two mules out of their misery. Then he joined the others on the road where Michael's ma was.

"Wait!" Walt stopped them. "We got to git Billy off the mountain."

"Go ahead," Michael told them. "I'm gonna stay with my ma."

Slipping and sliding their way up the hillside, they found Billy lying there. They picked him up and then slipped and fell and drug him all the way down. They kept telling Billy they were sorry, until they got him into the house and laid him next to Hugh.

They hurried out and up the lane to Michael again, and the girls.

Leah was lying under the blanket, which was getting covered with snow. Michael and the girls were getting covered as well; the men were all wet from sliding through the snow with Billy. Leah was the only one dry under her blanket.

Eddie cut holes in the blanket to thread the poles through. Then he tied ropes around the poles and back and forth between them for support, playing out the ends so the men could carry her instead of dragging the litter behind a horse.

They played out the ropes as far as they would go in each direction. Then they placed Leah on the litter and mounted up.

The girls climbed up behind them, and they positioned their horses around Leah, Michael handing each man his end of the rope.

They gently lifted her off the ground and had her suspended among them. Michael made sure she was covered well and tucked in, and, with his one good arm, mounted up and moved Cloud over so he could grab Cherry's reins. They all set out and up the road, away from the place.

It took them a little more than an hour to reach the wagons, walking the horses slowly with Leah swaying back and forth in their midst.

When they came into view of the wagons, all the rifles trained in on them until someone shouted, "It's the men!"

Everyone came running out to meet them. When they saw Leah under the blankets someone cried out she was dead. And everybody started moaning and sobbing.

It took the men several minutes to get them to realize that she was alive and that they covered her up because of the snow.

Settling her into her wagon, they made her as comfortable as they could and immediately began to work on her wounds.

Michael told them they were moving out right away, and he put Jacob in charge of setting up riders for the front and back and told everyone else to confer with Walt for any questions they had tonight. Then he climbed into the wagon with his ma and closed the back of the tarp.

***

The camp came alive with everyone getting the wagons ready. Though the mules were still harnessed, they had been fed and rested while everyone waited to find out about the men back at the fight. Now they were ready to pull them up and over the mountains.

19
Carson City

Back in Carson City the sheriff and his two deputies rode out for the pass as soon as they learned about the gun battle. They rode through the night and reached the station house just before noon the next day. As they came up onto the area of the fight, they saw two dead men still lying in the road, just as the freighter told him.

He led his deputies into the station house with guns drawn and found Harvey, Sergio, and Clem on the tables and a man, a lady, and a young man lying beside the wall. He spotted another man under another window and his friend Richard Gildenfor lying next to him.

He turned to look at the men on the table and then walked over to Clem and glared down at him. He grabbed him by the wrist and pulled him off the table, letting him bounce onto the bench, which toppled over and followed Clem down. He hit the floor and the bench landed on top of him.

The sheriff lifted the bench off of Clem and flipped it back onto its other side. It landed under the table.

The deputies watched in shock. "Sheriff! Whatta you doin'?"

He looked up at Joe, his chief deputy. "This animal got Richard killed. Mighta done it himself."

"We don't know that. Not yet. We don't know nuthin'. We can't treat 'em like this."

"Joe, you and Bub go search around; there's probably more than just those two in the road. Go look around and then come on back."

Joe glanced at the two men on the table and back at the sheriff.

The sheriff got a sour expression. "I'll leave 'em alone. Now go on before the snow makes it impossible."

Waiting until they left, the sheriff knelt down next to Clem. "I shoulda arrested you when I had the chance. I knew you were guilty as soon as I saw you. I let you go and now my friend's dead. And these others you got killed, who are they?" He stood up and kicked Clem in the side. Clem let out a groan.

He tried to talk but it wouldn't come out more than a whisper. "They attacked us."

Then he passed out again.

The sheriff bent over with both hands on his knees. "You better stay alive, mister, 'cause I'm gonna kill you, but first I'm gonna convict you of killin' my friend, and them at that flag of truce meetin', and these here men, and then I'm gonna hang you. I'm even gonna use an old rope so it'll break, and then I'll git to hang you agin."

He went to his friend Richard and told him he was sorry, that this was his fault, and then he looked at Yancy. "Sorry, mister, whoever you are. I presume you came in at the wrong time. He shot you in the back of the head? I'll hang him for it. Don't you worry."

He went over to examine the others.

First he looked at Sergio and then Harvey. "Who are you two?" They never responded. "My gut tells me you're part of his gang. I hope you die in bad pain."

He approached the ones along the wall and took his hat off in reverence. "Ma'am, who are you? I'm presuming you're one of the ladies from the wagons. Why would he shoot you? This here your son? He looks like he could be. I'm very sorry. And who are you two? You here to help? Which side?"

Stepping over to one of the tables by the bar, he sat down, trying to figure out what happened.

***

It was ten more minutes before Joe and Bub came back in covered with snow. Shivering, they stomped their feet and shook the snow off just inside the doorway.

Bub went to start up the fire while Joe gave the sheriff his report. "We found one behind the house and carried him over to the barn and laid him inside. Then we found two more up in the woods just off the road; we drug them down, and then we got them two off the road. There might be others but we can't search no more in this snow. We can bring 'em in here but, I mean, why? They're out of the weather and I don't think they care, and someone will jist have to carry 'em back out agin to bury 'em if we do."

The sheriff just stared at him, showing no emotion of any kind. "You stuck 'em in the barn. They might be heroes, maybe from the war. Never mind, you stay an' work on buryin' 'em when you can."

"What? Why me?"

"'Cause Mrs. Gildenfor can't do it by herself, and you're a lawman sworn to help others. Thank you for your service."

Joe grumbled something unintelligible and looked over at Bub, who was trying to hide his grin.

The sheriff was all about business now. "So there might be others out there, but if they are, they're dead, or soon will be. You can look again tomorrow if the snow clears away. We got the one we needed; now we need a wagon so we can bring him back into town for trial so we can hang 'em. That one wagon's all broke up. Hopefully one of them freighters will come along soon. We'll grab him and make him take the killer back."

***

Walt was leading the wagons now, staying about thirty yards ahead, when he saw a nice flat meadow with plenty of cover from the roadside.

The mules had been pulling the wagons for about eight hours

228

altogether, and he figured the meadow was a blessing from Heaven because the animals were just about to give out. First running from the fight after a long pull, then the last three hours without a change, they were exhausted.

He decided to make camp and had everybody eat cold food that night, no fires, and keep the wagons circled up to corral the herd. He set a watch near the road so they would know if anybody was looking for them. Freight wagons rumbled past a couple of times but nothing seemed suspicious.

The snow stopped about an hour after they made camp, just before the sun set and everything went dark.

***

Back at the station house, a wagon pulled into the yard to get out of the weather. The freighter first saw Mary's wagon overturned and broken up but didn't think much of that—accidents happen—but then he noticed the mules were still there in harness. That stopped him for a moment.

Then he remembered this place was run by two old folks and figured they must not have been able to move them yet, so he figured he would have to help in the morning.

Best to just pull the animals next to the wagon an' burn it all, right there. Easiest that way an' the stink wouldn't last long. He grumbled as he got down and unhitched his own animals.

When he moved his mules into the barn, he didn't notice the five bodies lying next to the wall in the dark. He loosed the mules to wander around and feed themselves. When he came out he noticed the corral was broken and hadn't been fixed, so he started wondering if the old gent was sick or maybe even dead. That would mean the widow would need a husband again. He surveyed the back of the station house. *Nice place.*

He ambled around to the front feeling pretty good until he entered the door and surprised the sheriff and deputies.

They all pulled pistols and aimed at him, hammers cocked, before he could get his hands up.

"Oh God, please don't shoot me. I've got young'uns—at least they used to be mine. Please, take the wagon! Nuthin' in it you'd want, but you can have it. Just please don't kill me."

The sheriff stared at the man. "Who are you, sneakin' up on us like that?"

"It's the snow, mister, makes ever'thin' quiet. I'm sorry. Please don't shoot."

"Shoot? What are you—" The sheriff realized he had his gun out and pointing at the man. "Oh, sorry." He and the deputies holstered their guns. "Come on in. There's a murder happened here. These here are the killers." He nudged Clem with his boot and thumbed over at the two men lying on the table.

He told the man the place was closed because of the murders, but he could get some coffee and bacon warming at the fire, and then they needed his wagon as soon as he ate.

The freighter learned he was driving them all out again together, down to Carson City with the prisoner.

The man started to protest. "But—but my job! And my boss!"

The sheriff walked up real close to him and said real quietly, "You're drivin' the wagon, or I'm leavin' you here with them and takin' it myself."

The man stopped. "Okay, let me get that bacon an' coffee an' we'll leave when yer ready."

"Good. I appreciate a man helpin' the law when needed."

He looked over at Joe. "Whenever Mrs. Gildenfor shows, she's gonna be heart-struck. Richard was a good man. You can dig a grave for him wherever she wants. If you can get another freighter to stop, you make 'em help by my order, or you can arrest 'em. I'll figure out why later. Then be sure to bury this lady and her son, and this one they executed, and the ones you drug down from the road." He shook his head at him sorrowfully. "Them others on the table, when they die, I say drag 'em out into the woods and leave 'em for the bears. That's good enough fer the likes of them."

"Why them? Sheriff, I don't understand, why you actin' this way?"

"'Cause, Joe, I hate these kind that'll take advantage of women and children, them that can't defend themselves. They're scum, animals, and they don't deserve nuthin' but a trash heap burial. Don't deserve that, but you got to do somethin' with 'em."

"Sheriff, you don't want to bring them all in?"

"No! Let 'em die right here. Otherwise the town will want my office to pay to bury 'em. I say burn 'em or let the coyotes and bears have 'em, and hope they don't get sick from it."

***

The sheriff had everyone leave just before dark, with Clem lying in the back of the wagon, Bub sitting beside the freighter, and the sheriff riding alongside.

The sheriff pushed them all night and all the next day. They arrived in Carson City just after suppertime, completely exhausted. The sheriff had them pull up to the doctor's house to deliver his prisoner.

The freighter and Bub dragged Clem in as the sheriff announced them and held the door.

The doctor was with another patient. They plopped Clem on the exam table with a grunt. The doctor hollered out to give him a minute and came in after saying his goodbyes to whoever was in the other room.

He examined Clem briefly and asked the sheriff the circumstances of the wounds and all. Then he reached up onto a shelf above the exam table for his scissors and cut open Clem's shirt.

"Been shot before." A drip of tobacco juice escaped and fell on Clem's chest. He wiped it off with the back of his hand. "Sorry, mister, bad habit. I would quit, but it calms me during operating. So, sheriff, you're not sure who shot him? Any dead?"

"Two more dead by mornin'. That'll make eleven all told, includin' Richard Gildenfor. It happened up at his place. A real battle, I guess. This one here's the ringleader of that gang that kidnapped them women from that wagon train. You hear about that?"

"Yeah. That's him? How do you know?"

"I know; got plenty of evidence. You'll learn soon enough."

The doctor probed Clem, lifting him and looking while talking. Every so often he had to lean over and spit toward his can. Most times he made it square. Either way afterwards he wiped his mouth with the back of his hand.

"He'll live, I think. He lived this long. It'll be 'bout two weeks before he can sit through a trial and not look like he's dying. I would say that would be better for your case. No sympathy for the wounded that way."

"Two weeks sounds perfect. When can I move him to my jail?"

"Give him a week here to rest and me to watch over him. The one bullet down here went clean through him. This other is still in there but I might kill him trying to get it out, so I'll probably leave it there."

"Good, killin' him's my job. I'll do it official."

The doctor looked up at him but didn't say anything. No need to argue, he thought. He leaned over and spit. Bull's-eye.

***

Walt had the wagon train all set to go before sunrise. Michael was ready but he asked Walt to take over.

Evie Hod and Jodi Mesto approached Walt just as everyone was prepared to start. Jodi spoke up first. "We've said our goodbyes to everyone here, so we need to say goodbye to you." She stuck her hand out to shake his. "Thank you, an' I mean it."

He was confused. He took her hand and she gave him a hearty handshake.

"We're headin' back to the house to help prepare the bodies to be buried, and we can give the names to whoever will be doin' the buryin'. Got to be someone there by now, or will be soon."

Evie held out her hand. "Thank you, Walt, for helping us. I really do appreciate everything you've done for us. I'm heading back with Jodi. We're going back to Carson City to make a go of it, like my Ed wanted. I'll help her and she'll help me. Cynthia is coming with us, but Eddie will stay with you and help where needed. He'll be just a few days away by stagecoach. So we'll be fine."

Walt was holding her hand as she talked, not realizing it. She looked down at her hand, and he looked down and then pulled his hand back. "Oh sorry. Well, there ain't much I can say. Thank you, to both of you, fer helpin' us all, an' good luck to you. I'll come back over after ever'one gits settled an' look in on you, I guess. Y'all take care." He touched the edge of his hat and waited while they walked away to Evie's wagon.

They climbed aboard and turned the mules out of line. He watched them pull out and waved with everyone else, and then he set about the business of getting the wagon train rolling again.

***

Back in Carson City the sheriff was trying hard to be professional and not brag too much about capturing the man who killed those men under the flag of truce that everyone knew about—and if there was someone who didn't know about it, they learned soon enough.

He was also charging the man with kidnapping. Somehow he had taken or coerced the women into staying with him, and those other men were obviously attempting to negotiate a release under that flag of truce when they were shot down in cold blood. An act that no decent man ever thought could have happened.

And there was a third charge of attacking and killing even more men recently in the mountains, including his good friend Richard Gildenfor, who owned his station house on the Henness Pass road.

***

Evie and Cynthia Hod and Jodi Mesto reached the station house early that afternoon. They found Mary and Tom Williams along with Hugh and Billy lying out in front of the building in a row with six other men they didn't know.

Then they noticed a man up on the hill behind the house digging a grave.

The deputy, Joe, saw them about the same time and came down to find out who they were and introduce himself. He explained that he was digging the grave for Richard Gildenfor and would take care of the others next, and that he had dragged the other bodies out of the house because he was afraid they would start to smell before he could finish all the graves. They assured him he did the right thing under the circumstances.

Joe mentioned there were two others in the house who were still alive, but barely. He didn't give them any chance to make it through the day, so they all walked inside to see who they were.

The ladies identified both Harvey and Sergio and determined the others must have been from the gang that attacked them. Jodi agreed with the deputy's assessment of their two friends lying on the tables. She gave Harvey a twenty percent chance of living and Sergio she put at forty percent. She recommended the deputy dig two more graves once he was done with the first group.

Then Joe made the mistake of telling them that the sheriff had taken Clem for the purpose of convicting him of the murders and having him hanged when it was convenient.

Jodi stood there, eyes widening and shaking just a little, trying not to lose her temper because she knew this was the law, and they had Clem. Evie reached over and took her hand. It had the desired effect. Jodi looked back at her friend, who was smiling, trying not to show her fear, and nodded that she was okay now. Then Jodi took a deep, shaky breath and calmly smoothed out her dress.

After she knew she had herself under complete control, she

looked up at the deputy and leaned slightly in toward him. In the calmest voice she could muster, she said, "Why in the name of ever'thin' that's good would that blockhead take the only good man left here alive? Is the man really that stupid or does he jist need someone to hang to polish up his badge? Runnin' fer mayor soon?"

Joe hadn't met many women like Jodi Mesto, and it showed. He tried to assure her that Clem would receive good treatment from the doctor there and they had nothing to worry about, until the trial anyways. She told the deputy what she thought of his assurances. She spent the rest of her time there glaring at him or rolling her eyes anytime he was forced to talk to them.

The deputy buried Mary, Tom, Billy, and Hugh on the other side of the clearing from Mr. Gildenfor. He buried the other four men inside the woods in a clearing in a common grave, dragging them there by horse.

The grave was fairly shallow, what with the deputy not caring to work so hard for them in the first place and being tuckered out from digging the other graves.

***

Helen Gildenfor arrived just after dinner was finished. She was delayed by the snow and near stricken dead herself when she found out about her Richard, who was resting peacefully in his grave by then.

The three ladies were still there because Evie finally had got Jodi to agree to stay until morning before heading into town to check on Clem. She knew that he would be at the doctor's for at least a couple of days if the doc was a man of any integrity, which the deputy had vowed that he was, and that the sheriff, in spite of Jodi's opinions, would wait to hold a proper trial so that justice would be served. It wouldn't be a lynching. This helped Evie, who knew it wouldn't serve Clem to have the "Mesto Brigade" come charging into a war with the sheriff, who was already on the wrong side of this.

Mrs. Gildenfor stayed in a state of half-consciousness for three days, eating and drinking whatever was brought to her without any acknowledgment of any kind—never saying a word or moving from her bed.

Evie went into town to check on Clem and learn what she could about any impending trial. Cynthia stayed with Jodi to take care of the three who were there, Mrs. Gildenfor in her bed and the two men lying on the tables—still there because Jodi expected them to die at any moment and she was not going to carry them upstairs to put into a bed nor drag a bed down for a couple of dead men. Even if they weren't dead yet. She did agree to bandage their wounds and keep cleaning their faces and arms regularly in spite of the great waste of time it was according to her.

On the fourth day Helen came out wiping tears from her eyes and introduced herself. She told them all about her Richard, and how she didn't want to start this place, that she told him it would be too dangerous, but she grew to love it so much that she decided years ago she wanted to stay.

Now that her Richard was gone she still wanted to stay.

Helen asked Jodi and Evie if they would be willing to stay for a few more days until they all knew what would happen next. Perhaps she could get someone from her family who would want to come live there with her and run the place as a co-owner. The women readily agreed because they knew Clem would be at the doctor's for at least a week and they wanted to stay with Sergio and Harvey until their end.

The ladies all moved into one of the upstairs bedrooms for convenience sake, and they moved Harvey and Sergio into the downstairs room.

The doctor did not come up because he had sent word that it would do the patients more harm than good to relocate them, and at this point there was nothing he could do for them that they couldn't do: providing rest and prayer.

236

***

Clem rested at the doctor's place for one week exactly, and then the sheriff insisted he transfer him to the jailhouse to await his trial.

Once he was situated in his cell, the sheriff let him know that his trial would take place the very next Saturday, five days away. *Perfect,* Clem thought. *The Sabbath, how appropriate they'd choose that day.*

As the days slipped by Clem had time to think about his past. His wife, Veda, and how she really did save him from a life without God. His three boys and how proud he was of them and the men they had grown up to be. He worried what they would think when word finally got back to them. He asked a couple of times for pencil and paper to write to them, but the sheriff made sure the deputies were under orders not to bring him anything. Not for any reason other than conducting him out to take care of himself or giving him his food and water.

He thought of Rabbi Weinstein and how he showed him how the Messiah never spoke against the Word God gave to Moses. He thought of the ladies. How proud he was of them. And his men. Those boys had really grown into men. They had to and rose to the occasion.

He missed Emmie. He felt really bad about what she would think when she was told what happened. He knew she would know the truth, but still he knew it would hurt her awful to hear what was said. That's what made him sad, so he tried not to think about that too often.

He prayed to God often, saying he was sorry for what he had done and thanking Him for the many blessings he had been given. He was content with his fate and determined to show this sheriff he was a man to the very end. He waited for the next Sabbath day.

20
And Justice for All

That Saturday arrived all too quickly for Clem, and he found himself sitting at the defendant's table bright and early on a sunny day. It would have been a beautiful day if not for the fact that the whole town was gathered there to kill him.

The courtroom was quite lovely. It was more ornate than what a person would expect to find. The building that housed it used to be a very grand hotel, and the room was the old ballroom. The hotel had been one of the nicer places in the new West. It had long windows on the south side letting the sun shine in, and two large chandeliers hanging from an elaborately decorated ceiling. The judge's bench was on a small raised platform built in the east end to give him his proper prominence with the witness box just beside him on the ground level. The jury box was also raised a little above the rest. Two tables just in front of the low fence separated the gallery from everyone who would be involved in the trial. The sheriff was at one table with the prosecutor, and his deputies were seated next to him in chairs against the wall next to the jury box. Clem sat alone at his table.

The trial would rely on the prosecutor building his case against Clem solely on circumstantial evidence. However, he had lots of it, mostly provided by the expert witness of Sheriff Augustus Thurmond. He also had a telegram, sent by the sheriff of Sacramento, California, that had been quietly given to him by Judge Ruud earlier that morning in the judge's chambers.

It seemed the Sacramento sheriff claimed to have had about thirty women storm into his office early that very morning after receiving a telegram from a Jodi Mesto, who had sent word to a Leah Knott, care of Sacramento general delivery.

The ladies demanded that he, the sheriff, send a telegram to Carson City asking the judge to postpone the trial to allow them to travel over and give their testimony.

The judge obviously wouldn't tell the prosecutor what to do with the telegram. He just wanted his man to have every bit of evidence at his disposal, no matter how circumstantial it might be, because ultimately he wanted to show the criminal element in the world that the law in Carson City was fair, but strict and swift.

The prosecutor thought the telegram would not have any bearing on the actual circumstances of the trial, being as it was only hearsay evidence. And they would need to postpone the trial by at least five days to allow the ladies to come over the pass with many stops to rest, knowing how delicate the fairer sex is and the extra time they would need to prepare themselves for an appearance in a court of law.

The judge agreed that to postpone the case would be ridiculous. They needed to move while the evidence in Sheriff Thurmond's mind was still fresh. And now that they had a jury, ready and willing, to ask them to wait five more days would be unheard of.

***

The room was filled to standing room only. The crowd wanted to see the man who murdered those poor souls trying to rescue their wives, up in the Henness Pass, and those others who died standing under a white flag of truce.

"Unbelievable" was the word used most often. Worse than that man who shot President Lincoln.

"He's worse than that man who..." And the storyteller would go on to recite some other tragic affair that he or she had heard about in times past. Many terrible stories were used to compare the worst man this town had ever had on trial.

They wanted to avenge every man who had ever trusted in the sacred honor of a flag of truce.

***

It was ten a.m. sharp when the Honorable Josiah Ruud rapped his gavel to start the proceedings.

"There are three counts against Clem Bentone," the judge informed the jury. "Decide on each charge in order, escalating with the severity of the crime involved."

He cleared his throat. "The first charge is kidnapping, and forcing the women to remain with him under some unknown duress.

"The second charge is murder, for the attack on the men up in Henness Pass.

"The third charge is murder under the protection of a flag of truce."

The sheriff was in the witness stand for over an hour giving detailed accounts of what probably happened.

Evie Hod was allowed to testify. She was not allowed to tell the jury about her family being rescued during the Indian attack; it was immaterial to the case before the jury. She was allowed to give her version of what happened outside of Fort Casper, and what happened at Henness Pass.

Jodi Mesto was allowed to testify only concerning the events in Henness Pass, having arrived after the first battle, or murder, as the prosecutor and sheriff referred to it.

She tried to tell the stories of the other ladies who told her what happened but was continuously blocked by the prosecutor. She was able to give great detail about the ambush up on the pass, but it appeared to all that the jury was unaffected.

Clem took the stand last and testified, attempting to recant the prosecutor's allegations and the evidence provided by the sheriff.

He had to defend himself because they could not find any attorney willing to help him.

He told of that first meeting, under the famous flag of truce, and what those men had planned for the ladies and all that had transpired.

He tried to explain what would have been the fate of the wagon train if he had given in to their demands, but he was continuously told to keep to the facts and stop trying to sway the jury with his imaginations of the so-called evil men.

He was able to explain what happened at the beginning of the attack at Henness Pass but couldn't recount much because he was shot in the beginning and still suffering from his wounds.

The jury was very proper and soberly listened to everything. They received their instructions from the judge concerning deliberations and retired to determine Clem's fate.

No one left the room because they knew it wouldn't take very long.

***

However, after three hours of waiting, the crowd was getting boisterous. The jury was still deliberating and no one could believe it!

The judged finally sent the sheriff in to see if they were going to be able to come up with a decision.

They admonished him to let them do their duty, and everyone could wait until they were all in agreement, or they could go home.

The judge ordered the courtroom cleared to allow everyone to go refresh themselves, and he would have it reconvened in two hours, decision or not.

There was a huge uproar about losing their seats until he calmed everyone down and had the deputies issue numbers as people left so they were assured of getting back in when they returned.

The crowd waited outside the doors for almost an hour when the deputies finally opened one door and insisted on escorting each person or couple back in individually.

***

The jury was seated and waiting for the judge to bring the court back to order and begin the proceedings.

After everyone was seated or standing in the same place as before, Judge Ruud gaveled the court to order.

"Foreman of the jury, stand and deliver the verdicts."

With a self-important air, the jury foreman rose and clasped his hands in front of him. "On the first count of kidnapping and holding the women under duress, the jury rules, not guilty!"

The audience erupted in anger.

It took the judge about three minutes to quiet them all down.

"There simply was not enough evidence to convict!" the foreman exclaimed.

He waited a moment before speaking again. "On the second count of murder, up in the Henness Pass: not guilty!"

The audience went wild this time. People shouted threats and curses at the jury. Hats were thrown in their direction.

Several of the jury members contemplated their escape after that last outburst, while others stood and yelled back at the crowd.

The sheriff and his deputies had to threaten both the audience and the jury members in order to help the judge calm everyone down.

It was several more minutes before the crowd finally did calm down again.

The judge issued a warning that people would be arrested in the event of another outburst, although he knew he would never enforce it.

The judge gave the foreman a hard look, then softened and asked him, "Is there anything we need to talk about, privately, before giving the last verdict?"

The foreman was indignant. "Your Honor, we reached our conclusions fairly." Then eyeing the sheriff and the prosecutor, he continued, "In spite of the lack of evidence provided by eyewitnesses."

242

Both men were completely unaffected by the implication.

The judge had to bring the court back to order again after yet another outburst, because the crowd fully understood the implications of what the jury foreman had just said.

Everyone was tense. The audience was ready to jump the rail between them and the trial area. The deputies had moved themselves to the inside of the rail in front of the jury after the judge and the foreman talked.

They were there, ready to repel boarders.

Clem was very aware that there was no one behind him in case of another favorable verdict.

The judge asked, "Do you have a verdict on the last count, murder, under a white flag of truce?"

The foreman never looked at the judge. His hands were balled into fists, and he glared at the crowd. They were defiant in their attitude back at him. "Yes sir, Your Honor. On the last count of murder under the white flag, we find the defendant, guilty."

The crowd didn't make a sound for a second that seemed like a minute; then it erupted into cheers! They tossed hats in the air again. They hugged and patted each other on the back and shook hands.

The judge let them go for several minutes, then abjectly rapped his gavel to bring them to order. He allowed them to quiet down slowly this time, letting them have their celebration.

He finally had to get more forceful to make them stop.

Once the crowd finally was quiet, the judge asked, "Tell me the circumstances on the last verdict."

Several men from the jury stood this time. One said, "It was the testimony of the accused himself. No one should be shot while under the protection of a white flag, no matter what the circumstances."

He sat down as the others were nodding in agreement.

The crowd erupted in another raucous celebration, and the judge let them go on.

Another juror who was still standing spoke up loudly over the noise of the jubilant crowd. "The mere threat of a kidnappin' does not mitigate him murderin' 'em. He's no better than they were."

Now the rest of the jury members who were still standing all sat down.

The sheriff walked over to Clem's table and leaned across it. "Yer gonna hang anyway, for one count instead of three," he said lightheartedly. "But it don't matter, the end'll be the same."

The crowd was finally forced to take their celebration out into the street, and most of the men headed for the saloon.

Clem had to wait until the courtroom was completely empty.

Many from the crowd pushed their way up to him on their way out, to give him a pat on the back, and well wishes for a nice trip to hell, and many such salutations.

Evie and Jodi waited until the crowd was gone. Even they got shoves and much jeering and laughter directed at them while the crowd departed.

They went up to Clem to say how sorry they were. They both had tears running down their cheeks. "We'll send word to California and let ever'one know," Jodi said with a tremble in her voice.

***

The sheriff took Clem out the back door trying to escape the crowd, but they saw him and surrounded them. They shoved and taunted Clem and the sheriff, with suggestions to hang him right then or drag him behind a horse, and many other thoughts to end this now. They were in a playful mood, so no one other than Clem was really worried.

The sheriff got him back to the cell and noticed he was bleeding again. "Don't bleed too much or I'll have to call the doc and charge the visit to you." He grinned. "I'll hang you next Saturday at high noon. Make a big show of it. And I'll use a new rope after all; I don't want to look bad in front of the crowd."

Clem wasn't paying attention; he had his own worries.

The town, now quieted down, returned to its normal routine. The jury members were forgiven as everyone came to understand their dilemma, about needing evidence and all, as long as they did the right thing in the end.

***

Jodi sent another telegram to Sacramento. The folks over there were keeping a rotating shift now, waiting to get the news as soon as it came in. It was Mrs. Hamilton who got the telegram, and she sent her children out with the news to tell everyone else. A meeting was planned for the next evening.

They all came together at the farm of Karen Roch. She had already found a place she was happy with.

They all felt an injustice was done but they had many different ideas what to do about it. Some were resigned to it being over, and others were trying to think of what they could do to stop the hanging and get a new trial.

Jodi and Evie were reunited with them now after taking a stagecoach back over to reach them. It was a special, and expensive, long and hard overnight run, with the coach stopping only to change out fresh horses and then off again.

Leah was not at the meeting. She was still recovering in Karen's house. She had been given a bed to rest on; otherwise everyone was there.

Millie Hafin had been talking with Jodi away from the others when she asked for everyone's attention.

"I have an idea I want to propose. But first, we need to have all the young people, men and women, leave and take the others over to the pond and stay there. No need for them to hear any of this."

This brought many complaints and arguing from those young people, what with all they had been through, then trying to determine just who was a young person and how young you had to be.

Finally, the boundary was set at being a parent; if you weren't, you left with the others for the pond.

Everyone who was left seemed willing to hear her out. Someone hollered, "Go on, what's your plan?"

"Now I must ask Walt to leave us. He would be the most likely accused if anything were to happen, so he must agree to leave now, and stay away, out in some very public place, where he could never be accused of anything that may or may not happen."

He started to argue but the looks he received from every face told him he had no chance. He gave up rather quickly and asked to be informed whenever they thought it was appropriate, and then with a big sigh he bid them all a good night and rode off into town.

Millie addressed the crowd. "I believe we need to mount a rescue attempt, just like he would do for us if the situation was reversed. If we don't, they will hang him. We all can say we owe our lives to Clem Bentone. So here's what I have in mind."

She laid out the plan to everyone and received many shocked looks, and several people were saying how it could never work. Others thought it was a great idea and the only thing that would work.

Still others started to come up with ideas of their own based on what Millie had brought forth, and in the end, they decided on a slight variation of her idea. Finally, there was a call for a vote.

"We need to know who will be with us in this," Millie said. "If they stop us, we'll probably end up in jail, and maybe worse, ourselves. We need to know that you will go all the way, or ask that you will hold your silence. So who's going to agree to the plan?"

Every hand went up.

***

Back in Carson City Clem was sitting on the bed in his cell when a man came down the corridor to stand in front of him. This was not so unusual. Several folks from town had been coming in every so often to gloat over him a little more personally.

This time the man looked back to make sure the deputy wasn't around.

"Hello, Ol' Leather."

Clem never moved. He knew this was one of them, but he didn't want to give the man the satisfaction of reacting.

"Oh come on, Leather, you recognize that name. You don't know me but obviously I know you. My name's Jed; I'm the one who organized the attack up in the mountains."

Clem looked up at him now.

The man smiled. Then his expression soured and he shook his head. "It didn't work out the way I wanted, but I still git away with 'bout seven thousand dollars, an' you git hung, so I guess I win. You got nuthin' to say?"

Clem just stared but didn't say anything. He was trying not to show any emotion. He knew that was why the man was here. Finally he cleared his throat. "You'll face yer judge when you stand before the judgment seat in the end."

"Oh yeah, but you'll face yers first." He laughed again. "Anyway I jist wanted to come introduce myself."

"Okay, I'm not impressed. You failed twice at attackin' a bunch of women an' children, an' we beat you both times. Yer a failure. Remember that the rest of yer life."

Jed quit smiling and his face hardened. "No, yer the failure. You'll die in a few days, an' I'll be there watchin'."

"I won't be lookin' fer the biggest failure in the crowd. Now git before I call the deputy."

Jed gave him a sneer and started to walk away but called back as he left, "Have a short life, Ol' Leather."

Clem resumed looking at nothing. Then he smiled and chuckled a little on his own.

21
The Ladies

On Thursday, two days before Clem's hanging and a little after ten o'clock at night, the deputy saw a wagon pull up in front of the office. He watched as two people got out and stepped up onto the boardwalk, then entered his office.

He was surprised to see it was two women, dressed for the night air in heavy coats, with shawls and scarves tucked in under big floppy hats hanging down in their faces.

"Ladies, what on earth are you two doin' out this late? And why are you here?"

The taller of the two spoke up. "We heered you got that man that took our sister. An' we been chasin' 'em clear 'cross the country, tryin' to ketch up, an' we jist now git here. So we wants to see 'em, an' see it's him."

"I'm sorry, ladies, but he's sleepin', and you should be too. You need to go get a hotel room and get out of this cold."

"No! Not till we see 'em. We ain't agonna leave nowheres till we see 'em."

"But—"

"No! No! We ain't agonna leave nowhere's till we sees 'em." This was the short one now. She stomped her boot into the floor and threw her arms out in emphasis.

The other one started getting loud again, jerking her hand at him and demanding to see the prisoner.

The deputy was taken aback looking up at these two obviously backwoods folk, and he could see they weren't going to leave until they saw the prisoner, so he sighed and pushed his chair back and said, "Okay, all right, calm down, he's this way. He's the only one we got here."

He led them down a corridor until he came to the last cell. Clem lay there in his bed snoring away. The deputy held up his lantern so they could get a better look at him.

"Open the door."

He turned to them. "What? No. We ain't gonna open no—"

Then he noticed they both had revolvers pointing at him.

"Open the door," the shorter one commanded. "Right now, open the door."

He stood staring at them until the taller one jabbed her gun into his stomach real hard. "Do it now or I'll shoot you in yer belly an' yer guts will muffle the sound. Now go on, do it! Now!" She jabbed him again.

The short one cocked her hammer back all the way. "Ain't agonna say it no more, mister—open it er die."

"Okay, okay, don't do nuthin', I'll open it." He turned to take the keys off the wall and unlocked the cell, then moved back into the corner of the hallway when he was prodded by the pistol again. He naturally raised his hands without being told; that made both ladies smile, showing dirty black teeth.

Clem was waking up during this. He sat up and it took him a minute to focus on what was happening.

The taller lady looked in at him and spoke. "We got you, Horace Claiborne! We got you an' yer agonna die, this very night! We got you, an' yer agonna die!"

She turned to the deputy. "Now you, git over in there an' sit!

Move the wrong way an' we shoot you afore we shoot him. Now move!" They followed the deputy into the cell.

He scurried to the stool in the corner and sat down, hands still in the air. "Yes ma'am! Don't shoot! But I think you got the wrong—"

"Hush! I'm gonna keel 'em, an' I can keel you too; don' matter ta me!"

"Okay, I won't, I'm not talkin'." He glanced at Clem, who was watching all this while still trying to make some sense out of what was going on.

The short lady pulled a small dirty handkerchief from a pocket and threw it at the deputy, who grabbed it and looked at it as if it were infected with something. "Steek it in yer mouth." She sneered at him.

He was horrified. He looked at her with a hope that maybe she could be talked out of this. But when she lifted her pistol and pointed it at his face, he shoved in the handkerchief. She barked at him, "Stand up an' turn roun'."

He stood up, staring at Clem as he turned around. Clem was staring at the ladies.

The short one jammed the barrel of her pistol against the back of the deputy's head, causing him to snap his head forward. "Don' move!" She pushed her pistol harder against him. He mumbled something from behind his gag that sounded like "I'm sorry."

The tall one pulled off her scarf and wrapped it around the deputy's head, stopping the handkerchief up in his mouth, while the short one backed away.

She turned to Clem and pointed her pistol at him before grabbing his arm. "Come on, Horace, yer agonna die. Le's go."

Pulling him up by the arm, she roughly yanked him out of the cell and propelled him down the corridor into the office.

The short lady poked the deputy in the side with her pistol. "You move back now, all the way." She stepped out of his path.

He shuffled backward, staring at her as she lifted her pistol and pointed it at his face. He hit the bars next to the door. "Stick yer hands back there an' don' move."

As he put them behind him, he felt the bars and stopped. He figured what was coming next but hoped it wasn't true; he was hoping they would just lock him up in there. He was wrong.

"Go on, stick yer arms through them bars." He obeyed and she walked out into the corridor behind him.

She pulled the handcuffs off the wall and locked him up with his hands sticking out. "Okay, so you can tell folks what happened. We agonna shoot Horace, then we agonna burn 'em afore he's even dead, 'cause he stole our sis an' sole her to a riverboat. So now he's agonna pay, thank you."

The deputy listened to her hurry down the corridor, and then he heard the front door open and close. And then he was alone, with nothing to do but sit on the floor and wait for morning.

***

The ladies hustled Clem out into the night and pushed him up into the wagon. Another lady who was lying in there immediately covered him with blankets. She tucked his head down and covered it too, telling him not to move.

The two climbed up into the box and snapped the reins. The mules jumped out and the wagon was gone, just like that.

***

Thirty minutes later, the ladies driving the wagon were still pushing the mules hard, making them run faster than they would have normally, especially considering they didn't have enough light for the driver to see. They were relying on the mules' better night vision to keep them in the road.

Clem for his part was riding along not sure what to do. He recognized Verlie Hamilton and Georgia Carsten in the jail. He still didn't know who was here with him in the back, but he would be patient and wait for them to let him in on their plan.

He relaxed and thanked Yehovah for the rescue and apologized for breaking the law, all at the same time.

Now they were heading up into the mountains and hardly gone far when two more wagons joined them. All three turned into a small cleft in the mountainside and stopped.

Clem had been bouncing around under the blankets but couldn't take it any longer, so he yanked them back and saw Millie Hafin smiling at him. She held her finger up to her lips, showing him not to talk. He smiled back, shook his head, and relaxed.

He heard people getting down, and then gun shots! Then he smelled fire, and whatever it was they were burning smelled horrible. He looked back at her, and she winked, stuck her finger to her lips again, and shook her head.

He let out a big sigh and lay back, gazing up at the stars. It was a beautiful night.

He heard the ladies coming and felt the wagon move as someone climbed in. He could hear others mounting up into their wagons, and they were off again.

He was out of jail, he knew that, but he couldn't figure out anything else that was going on, so he stayed on his back and enjoyed the ride.

They ran all through the night, and he could tell it was getting morning when they pulled up again. This time they climbed down and called to Millie to let him out.

He climbed out, steadied himself, and looked around. There was Millie Hafin, and there was Verlie Hamilton, and Georgia Carsten, and then there was Karen Roch, and Jodi Mesto, and Evie Hod and Lauren Wasterman. They all stood there grinning at him. Millie said, "Come on, let's get him inside."

He looked around again and realized they were at the very same station house where they had the gun battle not even a month ago. They smiled as they hustled him inside.

They walked him across a big room where he saw a new lady he never met before, smiling and leading the way into another room. Harvey and Sergio were there lying in beds! He didn't know what to think now. They made him lie down on a third bed and told him to get some rest.

He was trying to tell them he was fine, but they wouldn't have it. He had to rest because they were leaving again in just a couple hours, and that was that; he wasn't in charge anymore.

He turned over to look at Harvey and then at Sergio. They were both sleeping peacefully, so he decided he better try to do the same and closed his eyes. It wasn't too long before they woke him out of a very deep sleep and helped him up as soon as he realized he was awake.

He insisted on walking out into the big room by himself and sat down at a big table, and that new lady set a bowl of porridge before him, poured in cream, and then even sprinkled some sugar on top of that!

She told him, "You need to eat up 'cause you're all pulling out very soon. This might be the last warm meal you get for a couple days."

He stared at her trying to figure out who she was, but decided he needed to listen and ate it up happily. She talked with the others while he ate.

They took him back out and made him lie down in the back of his wagon again. Harvey was helped into another, and Sergio into the third. They were all lying on many blankets and had many more piled on top of them.

He was as cozy as he had ever been since he was a child, and soon enough they were off and running again. All through the early morning he bounced along in comfort, smiling and thinking how this was the most comfortable rescue he had ever heard of.

***

The sheriff showed up at the jail early that same morning to check on his prisoner. He was excited because he would get to hang him and couldn't wait to talk to him about it.

He didn't see Bub, so he went down the corridor searching for him and saw the cell door open. He thought, *He better have him out back*. Then he saw the hands sticking out between the bars, handcuffed together.

He ran to the cell and saw Bub struggling to get up. The sheriff dashed into the cell and frantically looked around at the ten-foot-square cell as if he just didn't see his prisoner.

He screamed at Bub, "Where is he?"

Bub was still trying to get up, but his legs were mostly asleep and his hands were behind him. Grabbing him by his shirt, the sheriff pulled him up and yelled again, "Where is he!"

Then he noticed that Bub had a scarf around his mouth, so he yanked it off and yelled at him yet again. Then he saw Bub trying to push the rag out, so he pulled it out for him. "Where is he!"

"I'm sorry, sheriff, they—"

"Who? Who's they?" He shook Bub by the shirt, banging him against the bars. "Where is he?"

"I don't know. Ladies—"

"Who? What ladies? Tell me now!"

"I'm tryin'. My hands, can you help me?"

"What? What? Oh good grief." He ran out and looked for the keys. He couldn't find them. He ran to the office and found a spare set in a bottom desk drawer. Grabbing them, he ran back and unlocked Bub.

Bub stood fully now and rubbed his wrists.

The sheriff came around and very slowly asked him again, "Bub, who came here, and when?"

"Two ladies, sisters of someone he took. They meant to kill him and burn him alive afterwards."

"What do you mean? Kill him and then burn him alive?"

"They said they was gonna shoot him, and then burn him alive before he died. 'Cause he stole their sister, and they been chasin' him all across the country."

"You don't know who they were?"

"No sir, never seen 'em. They wasn't part of that wagon train."

"Bub, how do you know?"

"'Cause they couldn't hardly speak English. They was from back in the hills; you know the kind, no learnin' a'tall. I could tell by the way they was speakin'."

The sheriff walked out and went down the hall into his office. He was pacing when Bub emerged, still rubbing his wrists.

The sheriff turned to Bub again. "When did they come in?"

"Last night, 'bout ten I 'spect. Not exactly positive."

"And you just let 'em take him? Why?"

"They had guns! Stuck 'em right in my face! I thought they was gonna shoot me right here."

"Okay, do you know, did you hear which way they were goin'?"

"No, nuthin' like that."

"You sure? Think for a minute. What else did they say?"

"They said he sold their sister to a riverboat but nuthin' else, other than sit here, and shut up, and that sort of thing. Oh, and they probably got the wrong man, but I figured it didn't matter."

"Whatta you mean, the wrong man?"

"They were lookin' fer a man named Horace Clay somethin'. I started to tell 'em they had the wrong man, but they stuck guns in my face, so I stopped. Figured it didn't matter anyhow."

The sheriff had to think about that for a minute. He started to pace again. "Okay, get Joe, and we'll form a posse and head out in all directions lookin' for 'em. What did they come in, wagon?"

"Yes sir, wagon, just one. And they was bundled up fer the cold too."

"Okay, go find Joe; he's makin' rounds by now. Then get back here."

Bub ran out the door. The sheriff continued pacing. Then he rushed over to the telegraph office.

He had to bang on the door to get the man up. The operator came out from the back, pulling up suspenders and sipping coffee.

The sheriff yelled through the door and shook it by the handle. That stopped the man, and he stood scratching his head trying to make out what the sheriff was saying. Then he realized the sheriff was about to break his door in, so he hurried over to open it.

The sheriff stormed in, grabbed his arm, and pulled him over to his desk, spilling his coffee all along the way and burning the man's hand while ignoring the hollering about the scalding.

"Sit down, I need this out right now! Emergency!"

He sent out telegrams to the sheriffs in Sacramento and Salt Lake City, telling them that his prisoner had busted out of jail, and to be on the lookout for two ladies in a wagon from the back hill country, probably Deep South, and possibly with the man who kidnapped those women and murdered everyone under the white flag of truce.

***

The sheriff in Sacramento was at his desk, boots up, drinking coffee and hoping this was going to be a good day.

The telegraph operator came busting through the door waving a paper in the air. The sheriff thought right then his day was shot. He took the telegram and looked at the man, thinking, *Why couldn't you of given me just one hour*. Very reluctantly he started to read the telegram.

He couldn't believe it. He sat up.

He read it again, then called in his deputy and sent him back to dispatch a note asking if the sheriff had really lost his prisoner? And was it really two ladies who stole his prisoner from him?

He thought for a moment after the two men left. *Maybe it's going to be a good day after all.* He smiled and laughed a little as he put his boots back up and sipped his coffee. *Looks like it's going to be a real good day after all.*

***

Sheriff Thurmond assembled four parties to go searching for the ladies and his prisoner. He had Joe take three men up the Donner pass. He sent Bub east with five men toward Salt Lake City. He sent another group of four, all volunteers, south toward the new community of Las Vegas Rancho.

He left by himself up the Henness pass on the off-chance they might have gone that way. Also it would give him an opportunity to check up on Helen and see how she was doing.

He reached the station house the next morning and walked in to find Evie and Jodi busily working away. He remembered them from the trial and was surprised to find them there. He was even more so when Helen told him they were her new partners. His surprise showed and made their whole day.

"Well, have you seen two ladies bundled up and drivin' a wagon yesterday, probably headed for California?" he asked.

They all claimed ignorance.

"You heard any news 'bout my prisoner escapin', with the help of two ladies?"

That stopped them all cold and produced mildly amused looks. Jodi asked, "You thinkin' Evie and me are the ones that broke him out? Maybe we have him hidin' upstairs right now?" They all were openly smiling.

He huffed and turned directly to Helen. "I'm sorry for your loss, Helen. You know I was a friend of Richard's. I'm goin' to be searchin' the area and I've got several men out lookin' in all directions." He turned to the other two. "We'll find him, sooner or later."

Helen spoke up. "Augustus, I've—we've known you a long time. Richard and I always held you in the highest esteem. I know you have a heart for justice, no matter what it takes to do it."

Evie and Jodi both gazed at her now as if she was talking about them; it seemed to the sheriff that they were slightly insulted.

She glanced at them and then back to the sheriff. "You know that I will always try to do the right thing. And if I learn of anything that you need to know of, I'll come down into town myself, I promise."

Jodi and Evie turned and left the room.

He watched them leave and had to work to keep from breaking out into a grin. "No need to say anythin', Helen; I know I can trust you. I'll be goin' now. I still got a lot of ground to cover, but it shouldn't be too long. Those two will stick out like sore thumbs around here."

"Two? Aren't you looking for three? The man, I mean."

He stared at the floor, now clearly uncomfortable. "Well, I believe they meant him no good. It seems they were after him because he might have taken their sister earlier and they were seekin' revenge. I'm tryin' to catch 'em before they get themselves into more trouble than they are right now. I would like to help 'em if I can. Justice is right, vigilantism never is."

"Vigilantism? They mean to kill him?"

"I'm afraid so."

"Well, I wish you God's good graces, Augustus."

He thanked her and left, riding back down the trail heading to town. By the time he got there, Joe was back and had sent out riders to fetch Bub and the others.

They had found their man, at least as far as they could tell. What they knew for sure was that a man had been drug up onto a woodpile and set on fire, and there was a good blood trail leading up to the smoldering body on the pile of embers.

That matched the description exactly of what those two ladies had meant to do to the prisoner. It was too much to be a coincidence.

Joe did not bother to go any further after that.

The sheriff sent a curt telegram to Sacramento and Salt Lake City informing the two sheriffs that the prisoner had been found, and was dead. It didn't mention anything else.

Sheriff Thurmond decided justice was done and he had no need to chase down two ladies who had been wounded by this man and did the job he was going to do anyways. He decided the case was closed and ordered Joe and everyone else to move on to the next day's affairs.

Epilogue

Many years have passed now since Sheriff Augustus Thurmond closed the case on Clem Bentone, kidnapper and murderer.

He has long since retired and his former deputy Joe is even now thinking that retirement is not far off. Sheriff'n is for the young.

Michael Knott married Marie Wasterman and now their oldest is talking about college.

Walt and Christine are living up near San Francisco with three children of their own, and her Jacob is talking about marriage and little Jennie has turned into a very successful seamstress.

Millie Hafin turned her freighter business over to her sons. They're sending wagons all over California, up into Oregon, and over into Nevada, many times on the very same trail that she and the others took so long ago on their rescue mission.

Harvey finally won Leah over, and they are planning another trip to Spain to visit Sergio before they all get too old.

Henry and Annabel's oldest, Margaret, is graduating this year near the top of her class. They live on the farm with Clem and Emmie, who just celebrated their fifteenth wedding anniversary.

Most everyone who came over on that wagon train is still living in the area and getting together every year on the anniversary of their first meeting with Clem, way back in Independence so many years ago.

That's why Michael was riding up the lane to Clem's this morning to talk to him about this year's party, because he knew Clem wasn't going to like it.

It was just as the sun was starting to peek over the Sierra Nevadas. It was too early to be calling on him normally these days, but he had errands to run, and supplies to pick up, and still so much to tend to back home.

Also he wanted to see if they needed anything from town.

As he came out of the lane, he could see they were on the front porch in the swing. *Must have slept out there again.* He laughed to himself when he saw them.

Emmie looked up and spotted him. She gingerly moved out from under the blankets, took her pillow, and stuffed it in next to Clem, easing him back down gently.

She stepped off the porch and slowly walked out to greet Michael, who stopped the buckboard well short of the house, not wanting to wake Clem either.

He leaned over and touched the edge of his hat. "Good mornin', Miss Emmie, how are you this mornin'?"

"I'm well, an' how is Marie?"

"She's beautiful." He smiled down at her. Then he glanced over at Clem, there in his swing, tucked under his blankets. "You two love sleepin' on the porch."

She looked back at her husband. "Yes we do; I do love him so."

His eyes returned to her. "I don't want to wake him, but I have to talk to him 'bout this year's party, an' he ain't gonna like it."

She was still gazing at Clem. "It won't matter, Michael; he ain't never gonna wake up agin."

She looked up at him now, tears running down her cheeks. "Would you please go git my Henry? I'll need him to help me, an' I'm gonna need you to tell ever'one. Can you do that?"

His heart started breaking. He looked back at his friend, then back down to Emmie.

"Yes ma'am, I'll start with my ma. She'll want to help. It all started with that first meetin'. They still argue 'bout it."

"I know, he really thought highly of her. Now go an' git my Henry."

"Yes ma'am."

Turning, she left him sitting there in the wagon and went back up onto the porch. She gently lifted Clem and slid in beside him, laying his head on her chest, and began rocking the swing and stroking his hair.

The End

Made in the USA
Columbia, SC
24 February 2019